The Black Sheep

Yvonne Collins and
Sandy Rideout

Hyperion
New York

For our fathers,
Jim Collins and Don Rideout

First Edition
1 3 5 7 9 10 8 6 4 2
Printed in the United States of America
Library of Congress Cataloging-in-Publication Data on file
ISBN-13: 978-1-4231-0156-7
ISBN-10: 1-4231-0156-1
Reinforced binding

Visit www.hyperionteens.com

Chapter 1

The doorbell rings twelve times in four quick bursts. I race into the dim front hall and skid to a stop, confused by the bright light bleeding in around the door frame and pooling on the floor. An alien on the doorstep? Unlikely. UFO sightings are pretty rare in Manhattan. A home invasion? More common, but what kind of robber carries a spotlight?

I don't need my parents, the Secretaries of Defense, to tell me that this is a security issue. Rule Number One in this house is *Never Open the Door to Strangers.* But what harm could it do to look through the peephole?

The light hits with such force that my eye practically explodes. I immediately break Rule Number Six: *No Profanity.*

There's a muffled laugh on the other side of the door. A voice mutters, "Quiet."

"Who is it?" I call.

Silence. Then the doorbell rings again. Three times. Three more times.

Now that I've broken rule six, breaking rule one doesn't seem like such a big deal. But there's also Rule Number Four to consider: *Think Before You Act*. Of all the house rules, I hate number four the most. Too much thought and not enough action leads to a very boring life. I should know.

I flip the locks and open the door, only to find the light is brighter still.

"Kendra Bishop?" a woman's voice asks.

I nod, one hand still over my exploded eyeball. All I can see with the other is a huge smile, like Donkey's in *Shrek*.

"Bob, get a close-up," the smile says. Someone reaches out and pulls my hand away from my eye. "Congratulations, Kendra, you are the new Black Sheep!"

Squinting, I make out a horde of people on the stoop. Front and center is the owner of the smile, a short, pretty woman in a suit, with shiny dark hair and rimless glasses. A massive bald man stands beside her with a camera on his shoulder, on top of which is the light. Another man shoves a microphone at me.

"The new what?" I ask. There must be some mistake.

"Black Sheep," she repeats. "The reality show. I'mJudyGreenberg. Oneoftheproducers." She speaks so fast her words run together.

"You mean I'm on TV?"

"You will be soon. Just give us a week to edit the footage."

I glance down at my blue-and-white Tommy Hilfiger

pajamas, which I put on right after school to save time later. My hair is in a stringy ponytail. "I should change."

"Don't. We want to capture the real Kendra."

She pushes past me into the hallway, followed by a small army hauling cables and equipment. They smile and congratulate me, and I thank each one. Rule Number Fourteen: *Respect the Guests.* "Excuse me . . . Judy, right? I don't understand what's going on."

She raps her knuckles on the wall. "Real marble?"

"I think so."

She turns to the big bald guy. "Close-up of the marble, Bob. Where are your parents, KB?"

KB? Rule Number Eighteen: *No Nicknames.* Kendra combines my dad's name, *Ken*neth and my mom's, Deir*dra*. "They're out for a run."

Judy clicks down the hall in stiletto boots and I rush after her, my socks sliding every which way. "Close-up on the family portrait, Bob," she says from the living room doorway. "Set it up in here, people."

"Set *what* up?" I ask, more alarmed by the second.

She points to the bust sitting on the grand piano. "Who's that?"

"Mozart." Duh.

"Bob—"

"—Zooming in on Mozart," Bob says, in a soft southern drawl.

Judy tosses her huge leather bag onto the oak coffee

table and I snatch it up again. Rule Number Thirty-three: *Watch the Finishes.* "Listen, Judy," I say, "I really need to know what you're doing here. Otherwise, I'll have to call the police."

"Careful with the tone, kid," she says. "This business is all about likability. But call the police if you must and I'll read them your letter."

"What letter?"

Her smile widens until it hooks over her ears. "The one responding to our ad in *Teen Nation.*"

Oh, *that* letter. "But that was months ago."

"One month, actually. Rememberhowtheshowworks?"

"No. And can you speak a little slower, please?"

Judy calls to Bob, who's trudging toward Mozart in dirty boots, "You'd better catch this." He trains his lens on me again, and she continues: "Kendra Bishop, you are going to sunny California to trade places with another frustrated teenager!"

The sound guy jabs the microphone at me again, but I don't know what to say.

"Give Judy a reaction, honey," Judy says. "Tell us how this news makes you feel."

"I can't go to California," I say. "I'm taking music theory class this summer. And economics. Plus I've got math camp."

"Sounds like we got here just in time!"

My brain buzzes like a trapped fly until I see an escape

route: "My parents would never let me go."

"Just leave your parents to Judy," she says. "I'm going to bust you out of here." She jerks her chin at Mozart. "No pun intended. You were so right about this place, KB. It's a mausoleum."

"I said museum." At least, I think I did. I barely remember the letter.

"Close enough. How long till your folks are back?"

"Maybe half an hour."

"Perfect. Just go about your normal business. Pretend we're not even here."

"Sure, I'll just kick back with a soda while you guys destroy my living room."

"Ha! You're spunky, I like that. Spunky gets ratings." She signals Bob to get another shot of me and studies my image on a portable television monitor. "Hair's a little dull, KB. Ever think about highlights?"

Of course I think about highlights. My hair used to be nearly white, but it gets darker every year and will soon match my parents' nondescript beige. "I'm not allowed. I can't get my ears pierced either."

She snorts. "Start packing, kid, it's time for a jailbreak. And listen, what's a producer gotta do to get a drink around here?"

After putting on a pot of coffee for the crew, I grab the phone and duck into the breakfast nook.

"Lucy, it's me," I whisper when my best friend picks up. "I'm in so much trouble. There's a camera crew in the living room."

"A camera crew?" she asks. "What for?"

"I wrote this letter and I've been chosen to be on this show and I can't and I don't know what to do. I've got to get them out of here before my parents get back." There is no air left in my lungs. My chest feels concave.

"Calm down," she says. "You're talking so fast I can barely understand you."

"You should hear Judy."

"Who's Judy?" Lucy is mystified.

"The producer on the show. It's called *The Black Sheep*."

"Hey, I read about that," she says. "I can't believe you get to be on it."

"My parents are more likely to send me up on the next space shuttle."

There's a pause on the other end of the phone and then, "True. So why did you write the letter?"

"It was just after Rosa left."

"Uh-oh." Lucy refers to this period as the time I "went dark." Despite her constant calls and instant messages, I didn't surface for seven days—the longest we've gone without contact ever. "Now what are you going to do?"

"I don't know. The crew's wrecking the place. Someone threw his jacket over Mozart."

Lucy laughs. "Breaking Rule Number . . . ?"

"Twenty-five: *Respect the Art.* My parents are going to kill me, Luce. I'm going to try to sneak out before—"

A bright light hits me in the face as Judy, Bob, and his camera join me in the breakfast nook.

Judy takes the phone out of my hand. "Lucy, am I right?" she asks. "It's Judy! KB told us all about you in her letter. We'd love to meet you. Come on over and we'll grab a few shots of you helping her pack. Great! See you soon!"

A guy wearing a headset is standing guard at my bedroom door while I make a show of packing. I know full well that this suitcase isn't going anywhere, but it's easier to stuff things into it than to argue with Judy. She's the one with the army.

"How about a little privacy?" I ask the guy.

When he turns his back, I grab my laptop computer, slip into the bathroom, and lock the door. My parents will be home in fifteen minutes, and although Lucy lives only half a block away, I know she'll take time to dress for the cameras. I have to think of a way out of this myself.

Obviously I can't go to California tomorrow. I'd miss the last two days of school. Besides, even if my parents agreed, I don't want to be on some lame reality show—especially if it means moving in with people I've never met. What was I thinking?

Sitting down on the edge of the tub, I flip open the laptop and scroll through my files until I find the letter.

Dear Black Sheep Producers:

Please choose me to be on your show. If you do, you will be rescuing me from the Manhattan Banker Duplication Program. My parents—bankers, did you guess?—are the co-presidents. They're not horrible or any-thing, but they are pretty weird. For starters:

• They look alike. They both have short, mousy hair and gray eyes. From behind, you can only tell them apart because Mom jacks up her hair with product.

• They run marathons. Over and over again. How many times do you have to prove a point?

• They have no friends. They say it's because they value their privacy; I say it's because they're antisocial.

• Their idea of a great family vacation is to visit golf resorts. Without me.

• They never argue. In fact, they barely speak. They're like the three-year-old twins next door who have their own form of language based on meaningful looks and monosyllables. A couple can be too close, if you ask me.

• They're obsessive and controlling. Yes, all parents make rules but how many keep a binder and update it constantly? I call it *The Binder of Limitations and Harassment*, or *The BLAH*. There are rules about what I can

wear (no ultra low-rise jeans, no short
tops, no cleavage), what I can do to my body
(no piercings, no body art, no dye jobs),
and who I can date (as if I don't have
enough strikes against me, going to a girls'
school and being a virtual prisoner except
for approved activities). It's like an Amish
settlement, only with more rules.

• They're workaholics. That's why Rosa,
my nanny, moved in when I was born. Someone
had to be around to enforce *The BLAH*.

• They're worrywarts. Mom frets if my
mind isn't being fertilized constantly, and
she's always enrolling me in classes. She
calls this "enrichment," and its goal is to
foster an international banking career.
Flute lessons make the cut only because
musical training apparently promotes excel-
lence in math.

Dad frets if I'm not active. He's been
trying to convince me to run for years, but
I've held out so far. "Marathons build char-
acter," he says. "You learn to set goals and
build capacity until you can achieve them."

Build capacity? My parents are such
banker-nerds they have dollar signs where
their pupils should be.

Still, even bankers need something to
talk about at client dinners, so Mom packs
her few free hours with culture. On the

third Sunday of every month—I call it
Torture Day—we have a mother-daughter bonding trip to the Met, followed by a quiz over
tea and scones. With my parents, everything
is "on the test."

Each morning, including weekends, Mom
prints out a schedule that breaks my day
into half-hour slots. (I've enclosed one in
case you don't believe me.) The "Comments"
column is for Rosa, and the reason it's
blank is because my parents recently fired
her. They didn't use the word "fired."
Rather, they said they were "downsizing" and
would "outsource" her duties to cleaning
and catering services. They offered her "a
package." That this happened right after
they learned Rosa was secretly giving me
"downtime" during educational slots was
purely coincidental, I'm sure. "Fun" is not
in my parents' vocabulary.

"You're fifteen," Mom said. "You don't
need a nanny anymore."

But Rosa wasn't just a nanny, she was the
only one standing between me and complete
banker domination.

"We can direct her salary into enrichment,"
Mom said.

Any more enrichment and my head will
explode.

"We'll come home a little earlier,

and cut back on running," Mom said.

They didn't. I ate my catered meals alone and went to bed alone. And less than a week after Rosa left, I found two entry forms for the Toronto Marathon on the hall table. My parents are so desperate to avoid me they're crossing borders.

Obviously, they shouldn't have had a kid. In fact, I think I was an "accident." Rosa didn't deny it when I asked her. She pursed her lips the same way she did every time she looked at my schedule and then gave me a big hug. The last time Mom hugged me was four years ago, before my first trip to math camp.

If my parents had been more careful about birth control, they could have directed their child-rearing budget into technology. They like computers, probably because they're reliable and you can upgrade them regularly. I'm less dependable. Although I mostly get good grades, I have to work my butt off and sometimes my system crashes for no reason.

Don't get me wrong, it's not like I'm starved or beaten or anything, and I know that from the outside it probably looks like I have it pretty good. But isn't a kid sup- posed to have some say in what happens to her? Isn't she allowed to "just say no" to

banking if she wants to? Aren't cults
illegal in this country?

And so it goes for another six pages. It's ugly. In fact, it's like a volcano erupted and spewed lava all over the keyboard. I remember how much better I felt after I wrote it. What I should have done—it's perfectly clear now—was obey Rule Number Four. I could have so easily hit SAVE rather than PRINT. Instead, I acted before I thought about it, and now I'll be in lockdown until college.

I broke the same rule again today, which is why Judy is standing outside my bathroom door spitting out an indecipherable question at high speed.

"I'm not feeling well," I say. It's a good answer to any question and also true.

"Nerves," she says. "Do you have the runs?"

That I can decipher, as I'm sure Bob can, too. "Just an upset stomach."

"Come out and we'll talk about your new family. That'll make you feel better."

I'm surprised at how quickly I've picked up her fast-talking. Enrichment must have given me an ear for languages. "I doubt it."

"You're buried alive here, KB. But never fear, Judy's going to dig you out."

Or if that doesn't work, maybe she can just stun me with her shovel.

* * *

"Bob, zoom in on the knob turning," Judy barks. Then she snaps her fingers at the young guy with the wild red hair who threw his jacket over Mozart. "Chili, get a wide shot."

The door opens and my parents stand blinking in the spotlight. They are built like greyhounds—long, lean, and muscular. Mom's hair is slightly ruffled from the wind; Dad's is as stiff as a hairpiece, although I'm pretty sure it's real. They look at each other and for once I understand exactly what they're thinking: what the hell is going on here?

Judy doesn't keep them in suspense for long. She introduces herself with a Donkey smile and tells them about *The Black Sheep*. Then she announces, "Your daughter has been chosen from ten thousand entries to trade places with a teenager in California for a month."

My parents' mouths open in unison, say "No," and snap closed. They cross their arms over their chests, a gesture that might be impressive if they weren't wearing matching tank tops.

I start backing down the hall toward my bedroom, but Bob turns to pin me in a circle of light. Chili stays focused on my parents, and a third crew member covers Judy.

She waits until her camera is rolling before opening a folder and producing a stack of pages covered in pink highlighter. "Let me read you KB's letter," she says.

"That's *Kendra*," my mother interrupts.

"Of course," Judy says. "I think when you hear what

Kendra had to say, you'll agree that some time away will do her good." She reads several paragraphs—the worst ones— aloud.

My mother gasps when Judy reaches the part about the Met. "Torture Day? I thought you loved that."

Judy pats my mother's arm. "Now, now. Every family has communication problems."

At the end of the letter, all eyes turn to me expectantly. I stare at the floor and mutter, "I didn't mean it the way it sounds."

"Speak up, honey," Judy commands. "Are you saying you lied?"

"I was mad when I wrote it, that's all."

"More like heartbroken." She signals Bob to get a close-up of the letter. "There are tearstains on the page."

That's almost as bad as suggesting I have the runs. I am not one of those girls who cry for no reason. "It's Sprite," I protest.

She wraps an arm around my shoulders. "That's your pride talking, kiddo. Are you telling Judy you don't want a vacation in California?"

I keep expecting my parents to toss Judy and her army out of the house, but they seem to be paralyzed. Sweat is dripping down my father's face, and my normally pale mother is flushed. "I'm telling you I didn't really think it through."

"That letter came straight from the heart," Judy insists. "I cried like a baby when I read it, and so will the rest of

America. That's how I knew we'd found our girl. This fine nation loves an underdog, and you can't beat a lonely child in search of love."

"I'm not a child," I say. "And I'm not lonely."

"You haven't been hugged in four years," she says, promptly hugging me.

I wriggle out of her grasp. "I have, just not by them." I point at my parents, willing them to take charge, but they continue to stand there on stick legs, silent, bland, and beige.

Judy continues as if I haven't spoken. "You need a break. And fortunately, there's another unhappy teenager who needs a break, too."

She tells us about Maya Mulligan, a fifteen-year-old from Monterey, who has written an equally long letter to complain about her family. Maya says her parents are hippies who are into saving the planet and leaving a "small footprint." Whatever that means. She wants to experience life in Manhattan with a "normal" family.

"Normal?" I ask. "You'd better keep looking, Judy."

"Normal is all in the eye of the beholder," she says. "And as a contestant on *The Black Sheep*, you'll have a chance to see that for yourself."

My father finally finds his voice. "Our daughter is not spending a month with beatniks."

"Why not?" I ask, although I don't even want to go. "I'd be back before you even noticed I was gone."

"Kendra," my mother says, "enough."

"I'm just communicating," I say. "Unlike you two, I actually like to talk. I'm sorry if it embarrasses you."

"Atta girl," Judy says. "Let it out." I notice that her head is twitching repeatedly to the right, and I wonder if it's a nervous tic. Then I realize she's signaling Chili to zoom in on my parents' reaction. "Your daughter is telling you that she's miserable."

My parents exchange a meaningful glance, and Dad asks, "Are you miserable, Kendra?"

I waver for a moment before pulling my punch. "Not *all* the time."

Judy wraps an arm around each of my parents. "Ken. Deedee." Mom opens her mouth to protest but Judy picks up speed. "I know how tough it is to raise a teenager today, but it's obvious that you've hit a roadblock here. Kendra deserves to experience a family that has time to spend with her. She needs to explore her own interests. Do you have any interests, Kendra?"

I think about it for a moment. "I like to play the flute— or at least I don't hate it. And I, uh, like to shop." Then I shrug to let her know I'm out of ideas.

"I rest my case. Your daughter's growing up without a personality to call her own."

"Hey!" I have a personality. Whose side is she on, any-way?

Silencing me, Judy continues. "Here's your chance to do

right by Kendra and give another kid a break in the process."

My parents shake their heads as one.

"Why not?" I ask again. "This Maya might actually like living in a museum."

"What are you afraid of?" Judy asks my parents. "That you'll lose Kendra forever? The truth is, letting her go is probably the only way to keep her."

My mother's mouth twitches, and I think for a moment that she's going to laugh. Dad drapes an arm around her and turns to Judy. "Please collect your gear and go. You'll be responsible for any damages to the furniture."

Judy backpedals quickly. "Think of *The Black Sheep* as a student exchange program. It's a developmental opportunity for Kendra and for poor Maya, who longs for all you have to offer here." She points at the wall. "Maya has never seen a Monet."

"Matisse," I say.

"It's just a print," Mom says. Her voice sounds faint and faraway. She leans around Bob to get a good look at me. "Is this really what you want, Kendra?"

Now that she's opening the door, I'm not sure I want to walk through it.

Judy saves me the trouble of deciding. "Of course it's what she wants. It's the opportunity of a lifetime."

Dad says, "I'll need to know more about these Mulligans. Are they professors?"

"Not exactly," Judy says, "but they're upstanding

citizens." She snaps her fingers at a man in a suit. "Stan, our attorney, will tell you all about them."

Stan leads my parents to the stack of permission forms on the desk.

"Wait a second," I say. "I haven't said I'll go."

Judy hands me an envelope containing a plane ticket. "Finish packing, kiddo. The limo will be here early."

"But—"

"I know you're scared, but don't worry. Judy will be holding your hand every step of the way." The doorbell rings. "Lucy, I presume?"

Chili trains his camera on Lucy, who smiles and waves as she steps into the house. As I suspected, she dressed up for the occasion in white jeans and a halter top.

The army packs up and disperses. Finally Judy hugs me again and heads for the door. "See you tomorrow, KB."

I wait for my mother to correct Judy, but she doesn't. Instead, she steps aside as Chili dashes back into the apartment to pluck his jacket from Mozart's head.

Chapter 2

In the arrivals area of the San Francisco airport, a group of people waves a sign at me. Fluffing my hair nervously, I hurry toward them, only to discover that the sign reads, WELCOME, FERGUS. There's no way I look like a Fergus, even from a distance.

It's the latest in a series of disappointments today. First, my parents didn't come to see me off because they had to pick up Maya Mulligan at another airport. Then, my hopes of being seated next to a hot guy fizzled when a middle-aged nun in street clothes sat down beside me. She didn't admit she was a nun until halfway through the flight, and I spent the next half trying to remember whether I'd said anything offensive. And finally, no one, not even the nun, showed the slightest interest in why I was flying alone. I may not be thrilled about participating in *The Black Sheep*, but it's the most exciting event of my life so far.

Deciding it's better to look nonchalant when the Mulligans arrive, I turn to find a seat. A now-familiar light assaults me.

"Welcome to California!" Judy says. Today she's West Coast casual, in jeans, a white T-shirt with a fuzzy black sheep on the front, and flip-flops.

"What are you doing here?" I ask, too tired to be polite. Lucy called me at 4:45 A.M. to make sure I was up. As if I could sleep when I was about to fly across the country to live with strangers. I've never been away from home for a month before and Judy has the option of extending my stay to six weeks.

"Is that any way to greet your peeps?" Judy says, signaling Bob to walk backward ahead of us as she leads me to a bench. "You'll have to get used to the bright lights, kiddo: the eyes of the nation will soon be upon you."

The eyes of many people in this lounge already are. They're gathering in clumps and staring, wondering whether I'm "somebody." I shake my head to let them know I'm not. "Where are the Mulligans?" I ask Judy.

She shoves a bystander out of the way. "Don't worry, they'll be here. And listen, KB, we'll have to discuss your wardrobe. Some colors and patterns don't work on camera. Your red T-shirt is pulsing."

I wonder if it's my racing heart that she sees through my T-shirt. She presses my shoulder until I drop onto a bench and then shows me the portable monitor. On the screen, my T-shirt appears to be dancing.

Judy turns to her army and shouts, "Tess, we've got some shine here!"

A woman I didn't notice yesterday comes at me with a powder puff. "Oh, no," she says. "She's breaking out."

Leaning in to inspect me, Judy says, "No worries. Viewers won't get past her pulsing T-shirt anyway."

The crew laughs, like they laugh at all of Judy's jokes. I, however, refuse to suck up to her, especially since the jokes are at my expense. Rosa was always after me to stand up for myself, and there's no time like the present to start trying. "Excuse me," I say, rising with dignity. "I'm going to the restroom."

"Not now," Tess says. "The Mulligans will be here any minute."

"You can't tell me when I can use the restroom," I protest. But the crew closes in to block my exit, and I realize that for the next month, they intend to control my bladder and the rest of me, too. Panic begins to flutter in my chest. "Let me go."

Judy snaps her fingers and the crowd parts.

So much for showing them who's boss.

"Kendra, what is it about you and restrooms?" I peer under the cubicle wall and see Judy's flip-flops outside my stall. There's no spotlight, so I guess her sidekicks actually respect the gender barrier. "Any health problems I should know about?"

"I want to go home," I say.

"Come on, where's your sense of adventure?" she asks.

"Your letter said you were dying for something to happen in your life. Now it has."

It's true that I crave adventure, but I was thinking more along the lines of bumping into Prince William in Hyde Park while my parents ran the London Marathon.

Judy moves over to the sink and washes her hands. "Think about the stories you'll be able to tell when you're back at school," she says. "No one will have anything on you. Judy's going to make you a star."

"I don't want to be a star."

"Everyone wants to be a star."

"Not me," I say. "I just wanted more independence and to have some fun."

"Well, think of all the fun you can have with twenty-five thousand dollars. That's how much each family will receive when the show ends."

"Really?" That's a lot of money. No wonder my parents agreed to participate.

"Really," Judy says. "Although, Maya will ultimately decide how your family spends the money."

Naturally. There's always a catch.

"And you'll get to decide how the Mulligans spend theirs," she says.

Whoopie.

"Plus, you get to keep the eight hundred dollars a week you earn, and spend it any way you like."

Now she's talking. Even if we only go four weeks, I'd

earn over three grand, which would finance a lot of trips to Sephora.

"See, it's all good, KB," Judy continues. "The Mulligans are a blast. And your parents are going to see the show and realize how grown-up you are. When you're back in New York, they'll give you more freedom."

"You don't know my parents."

"I know how all parents think," she says. "Once you've proven you can survive without them, they always loosen the reins."

That does make sense. "Are you sure?"

"Trust me," she says.

I open the stall door, and Judy is right in front of me, every tooth on display. She ushers me out of the washroom and dismisses the crew with a flick of her fingers. Setting her shoulder bag on a bench, she sits down and pats the place beside her.

"Take a moment to regroup," she says, rifling through her bag.

"I hear what you're saying. I'll use this time to prove to my parents that I'm mature enough to make my own decisions."

She brushes my hair back over my shoulder. "They'll be amazed at your transformation."

Up close, her smile is terrifying, but it's not her fault she has such big teeth. And it's nice that she's being supportive.

She continues to fiddle with something in her bag until there's a flash of bluish white light.

"Is that a camera?" I ask, stunned.

"Of course it's a camera," she says, plucking a tiny camcorder out of her bag and switching it off. "You're on a reality show. How do you think they get made?"

"But this was supposed to be a private moment."

She stands and pulls her shades down over her eyes. "Say good-bye to those, kid. You're public property now."

"But . . ."

"Enough whining, Kendra. America loves a sweetheart."

I stare at her, realizing that I'm in deeper than I thought. "I can't do this, Judy."

"Excuse me?"

"I can't go through with it. I'm sorry. You've got the wrong girl."

She pulls a stack of papers out of her bag and makes a show of examining them. "Nope, that's your name on the contract. Judy's definitely got the right girl."

A dilapidated, powder-blue van covered in decals pulls up in front of the terminal. I only have time to read two of them—SAVE OUR SOUTHERN SEA OTTERS and OIL: THE SPILL THAT KILLS—before the sliding door on the side creaks open and people start pouring out.

"Bob," Judy says, "close-up on the Mulligans. Chili, you cover Kendra."

A woman wearing a beret over long, graying hair wraps

her arms around me and nearly crushes my rib cage. "You must be Kendra," she says.

"Nice to meet you, Mrs. Mulligan," I say, when she pulls away.

"Call me Mona," she says. "No one calls me Mrs. Mulligan—especially because my last name is Perlman. I never married Max, you know." She turns to smile at a balding, paunchy man who has a large octopus tattoo on his forearm. "I like to keep him on his toes."

Max shakes my hand. "We don't need a piece of paper to prove we're meant for each other. Been together thirty-eight years."

"Thirty-eight?" I ask. "You're kidding." They look old, but not *that* old.

Mona laughs. "We were barely teenagers when we met at the Monterey Pop Festival in '67. It was the Summer of Love that never ended."

"We've got six kids to prove it," Max adds, giving his wife's bottom an affectionate slap.

"Daddy, please," says a skinny girl of about ten who's standing behind them holding a baby on one hip. Next to her, identical twin boys of about seven peer at me shyly.

Mona says, "Sorry we're late, Kendra. Max was snaking out someone's pipes. He's the most popular guy in the neighborhood."

"Everyone loves a plumber," Max says, starting to herd everyone into the van.

I hang back, but Judy prods me with her pitchfork. My eyes are riveted by Mona's outfit—a tie-dyed blouse and long skirt over Birkenstocks. I don't think she's wearing a bra, and after six kids she should be.

She points to the little pin on her chest. "I see you've noticed my otter. I'm obsessed with them."

"It's so pathetic," the girl says.

"Meadow, hush," Mona says, settling into the passenger seat.

With Judy propelling me forward, I climb into the rear seat and take the only spot available—on an exposed spring between Meadow and one of the twins. The baby is sitting on Meadow's lap.

"Shouldn't he be in a car seat?" I ask, fumbling for my seat belt. My search turns up a couple of dog biscuits, which the baby promptly grabs. Meadow doesn't even try to stop him from shoving one into his mouth.

Mona calls from up front. "He'll be fine, dear. Max has never had an accident."

The rest of the crew piles into a second van bearing the *Black Sheep* logo, but Judy joins us, sitting in the middle seat beside the other twin. She winks at me before raising the camcorder to her eye. I scowl back at her.

"Likability, KB," she says.

I don't care if America likes me. I may have a contractual obligation to be here, but ratings are Judy's problem, not mine. She's got her work cut out for her, because I can already tell this show is totally predictable. They're going to dump the Manhattan girl into a hillbilly shack and watch her squirm. Or maybe we'll all live out of the van.

Meadow plops the baby onto my knee. "This is Egg," she says.

I balance the rubbery little thing on my lap for a few polite moments before trying to slide him back to Meadow.

"You don't like babies, Kendra?" Judy asks, swinging her camcorder to catch the family's horrified reaction.

"Of course I like babies," I lie. "Mona, your grandson is very cute."

Everyone laughs uproariously until Mona finally gasps, "Egg isn't our grandson, dear, he's our son."

"I'm so sorry," I say, horrified at my gaffe.

"Don't be," Max says, not offended in the slightest. "We started late."

"After we got tired of trying to change the world," Mona adds.

"Egg is an unusual name," I say, to change the subject.

"It's really Milo, but we call him 'Last Egg' for fun," Mona explains. "I thought I was starting menopause but somehow Egg slipped in under the wire."

Max gives Mona's thigh a squeeze. "Remember where it happened, sweetie?"

The twins answer for her: "The Save the Cormorant rally in Santa Cruz."

Meadow flushes and says, "Don't talk about that on camera."

"Oh, honey, relax," Mona says. "The moment of conception is something to be celebrated. If you're in a committed relationship, that is. Why, I remember exactly where we were when you—"

"I know," Meadow interrupts, exasperated. "The anti-sonar protest near Mendocino."

Mona turns in her seat to grin at me. "Happens every time we're at a tent rally. Something about all those people coming together for a cause."

"I don't get it," one of the twins says.

Judy trains her lens on me as I silently pray they'll resist the urge to explain the facts of life to their son. I didn't learn them from my own parents and I don't want to hear them now. That's what television is for.

After a pause, Max says, "We'll talk about it at home, son."

I sigh with relief, and Judy's mouth forms a huge crescent under her camcorder. There must be more than the standard thirty-two teeth in there.

Meadow stares at me, unblinking, until I raise my eyebrows at her.

"How come you're so skinny?" she asks.

"I'm not skinny," I say. I am slim. And I might even be muscular if I ever lifted anything heavier than a cell phone.

"You're skinnier than me," she says. "And I'm only ten."

I am not skinnier than a ten-year-old. And why isn't someone telling her she's rude? Rosa would have escorted me to my room by my ear if I'd spoken to a guest like that. Judy, of course, is loving every minute of it.

"Can I try on your watch?" Meadow asks.

"Sure," I say. Anything to shut her up. I slip it over her wrist, and Egg immediately clamps his mouth on it. "You can keep it for now."

By the time we pull into the Mulligans' driveway, it's almost dark, thanks to an unexpected delay on the side of the highway after the van died. Max, who seems to be more talented with drains than carburetors, took his sweet time to fix it.

Judy didn't mind at all. We could have flown into the Monterey airport in the first place, but she was anxious to document our "honeymoon drive." She's spent so much time leaning in for close-ups of me that, if there's any justice in the world, her neck will seize up tomorrow.

Happily, the Mulligan house looks normal enough. It's not the beachfront cottage I'd initially hoped for, but it's not the rundown shack I'd feared, either. Rather, it's a tan stucco two-story on a quiet cul-de-sac. Toys are scattered across the front lawn, and a dog is barking inside.

Meadow and the twins, Matt and Mason, surge ahead of us into the house, and Max follows with Egg and my suitcase. Mona drags me into her front garden. "It's my pride and joy," she says, kicking a soccer ball out of a flower bed.

"If only you'd been here a little earlier in the season. My tulips are cups of light."

Cups of light? I may throw up before I make it into the house. Seeing as Judy is recording this moment for America, however, I make appropriate gurgles of admiration. It turns out to be good training for keeping a straight face once we go inside, where all resemblance to normal ends. An upended rowboat forms the hall closet and there's a mural of whales covering two walls of the living room.

"Max is an artist as well as a plumber," Mona says, leading me into a room that must have been a dining room once, but is now a very messy office. "Welcome to Save Our Sea Otter Central Command."

Our grand tour skips the room I most want to see: my bedroom. I finally ask about it, but Mona is too distracted by kitschy artifacts to answer. "This is the otter cushion Maya bought me with her babysitting money," she says.

She yanks me aside as a large dog barrels toward us in pursuit of a small silver creature.

"A rat!" I yell, leaping onto the closest chair.

Bob zooms in on my terrified expression. "Chili thought so too," he says. "He nearly fainted."

"It's not a rat, dear, it's Maya's ferret," Mona says, helping me down.

The ferret arches and hisses, his tail sticking straight up like a bottle brush. The dog backs up until his wagging tail swipes a glass otter off the coffee table. It shatters on the floor.

"Not another one," Mona sighs, pushing the shards away with her foot as the ferret scrambles onto a bookshelf. "He's a troublemaker, but Maya adores Manhattan."

It takes me a second to clue in. "That's the ferret's name?"

Mona nods. "Maya's been dreaming of visiting New York for years."

"There are a lot of M-names around here," I say.

Delighted that I noticed, Mona says, "It's our thing. You know—how every family has its thing?"

Mine doesn't have a thing. Unless you count the rules.

Manhattan deliberately brushes against my shoulder from the shelf. With Meadow now standing beside me grinning, I try not to squeal. My mother claims to have allergies, so I've never had a regular pet, let alone an exotic one.

"Wow, Manhattan usually isn't that nice," Meadow says. "He has Maya's personality."

Mona clucks disapprovingly and leads us through the kitchen and out the patio doors. As I emerge, more than two dozen people yell, "Surprise!" Stretched between two trees is a banner reading, WELCOME, KENDRA, OUR BLACK SHEEP!

Although I'm embarrassed at having so many eyes upon me, I can't help but smile. I've never had a surprise party before.

And a party it is. The barbecue is smoking, the stereo is cranked, and there are two picnic tables covered in salads and a huge array of the snack foods I never get to eat at home. Soon I am feeling so much better about this whole adventure that I barely grumble when Tess jumps out from behind a shrub to powder my blemish. Bob and Chili are too busy clear-cutting the table to bother capturing the moment.

Judy comes toward me with a girl about my age. "This is Carrie Watson," she says. "Maya's best friend. She lives next door."

It occurs to me that someone may be introducing Lucy to Maya in New York right now. I don't know whether to be happy, because Lucy can tell me all about her, or jealous. They'd better not hit it off.

Carrie offers me a soda and waits until Judy is out of earshot before saying, "Maya and I aren't best friends anymore. She hasn't wanted to hang out for a while."

"Why not?" I ask. Carrie seems nice to me. She's dark and pretty in a sporty way, and her denim capris and lululemon hoodie reassure me that Monterey isn't some remote outpost beyond the reach of fashion.

Meadow pulls her head out of the Cheetos bowl long enough to answer. "Because Maya's a bitch."

Mona appears out of nowhere. "Now, Meadow. Maya's been frustrated lately, that's all. She'll come back from New York her old self."

"Don't count on it," Meadow says.

"I'm so sorry, girls," Mona says, towing Meadow away.

"This is what happens when I let them eat junk food. Normally we have a very healthy house."

Another hope dashed. "Is Maya really that bad?" I ask Carrie, piling Cheetos onto my plate while I have the chance.

Carrie nods. "But Mitch makes up for it. He's sweet."

"Who's Mitch?"

"Maya's older brother. He's hot, too."

"Really." I toss my Cheetos into the trash. A hot older brother is so much better than junk food.

"Yeah, but he's pissed about the whole *Black Sheep* thing. He asked my brother if he could stay at our place while you're here, but the Mulligans refused. He's boycotting the barbecue, though."

Well, that's just great. I've driven a sweet, hot guy out of his own house before he's even met me. "It won't be so bad," I say. "The crew is really nice." The lie sticks in my throat with the Cheeto dust.

"Mitch will come around," she says. "It's got to be easier than living with Maya."

I squeeze her arm to silence her because I notice that Judy and Bob have crept up to record our conversation. Carrie's mouth forms a perfect O as she realizes what she's just told America.

Turning to Judy, I ask, "You can edit Carrie's comments, can't you?"

She shakes her head. "The neighbors signed waivers."

"But Carrie didn't realize, and she has to live here after we're gone," I insist. "Can't you give her one free pass?"

Judy rolls her eyes at Bob. "Free passes don't equal good ratings, KB."

I switch off the lamp on the bedside table, and it immediately flicks back on. Now I fully understand why Maya is A) a bitch, and B) sleeping in my bedroom (with *en suite* bathroom) in Manhattan right now.

Meadow is staring at me from the other twin bed. "I'm not tired yet," she says.

"Well, I am. It's been a really long day."

I click off the light again, pull the homemade quilt under my chin, and try to relax. I'm a little nervous in this house. Even this late at night, there are distant rustling sounds. And it smells of . . . people. Not unpleasant, necessarily, but lived-in.

There's a soft thud as something lands on the bed. I scream, and Meadow turns the light on. "Relax, it's just Manhattan."

The little beast puts two paws on my stomach and stares at me with shiny brown eyes. "Can you get him off me?"

Meadow shakes her head. "He always sleeps with Maya. If we shut him out, he'll just scratch on the door." She switches off the light again.

The ferret steps onto my chest and stands there for a few moments, confirming the location of my jugular. Eventually he turns a few times and settles down. Pretending to be asleep. Waiting.

Meadow's voice comes out of the darkness. "Kendra?"

"What?"

"Can I borrow your jeans tomorrow?"

"They wouldn't fit you, Meadow."

"Sure they would. I'm as big as you. And I can roll up the legs."

I grit my teeth. "I'll think about it. Now go to sleep."

She's quiet for a few minutes and then, "Kendra?

"Yeah?"

"What are your parents like?"

I consider for a moment. "Busy. They work a lot. They run marathons."

"But are they nice?"

That's a good question. I don't know the answer to it. "I guess so."

"Will they be nice to Maya?"

I reach over to turn the light on, careful not to disturb the ferret, who's curled in a tight disk. "Are you worried about your sister?"

Meadow wrinkles her nose in disdain. "No."

"She'll be fine. I'm sure she's sound asleep right now, and I bet she likes my bedroom."

"She'd better not get any ideas about staying there."

I smile at her. "I thought you said she's a bitch."

"But that doesn't mean I want her to go for good."

"Don't worry, she'll be back before you know it." I switch the light off.

"Kendra?"

"Now what?"

"Have you had your period yet?"

"I'm fifteen, what do you think?"

"I heard that if you're too skinny, you won't get it."

"You'll get it. And it's no big thrill, believe me."

"Do you have a boyfriend?"

"Not right now," I say. No need to tell her the truth, which is that with the Secretaries of Defense on duty, I hardly ever meet guys, let alone go out with them. So far, the closest I've come is with Jason, a guy I met in music history last year. Rosa let me go to Starbucks with him after class, but for reasons of job security, she sat at another table—close enough to hear me scream for help, but far enough away that I had the illusion of independence.

We did this for a few weeks and Jason never knew we had a chaperone. Finally, at the exact moment he officially asked me out, I realized that I didn't even like him because all he ever talked about was himself. Rosa sensed the change instantly. She walked over to the door, pulled her cell phone out of her bag, and called mine. I picked up and she said, "Tell him you really like him as a friend, but you're not interested in him *that* way. Then excuse yourself."

Having my nanny coach me on how to dump a guy doesn't rank among my proudest moments, but it worked.

Meadow flicks the light on and props herself on one elbow. "Have you ever kissed a boy?"

I flick the light off. "You're not supposed to ask people questions like that."

"Maya has," she says into the darkness. "Lots of times."

"Well, that's nice for Maya."

"You haven't, I can tell. Mom says I can read minds."

"Yeah? What's my mind telling you right now?"

"Fine," she says, sounding miffed. "I'll go to sleep. But just remember, I can make or break your stay here."

I snort and roll over onto my side—gently, though, so that Manhattan slides off me and onto the bed without even waking.

That's when I notice the red eye of the camera gleaming from the corner above the door. It keeps me awake long after Meadow's chatter finally ceases.

Chapter 3

I'm barely out of the shower when Mona knocks on the door. "Kendra? I hate to rush you, but Max needs to get into the bathroom. He's going to be late."

"Could he use another one?" I ask, toweling off. "I just got started here." Judging from the fur growing on her legs, Mona has no clue how long it takes to pull a polished look together.

"There's only one, and it's a popular place in the morning," she says. "Remember I pointed out the roster? Everyone gets fifteen minutes. I'm afraid you're running over."

"Sorry," I call to Mona. "I'll be right out." I hope I didn't sound all uptown-snob there, but it never occurred to me they'd only have one bathroom. Max is a plumber: he should spend less time Saving Our Sea Otters and more on the bathroom crisis in his own home. Had I realized, I wouldn't have wasted half my allotted time on a security sweep to see if Judy had installed tiny cameras in the showerhead or toilet tissue roll.

Throwing my pajamas back on, I hurry down the hall to the bedroom. Though Meadow was sound asleep when I left, she managed to get up and out while I was gone. At ten, I probably wasn't concerned about personal grooming either. Now, as Maya's mirror verifies, I need to be concerned. My limp, lifeless locks can only be salvaged with volumizer and a blow dryer, both of which I left behind in the bathroom.

Limp hair isn't my only challenge. I have my parents' dull gray eyes (although theirs are beady and mine are normal-size), and I'm prone to breaking out at the worst possible times, such as after learning that I'm starring in a reality show. Fortunately, I also have good bone structure and a nice smile. My parents came through there.

I wait a full twenty minutes before skulking back down the hall to the bathroom. The door is closed, but when I call Max's name, there's no answer.

I push the door open, step into the bathroom, and freeze. Standing in front of the sink brushing his teeth is a naked man. It isn't Max, unless Max has lost forty pounds and gained a full head of hair overnight. Nor is Max likely to have such pronounced tan lines.

By the time my eyes make the long climb from the guy's hip to his face, he's turned to stare at me in the mirror, toothbrush suspended in midair. It must be Mitch, I realize, because he's not much older than I am.

"Excuse me," I say, still frozen to the spot.

"Do you mind?" he asks through a mouthful of tooth-paste.

Keeping my eyes well above sea level, I reverse course until something blocks my exit. Make that some*one*: Judy.

"Morning, KB!" she says, flashing me a grin as she steps aside to give Bob a clear shot. "I see you've met Mitch."

"Not exactly."

She grabs a towel off the rack and tosses it to Mitch. "Put something on, cutie, this is a G-rated show."

He rinses his mouth before putting the towel on, and I sneak another look at the tan lines. I've never had the opportunity to examine the male form at such close range before, unless you count the marble sculptures at the Met.

"Bob, zoom in on Mitch, but stay off Kendra. She looks pretty rough today."

Mitch laughs, although he doesn't show any teeth. "It's nothing her make-up artist can't fix," he says.

"Tess has already gone back to L.A.," Judy says. "Poor Kendra's on her own from here on in."

I glare at Mitch. "When you've finished mocking me, maybe you could hand me my blow dryer."

"When you've finished invading my privacy, maybe you could close the door behind you," he says, handing it to me.

I turn to go, giving the door a good slam on my way out. It might have made a bigger statement to Mitch if Bob and Judy weren't still inside.

Mitch may be hot, but he's not sweet at all. And he's not

40

very bright, either, as those tan lines certainly prove. Melanoma is no laughing matter.

Mona is lifting slices of French toast out of a skillet when I come into the kitchen, and the crew is crowding around the counter, plates outstretched. Now I can see why they selected the Mulligans as my host family: Mona is used to feeding an army. The crew in New York is going to starve to death; my parents don't even know where the kitchen is.

Meadow, who is dipping the bread into the egg mixture, gives me a smug smile. She's wearing my jeans.

"What are you looking at?" she asks.

"The egg splatters on my jeans," I retort.

Mona turns to her daughter. "Did you take Kendra's jeans?"

The defiance on Meadow's face evaporates. "She said I could."

"I didn't say she couldn't," I say. "But I said they'd be too big, and they are."

Meadow snorts. "I didn't even need your belt."

"Don't push your luck," Mona tells her.

Noticing that Meadow's bony wrist is bare, I ask, "Has anyone seen my watch?"

The Mulligans look at each other before chiming, "Manhattan." It takes me a moment to realize they mean the ferret, not the city. Mona sends the twins to hunt for my watch in Manhattan's favorite hiding places. Then she offers me three slices of French toast.

Egg lets out a screech as I pass his high chair.

"How cute," Judy comments from the table. "The baby wants to say good morning. Give him a kiss, KB." She nods at Chili, who drops his fork and picks up his camera.

Egg's round face is covered with syrup and crusty bits. It's not an inviting prospect, but I feel obliged to lean over and plant my lips on the cleanest part of his cheek. He promptly grabs a clump of my hair and squeals with glee.

I squeal myself, but it isn't with glee. Meadow giggles until Mona shushes her. "Kendra isn't used to being around babies," she says, prying Egg's sticky fingers off my hair one by one. "I hear you met Mitch this morning, dear."

I dart a glance at Judy. "What did he say?"

"Nothing," Mona says. "Judy mentioned you ran into each other."

Judy winks to let me know she hasn't provided details, and kindly changes the subject. "So, what'll it be today, folks?"

"I thought we'd go sightseeing," Mona says. "What do you like to do, Kendra?"

Before I can answer, Meadow recommends a local amusement park.

It sounds all right to me, but Mona frowns. "We can do better than that. Kendra's here to learn about Monterey's history and discover our beautiful coastline. Let's take a hike."

The prospect of discovering the coastline with Mona, Meadow, the twins, Egg, and the entire crew in tow isn't very appealing. Besides, I've never been on a real hike. It sounds like work. As does the history lesson.

Judy suggests a bike ride instead. "You could check out Cannery Row and Fisherman's Wharf." I start to protest but then she adds the magic words: "There are stores."

That's different. Shopping is something my parents actually permit occasionally, because banker clones need to present well. In fact, before I left yesterday, my mother tucked a credit card into my hand "for emergencies." My favorite jeans are a mess, which constitutes a fashion emergency, if you ask me. "Sounds good," I say.

"A bike ride it is," Mona says. "But first our chores." She points to the roster on the refrigerator. "Kendra, you're taking over Maya's, which means you're on dish duty."

Chores? The whole point of this trip was to gain freedom, not more work. But it would be rude to complain. "Sure, where's the dishwasher?"

Mona puts the dishcloth in my hand and pats my back. "Right here."

Though normally in a tearing hurry, Judy has all the time in the world to shoot me cleaning up after the crew. Finally she cuts the camera and says, "Let's go, Cinderella."

I toss the dishcloth at her, but Bob gallantly reaches out and intercepts it.

* * *

I haven't been on a bike in a few years. Opportunities to ride are few and far between in New York. Dad, usually so anxious that I get proper exercise, is more anxious still about my risking death under a cab's tires. He's invested fifteen years in me and won't relax until I'm safely locked up in some office tower.

Maya looks normal enough in the family photos, but she must have an oversize cranium, because her bike helmet immediately tips forward and covers my face. Once Meadow stops laughing, she offers me hers and digs up another for herself. So not only do I have the physique of a ten-year-old, but I have a pinhead as well?

"Be grateful, KB," Judy says, sensing my thoughts. "It could have been Egg's."

I set off down the street without answering, and Meadow pedals madly after me with the twins. Mona brings up the rear, her genie pants billowing in the wind. Egg is in a seat on the back of her bike. Having been trained by my father, I follow standard safety rules, including using lame hand signals. The twins laugh so hard at this that they veer into traffic and Mona screams. As if we weren't causing enough of a commotion, what with Judy and the crew following in two white vans.

Roaring up beside me, Judy shouts, "Slow down and chat with Mona." She raises a walkie-talkie to her lips to communicate with the crew in the second van. "This is Wolf One to Wolf Two. Get a close-up of the mutton. I'm sending the lamb back there now. Over."

"What am I supposed to talk to Mona about? It's not like we have anything in common."

"Talk about anything. Be spontaneous."

I may know the hand signal for a left turn, but I suck at spontaneous. Plus, my last impulsive moment got me into this mess. Fortunately, I know Judy well enough by now to realize she has something specific in mind. "Give me some ideas."

"Ask her what she likes to do in her spare time," she prompts.

I let Mona catch up to me, and while Bob leans out of the van to capture the moment, I ask, "Do you have any hobbies, Mona?"

"Oh, yes, I love quilting," she puffs, pedaling hard to keep up. "And macramé. But I hardly have time for them anymore because of our work with SORAC."

"SORAC?"

She nods. "The Sea Otter Research and Conservation program at the Monterey Bay Aquarium. Southern sea otters were almost extinct at one time, and we're helping them fight their way back."

"Interesting," I say, although it's not. I'm open to learning about marine life, but only if it features cute guys on surfboards.

"The entire family is involved, even the little ones. Max is on several committees, I teach public education courses, and Mitch is a tracker."

"What does he keep track of?" I ask. How many house-guests he insults?

"Rehabilitated otters. After they're released to the wild, someone needs to keep an eye on them for a while to make sure they stay healthy. He's been doing it for years."

That doesn't sound like the jerk I met in the bathroom this morning. Someone in this family has a split personality. Or maybe he just prefers animals to humans.

"Anyway," Mona continues, "this is a cause dear to our hearts, and we're hoping you'll help out while you're here."

"Help *how?*" I ask suspiciously. I knew Judy had something up her sleeve. The Mulligans must be recruiting for SNORAC.

"For starters, I was thinking you might come to the aquarium tomorrow. I volunteered to work with some otters that got caught in an oil slick."

I ponder for a moment. "Do they bite?"

Meadow, now riding so close to me that we risk locking pedals, says, "Maya isn't afraid of anything."

I'll bet she's afraid of my parents.

Mona ignores Meadow. "Not to worry, you're too young to handle the wildlife anyway. What we really need is help cleaning out the kennels."

"I have plans for tomorrow." I respond.

Judy shouts from the van, "Yeah, plans to clean kennels."

So much for spontaneity.

* * *

By the time we reach Fisherman's Wharf, our party of six has become a virtual parade. Over a dozen kids have joined us en route, attracted by the cameras.

Noticing that I'm at the center of the action, someone asks, "Hey, are you making a movie?"

Meadow saves me the trouble of answering. "We're starring in a reality show called *The Black Sheep.*"

We?

The kid races around to tell everyone else. Some pull out cell phones to call their friends.

Judy herds everyone out of the way, explaining that this is supposed to look like a *natural family outing.*

"Please. You called in the whole crew to capture our arrival," I say. "There's nothing natural about it."

"Natural doesn't make for good TV," she agrees. "Television shows need structure and a story line."

"What's my story line?" I ask, a little worried.

She smiles enigmatically. "It's evolving as we go. I'm hoping you'll get off your butt and do something interesting."

"Wait till you see what I can do with a credit card."

"I mean something film-worthy. No one's going to tune in to watch you shop."

"But they're going to tune in to watch me being savaged by otters?"

"Exactly."

I sigh. "I bet Maya has it easier."

"She'll have her share of conflict, don't you worry."

"Conflict?"

"Too much peace and harmony puts viewers to sleep."

"You're the one who told me to be likable."

Judy pretends to nod off. "I didn't tell you to put the entire country into a coma."

I might have gotten something out of Cannery Row had I read any of John Steinbeck's novels. Literature is not a high priority in the Banker Duplication program. Although my parents endorse basic literacy for the purposes of reading stock reports, beyond that, reading simply consumes time that would be better spent on more practical pursuits. Like math.

Mona mentioned that she owns Steinbeck's collected works and suggested I read them while I'm here. I guess it couldn't hurt. It would give me something to talk about at parties. I wonder if it's possible to become well-rounded in a single month? More important, I wonder if there will be any parties to look well-rounded at?

Mona didn't have much patience for shopping, and kept muttering asides about commercialism. She probably would have enjoyed it more if she weren't carrying a backpack large enough to contain her missing seventh child. When I suggested stopping for fish and chips, she was aghast. "Eating out is a big treat for us," she said.

I felt terrible, but Judy looked happy about the exchange. I guess that's the type of conflict she's looking for. It made me change my position on being likable: I'd far rather be America's sweetheart than pick fights to keep viewers awake. Let Maya fill the show's bitch quotient.

To prove how sweet I am, I make an extra effort when we stop at a park for a picnic lunch. I rave about Mona's egg salad sandwiches, even after learning it isn't real egg, but tofu in disguise. I play tag with the twins, even though it means running on camera, which might give my parents false hope. I stop Egg from eating a thistle, even though it's tempting to let him go. And I offer to let Meadow wear my jeans to her friend's birthday party.

Judy doesn't complain, but her twitchy eyelid hasn't winked in a full hour. Suddenly she brightens. The twins are racing toward their brother, who is approaching with two other guys.

Bob trains the lens on me, and Chili closes in on Mitch.

"You brought your friends to meet Kendra," Mona says. "How sweet!"

Mitch looks at her as if she's lost her mind. "I came to borrow some money. We're going to play pick-up basketball at the rec center."

Judy gives Mona an exaggerated wink, and Mona says, "Why don't you take Kendra along?"

His face drops. "Forget it."

"Mitch, she's our guest and you will be polite."

He swallows hard. "Fine."

I reluctantly fall into step with the guys. On Judy's command, Bob darts in front of us and turns to walk backward.

By way of introduction, Mitch tells his friends, "Keep your curtains closed, Miss Big Apple's a voyeur."

Realizing that any response I give will feed Judy's hunger for conflict, I settle for huffy silence.

He continues to goad me. "Nice hair. I see it all worked out this morning."

My face ignites because my hair looks awful and I know it. No blow-out can survive two hours in a ten-year-old's bike helmet. Besides, there's Egg's sticky clump on the side that Judy wouldn't give me time to fix.

Fortunately, it isn't far to the recreation center, and the guys immediately abandon me at the bleachers. Not that I am truly alone. The cameras capture me from several angles and are still rolling when a basketball hurtles toward me. It misses my head by inches and crashes against the wall.

Mitch runs over to collect it. "Sorry," he says. "Lost control of the ball."

I do what Rosa always told me to do in times of stress: "Send good thoughts." Although it hurts even more than offering Meadow my jeans, I say, "No problem."

Undaunted, Mitch tries again. This time the basketball comes so close that only the syrup keeps my hair from blowing back from the force. I manage a weak smile because I know it will frustrate both Mitch and Judy.

Before he can have another go at me, Carrie arrives. Despite her rude initiation to reality TV yesterday, she gives me a hug and introduces me to her friends. I'd be more flattered by their attention if they hadn't arranged themselves in a semicircle for the cameras. Still, I'm happy to have a distraction.

Soon I am too caught up in conversation to care about Mitch, and I almost—but not quite—forget about the crew. The girls offer to show me the "real sights," starting with a trip to the Del Monte Center, a huge shopping mall.

When we finally come up for air, the guys are gone.

Under Mona's watchful eye, I am learning to chop vegetables. Max is teasing me about my lack of dexterity, but I'm too tired to dish it back. Between the jet lag and exercise, today has felt like the longest day of my life. Maybe time just slows down in California. I can't be sure: my watch is still missing.

Giving up on me, Max chases the twins around the kitchen, roaring. As if they need to be revved up any more than they already are. He throws Egg over his shoulder and charges at Meadow, who shrieks and hurls a red pepper at them.

"Focus on the knife," Mona says calmly, as if this ruckus were perfectly normal. If it fazes her to have Bob and Chili watching us through their lenses, it doesn't show.

I focus on chopping the carrots into tiny, uniform squares.

"They don't have to be perfect," she says. "There's no test, dear."

I glance up at her, realizing that she would have read the letter I wrote to the *Black Sheep* producers. She probably thinks I'm a spoiled whiner.

Max leans over Mona and blows a loud raspberry on her neck. She giggles, but I shoot him a disgusted look. Chuckling at my expression, he says, "It's just like having Maya here."

Living life in front of the camera clearly isn't fazing Max, either. I'm sure my father isn't chuckling as cameramen chase him around the house. Come to think of it, Dad is already asleep; my parents need their shut-eye to ensure optimal running performance.

Dinnertime at the Mulligans' is frantic. Everyone has a task except Mitch, who called to say he was eating at a friend's, and Egg, who is confined to his high chair. When I finish the carrots, Mona sets me to work on the yams.

Rosa never let me help with dinner, but she liked it when I sat on a stool by the counter and told her stories about my day. Even when she was cooking something complicated, she managed to ask the right questions and roll her eyes at the right places. Then she'd give me the first taste of whatever she was making, as if my opinion really mattered. "Just a little more basil," I'd say. We put basil in everything because Dad banned real spice from the house after his ulcer nine years ago.

Mona beckons me to the stove. "Taste this for me, will you, dear?"

I taste the grain dish she proffers. "It's good. Maybe you could try a little basil."

She snips a handful of leaves from a plant on the windowsill, adds them to the pot, and tastes it. "Good call."

I'd be pleased, if Judy weren't sitting at the kitchen table, flexing her Donkey smile. She's made me mistrustful of everything. This, too, could have been staged.

When Max heads into the backyard, Bob and Chili instantly lose interest in me and join him at the barbecue. Mona and Judy follow a moment later.

Seizing my chance, I sneak upstairs to the bedroom and dial Lucy's number.

"Hey," she says. "I thought you weren't allowed to make calls."

"I'm not, but I wanted to say hi. I miss you."

"I miss you too. How's it going?"

"Not great. The cameras are freaking me out, and I don't know how to act."

"Maya's finding it hard, too," she says.

"So you've met her?"

"Yeah. Katie invited me over. She's really cool."

That figures. Maya gets a really cool producer, and I get stuck with Judy.

"Well, what's Maya like?" I ask. "Everyone at this end says she's a bitch."

"Really?" Lucy sounds surprised. "I like her."

This can't be happening. I've been kicked out of my own home and my replacement is stealing my best friend. "Luce, she keeps a ferret!"

"I've seen pictures. He's adorable."

"Are you kidding? It's a rat with a better stylist. What kind of a person sleeps with vermin?"

"An animal lover, I suppose. Hey, guess what? Your mom took Maya to the Met."

I gasp. "How could she?"

"You hate the Met."

"Of course I hate the Met. That's not the point."

"Well, if it makes you feel any better, they didn't go for tea afterward."

"They didn't?" That does make me feel better.

"No, Katie wanted me to take Maya shopping instead."

And that makes me feel worse. Shopping with Lucy is my biggest pleasure in life, and now Maya has ruined it.

"I didn't take her to any of our favorites stores," Lucy says. "She wouldn't like them anyway. Her taste is a little . . . crunchy granola."

I heave a sigh of relief. "The Mulligans are hippies. Their kids were born tie-dyed."

She laughs. "I'm trying to offer some guidance. The show gave her a clothing allowance."

"What?!"

The door opens and Judy and Bob step into the room. Judy's lips are sealed in a thin line.

"Gotta go, Luce," I say, pushing the end button. I bet Katie allows phone calls.

"Kendra, you know the rules," Judy says. "No contact with friends or family. That's why you had to leave your cell phone at home."

I decide to go on offense. "How come Maya gets a clothing allowance and you wouldn't even buy me a souvenir T-shirt today?"

"You have all the clothes you need, and the Mulligans are on a tight budget."

"But I don't get paid for the show until it's over and my parents aren't sending my allowance. It's unfair." I toss the phone onto Meadow's bed and it bounces to the floor.

Judy studies me. "What's really bothering you?

I see her tap her temple, a sign I now recognize as "zoom in," but I ignore it. "Katie sent Maya shopping with Lucy, and she's *my* friend."

Judy shows her teeth again. "Someone sounds a little threatened."

"I'm not threatened," I lie. "But if Maya's own family says she's a bitch, she shouldn't be hanging with my best friend."

"You're exchanging lives. That includes families *and* friends." She throws her arm around me and pulls me toward the door. "Why don't you stop thinking about what you left behind and start thinking about the fun you'll have here?"

A silver blur races past us and leaps onto the bed. Manhattan has my watch in his tiny jaws. Taunting me, he bolts for the door.

Judy laughs. "See? It's symbolic. There goes your old life."

Bob gives a little yelp as my old life rubs against his leg on the way out.

Chapter 4

Unlike most of my friends, I've never dreamed of being a star of any kind—not a rock star, an actor, a model, or even an athlete. That's probably because of the programming restrictions of my urban-Amish upbringing. If it weren't for Lucy, who lives a fully normal life, I'd be shockingly ill-informed about celebrities. She does her best to keep me up-to-date with what the average person knows, but I still frequently draw blanks when the girls at school are discussing some hot new actor or band. As a result, Lucy and I developed a signal that lets her know I'm in the dark. When I tinker with my earring, she jumps in to provide information about the topic, thereby saving me from looking like a total loser. That's what best friends are for.

All I have to offer Lucy in return is help with her math and computer science homework, but she seems to think it's a good trade-off. Lucy isn't much of a scholar. Her ambitions run the gamut from fashion design to film production to choreography. Lucy's parents don't complain. That's partly because Lucy's grandmother, Nana Russell, is a big believer in letting kids explore any and all interests, no matter how seemingly unrealistic.

Nana Russell wants to save me from becoming a banker. She's always urging me to "think big," but that's hard to do when you live in a small cage. Even if I had more freedom to develop my own interests, I doubt I'd have considered a career in television. Living in the public eye isn't in my genes. Being practical is.

Now, thanks to one reckless moment, I am bent over, scraping oily residue from a stinky otter kennel while a couple of cameras zoom in on my backside. Something is so wrong with this close-up. Where is the fun Judy promised? Where is the independence?

And where is the break from nonstop education? Mona couldn't just hand me a hose and scrub brush. Oh, no. First she had to lecture me about otter pelts. I know it's horrible that people made coats out of them for centuries, but I couldn't care less how many hairs they have per square inch.

I tried to derail Mona's enthusiasm by staring off into space while she listed the biggest threats to otter welfare, but all that got me was skill-testing questions when she was done. Take away the beret, throw in a sensible bra and some scones, and it's Torture Day all over again. Having been well trained by Mom, however, I quickly regurgitated the key facts: oil spills kill otters because they destroy the insulating properties of the fur and leave the animal vulnerable to the cold; only quick cleansing of the fur prevents death by hypothermia. Mona looked surprised. Maybe her kids haven't mastered the fine art of processing information efficiently while totally bored. She took off pretty fast after that, leaving me to break out the rubber gloves.

I'm on kennel number two, when a muffled voice says, "Hey."

I look up to see someone draped in a black cape blocking the doorway. His face is concealed by a metal mask.

I raise the hose. "Don't come any closer, I'm warning you!"

Darth Vader takes a couple of steps toward me. "Wait a—"

I blast him square in the face mask. He backs off immediately, but I keep the hose going while letting out a scream so piercing it startles even me. Growing up in the big city has made me a survivor.

Chili bursts into the room, camera running. Obviously my welfare comes second to a good shot around here.

"Turn off the damn hose," Darth yells, his voice now much higher pitched. He removes the mask, revealing a scowling woman in her early twenties.

Chili swings his lens from me to the woman, and I notice that's where it stays. Even damp and disheveled, she's attractive in a hug-a-tree, no-makeup sort of way.

I lower my weapon. "Isn't it a little early for Halloween?" I ask.

"Who are you?" she asks.

"Who are *you*? You're the one scaring people."

"I'm Lisa Langdon, the aquarium's director of volunteers, and acting manager of the SORAC program."

She doesn't look old enough to be that important. The title probably sounds better than it actually is. "I'm Kendra Bishop. I'm staying with the Mulligans."

"Oh, right," Lisa says, pulling the dripping poncho over her head, "The movie star wannabe."

"Excuse me? You don't know anything about me."

"I know that your entourage is making it hard to get anything done around here."

"But my entourage could also bring some great publicity to your program, right?"

"Publicity brings people, and people threaten marine habitats," she says. "But if we're stuck with you, you might as well learn something."

Of course. Why go an hour without a lecture?

Lisa leads us down a long corridor and into a dim room full of monitors. Each displays a different otter, some in kennels, some in small pools. I'd envisioned a ferret on a larger scale, but they're actually very cute, with sleek dark fur and whiskery faces. One of the otters has an auburn face and a bandaged paw.

"Snagged by a fishhook," Lisa explains. "He almost lost that paw."

She offers a similarly depressing story for every otter we

look at, and I start to see one advantage to the Banker Duplication Program: ignorance. Not knowing means not having to care.

"Will he be okay?" I ask, pointing to the otter with the sore paw.

She nods. "We'll probably release him in a week or two."

"What's his name?"

"I don't name the animals I treat," she says, pursing her lips disapprovingly. "They're not pets. This is number 201."

"I bet he'd heal faster if he had a name. He looks like a Maurice to me."

Ignoring this, she says, "If you're staying with the Mulligans, you must know Mitch. He's volunteered here since he was ten. I can't tell you how many nights he's watched over sick animals.

"He's great with the kids in our education programs, too," she continues. "Mitch is the best tutor we have. Did you know he's entering the marine biology program at UCLA next fall?"

Why doesn't she start a fan club and be done with it? "We haven't had much time to talk."

"He is busy," she agrees. "He volunteers in half a dozen places and works to save for his tuition. I'll bet he misses Maya, though. They're very close."

"Does she volunteer here too?"

"Used to," she says. "She's lost interest lately."

As soon as I can, I escape to the administrative office to

wait for Mona. Someone asks me to help with a computer problem, and I fix it in a second. The Banker Duplication Program promotes exceptional technical skills.

Mitch's biggest fan eventually finds me and hands me a magazine, in which she's flagged an article. "How about summarizing this information for a fact sheet?"

It's a study of sea otter demographics in central California versus those in Washington and Alaska. I recognize another "teaching moment," but at least it's a change from my parents' curriculum, which doesn't cover anything nature-oriented.

Chili films over my shoulder as I type my summary. After he turns off the camera, he corrects my grammar.

Since Carrie isn't wearing a bicycle helmet, I break Rule Number Twelve—*Safety First*—and leave mine behind as we set off for the mall. Without my parents or Rosa around to enforce *The BLAH*, it's becoming more a set of guidelines than actual rules—guidelines that I can follow at my discretion. Judy gives me an encouraging wink, probably to suggest that serious head injury or death on the streets of Monterey could boost ratings.

Whatever. I want Carrie's friends to like me, and that will be harder to do if I have helmet head. Besides, we might run into some hot guys at the mall. One of Mitch's friends was seriously cute, and he looked intrigued when Mitch said I was a voyeur. It's rare for someone to think I'm more interesting than I really am.

Thanks to the camera crew, the salespeople trip over each other to help us in every store. Some even offer us special deals. Carrie's friend Tia gets a denim skirt at half price and is so excited that she hugs me. I know I don't deserve the credit, but I feel proud just the same. It's like I'm hosting a party where the guests are having a good time. Finding a cool T-shirt and a great pair of jeans for myself is an added bonus.

We spend so long choosing lip gloss that Judy taps her watch, but she doesn't protest when I offer to treat everyone—including the crew—to ice cream.

I hope they don't cut the shots where I'm whipping out my mother's charge card every five minutes. I want her to see I've found a way to manage without my allowance. She's far too cautious to cancel the card on me anyway.

We're sitting at a table in the courtyard when Tia asks how Maya is doing in New York. "Apparently she's fitting right in," I say. "Who knows, she may end up running marathons with my parents."

Carrie says, "She'd love that. Maya runs track."

I feel a prickle of resentment, but swallow it before Bob abandons his banana split to zoom in on my reaction. I'm getting better at this game. "My parents have a lot of rules and they're goal-oriented," I say. "She won't have a lot of freedom."

"That won't bother Maya," Tia says. "She's an A-student and totally focused. In fact, she's too mature for her own good. Her parents give her a lot of freedom and she doesn't even take advantage of it. Last month they let her take the train into San Francisco, and she wasted the day at some art gallery."

The stork must have switched us at birth, because Maya sounds like the daughter my parents really wanted. Unfortunately, her visit will make my shortcomings all the more obvious when I get home.

Carrie continues, "Maya used to be into environmentalism, but she's gone off it. She hates the way her parents are always chasing some cause. And they embarrass her all the time."

Tia nods in agreement. "Before Maya left, Mona put a box of condoms into her suitcase and gave her the 'safe sex' talk. The crew caught it all on film and Maya wanted to kill her."

The Mulligans might be eccentric, but they're also well-meaning and laid back. If Maya decided to drop out of school to become an astrologer, for example, her parents would probably rush out to buy charts of the cosmos, whereas mine would most likely have me hospitalized.

Since the conversation is killing my good mood, I change the subject. "What's with Mitch? He's been kind of mean to me."

"I told you how he felt about the show, remember?" Carrie says.

"Yeah, but it's not my fault Maya applied. And if he's so miserable, Max and Mona should just let him stay at your place."

She shakes her head. "He had to participate. It was part of the deal."

I glance at Judy, who's suddenly riveted by her ice cream. Before I can explore the issue further, however, some guys the girls know from school arrive. This time I really do forget about the cameras for a moment. One of the guys, Aaron, invites us to a party this weekend, saying his parents will be away.

I'm going to a party with my new friends! A party without parents! I'll be breaking at least six of the top twenty rules, and my parents will get to witness it on TV.

It's Maya's turn to have her mature, A-student, art-loving spirit crushed under the weight of The BLAH.

I chopped all the vegetables for dinner and mixed my first vinaigrette. It took a while, but I painstakingly layered equal amounts of cubed beets, carrots, cucumbers, tomatoes, and peppers over two kinds of lettuce. It was a marvel of precision. Max commented that he'd never seen a more attractive salad, before grabbing a pair of tongs to give it a hearty toss.

He was probably worried it would steal the glory from Mona's tofu loaf, which looked like dog food straight from the can. It was surprisingly tasty, though, because she used so much garlic and spice. You could season a dead ferret like that and no one would recognize it. Not that I hate Manhattan as much as usual tonight: the twins found my watch under the anti-sonar placards in the closet, and I was able to wear it to dinner. I'm never taking it off again.

I tell Mona and Max about the party invitation, coming clean about the absentee parents. It's the right thing to do. Besides, Judy will tell them anyway.

Mona's usually genial face clouds over. "We're going to the same rally as Aaron's parents, dear, and we hoped you'd camp out with us."

Max's eyes light up at the thought of the tent rally and one hand disappears under the table. Mona giggles, and Meadow and I, in agreement for once, roll our eyes.

"Please, Mona?" I ask. "This is a huge opportunity for me. I never get to go to parties at home."

She ponders as she rises to clear the table. "Well, I suppose there will always be another rally." My heart soars, until Max gives her nudge and tilts his head toward Chili's camera. Suddenly mindful of the fact that she's on national television, Mona adds, "But I'm not happy there won't be any adults in attendance. It's easy for parties to get out of hand."

So much for all that freedom I keep hearing about. "I'll be with Carrie, and I can be home early."

Mona looks at Max and he shakes his head. "We can't let you go alone."

"But—"

She holds up a hand. "It's settled: Mitch will take you."

"Mitch!" I'm horrified and I sound it. "There's no way

he'll agree to go."

"He'll go," Max says, his tone indicating that it really is settled.

Why did they have to choose this moment to get all normal?

After dinner, Mona, Meadow, and I make chocolate-chip cookies. I've never baked before, but I find precision comes in handy, especially when you're quadrupling the recipe. My biggest challenge is keeping the twins' busy hands out of the chocolate chips. Finally I promise the biggest cookie to the twin who can track down my watch. It went missing again when I took it off to scoop the flour.

"More chocolate chips," Meadow commands. "You need to gain a few pounds."

"Then you wouldn't be able to steal my jeans," I say. Not that I want them back, after the damage she's done to them. They're hers now, and her smile says she knows it.

Mona cranks up the stereo and hits repeat on Joni Mitchell's "Big Yellow Taxi." She teaches Meadow and me the words and soon we are all bellowing, "They paved paradise and put up a parking lot."

A shout drifts up the basement stairs. "Mom! Will you quit it? I'm trying to study!"

It's Mitch. I didn't even know he was home. He usually leaves before I'm up and returns when I'm in bed. "Studying?" I whisper. "School's over. He graduated."

"Mitch is always studying," Meadow says. "He's getting a head start on college."

Who knew nerds came in such nice packaging?

"Did you know he's already been published?" Mona asks. "He wrote a first-hand account of his tracking experiences for a local travel magazine."

Mitch sticks his head out of the stairway. "Don't talk about me."

Too bad the packaging can't hide the personality.

"Lighten up, honey," she says. "Can't a mother be proud?"

"Just cut out the yodeling," he says, disappearing as fast as he came.

Mr. Likable is going to be thrilled to hear he's escorting me to a party.

"I'm not doing it," I say.

Judy stacks warm cookies onto a plate. "What's the big deal? Just go downstairs, offer Mitch a cookie, and have a little chat."

"Forget it. He tried to kill me with a basketball."

She throws an arm around me. "That's how boys show girls they like them."

"Not in a civilized society," I say.

Mona laughs. "There's nothing civilized about teenage boys, Kendra."

"I'm not chatting with him," I say. "He's rude."

"My point exactly," Judy says. "Judy thinks you two got off on the wrong foot and you need to smooth things over."

I step out from under her arm. "I thought Judy liked conflict. Ratings, remember?"

She shifts gears with her usual split-second timing. "Sure, but too much conflict about the same thing gets old fast. Viewers have short attention spans."

"Mitch isn't so bad," Mona assures me. "He's just cranky about the cameras. No offense, Judy."

"None taken," Judy says.

"I'm not a fan of television myself, to be honest," Mona continues. "Ours broke a year ago and I had no intention of repairing it." She turns to me and shrugs. "Judy arrived with a new one and I've hardly seen the kids since."

Judy puts the plate of cookies in my hand and propels me toward the stairs. "Think about how much easier the party will be if you're getting along. Go patch things up."

"Only if you and your cameras stay up here." I brace myself in the doorway with one elbow and my free hand as she pushes.

"It's all fair game, KB, you know that."

"I can't patch things up unless you back off."

"Fine," she says. "Have it your way." She presses the button on her walkie-talkie. "Attention, *Black Sheep* crew." Several crew members are in the kitchen with us, and their walkies squawk because of the close proximity. "We're standing down on the lamb. Repeat: stand down on the lamb." Taking her thumb off the button, she says, "Consider this your one free pass, KB."

Halfway down the stairs, I turn and run back up to make sure they're keeping their word. Mona has left the kitchen and Judy is kicking back at the table with the rest of the crew. The cameras and mikes are on the floor. "Go," she says, around a mouthful of cookie.

I start down the stairs again, feeling a little nauseous, either from nerves or from eating too many cookies. Winning Mitch over is one of the tougher challenges I've faced in my life, but I'm sure he'll come to like me when he knows me better. It's not like he has a good reason to hate me.

When I reach the bottom of the stairs, Mitch is parked in front of a large plasma-screen TV watching a basketball game. I hold out the plate of cookies and offer a faint "Hi." He doesn't respond. He doesn't even move his eyes from the screen.

This is going well. "I thought you were studying," I say.

He turns to see if the crew is behind me. "And I thought you were upstairs milking your fifteen minutes of fame."

I consider throwing the cookies at his head, but that would be a sad waste of my newfound talent for baking. "The same way your sister is milking it in New York."

"Her choice, not mine," he says. "I want no part of it."

I point at the TV. "Except for that, you mean. I hear it's a gift from the show."

He flushes, then looks away. "How about you stop

barging into every room I'm in?"

"How about you stop throwing things at me?"

"What are you talking about?" A smirk plays on his lips.

"I'm talking about the basketball."

"It was an accident."

"Accidents don't happen twice."

He stares at the screen in silence for a full minute before finally flicking his eyes at me. "Are you still here?"

Setting the plate of cookies on the coffee table, I sit down on the couch across from him. If it weren't for Aaron's party, I'd walk back up those stairs. But I have to win Mitch over. I can only stand having one enemy in the house, and that role belongs to the ferret. "Look," I say, "I didn't get you into this, Maya did. And it's only a month out of your life."

He ignores me.

"It was really nice of you to agree to participate for her sake," I add.

He turns up the volume on the television.

"She's going to have a great time in Manhattan," I shout above the TV. "For the first few days. Then my parents will get progressively obsessive and controlling until she's begging to come home early. You can expect that call by the end of week two."

Although he doesn't turn his head, Mitch does lower the volume slightly. I take it as a good sign and continue. "My house is like a high-security prison," I say. "There's a binder of rules *this thick*."

Mitch rolls his eyes sideways to see how thick. "A binder?"

"Now you see why I like *your* parents." Since he's starting to thaw a little, I say, "I applied to be on *The Black Sheep* because I was having trouble at home. I just wanted to try something different."

"You could do that without dragging your whole family into it."

"For your information, I had a really good reason for being upset with my parents."

"Yeah, what did they do? Reduce your shoe allowance?" He raises a hand to his mouth in mock horror.

"It's personal," I say. There's no way I'm admitting I lost it because they fired my nanny. "But I did have second thoughts. By then it was too late, I'd signed the contract."

He turns up the volume again.

"Anyway, I don't have much of a family to inconvenience," I yell. "I'm an only child." I wait for him to say something, and when he doesn't, I continue. "My parents obviously didn't go to enough tent rallies."

Mitch laughs his odd, barky laugh—and looks startled that it slipped out. "My parents are so embarrassing," he mutters.

"They're funny," I say, choosing the word carefully. "Funny" can go either way.

He grunts noncommittally.

"I was at the aquarium today," I tell him. "Some woman

there thinks you're God's gift to salt water."

He looks at me again. "Yeah? Who?"

"Lisa. She wouldn't let me name the otter with the sore paw: *'They're not pets, you know.'*" I use my uptight teacher voice and he laughs again.

"Lisa takes everything seriously. She's an academic."

"An academic? Already?"

"She's doing her Master's thesis on how toxins are affecting the ocean's food chain."

And Judy thinks *I'm* boring? "Well, I didn't mean any harm by naming Maurice."

"Maurice? Please."

He sounds somewhat entertained and, figuring he's in as good a mood as he's likely to get, I deliver the bad news. "Carrie's friend Aaron invited me to a party and your parents will only let me go if you'll come, too."

"What about your entourage?" he asks, raising his eyebrows.

"I don't have any choice about that. I just used my one free pass to come down here without them."

"Aaron's a loser," he says. "But I'll think about it."

Knowing I've pushed my luck far enough for one night, I stand to go. "Okay. Thanks."

Mitch says, "His name is Fred."

I'm confused. "Whose?"

"The otter's."

"Shouldn't it start with an 'M'?"

He smiles—not *at* me, but in my general direction. I smile too. He can't be all bad if he names the wildlife.

That's when I hear a creak on the stairs. We turn at the same moment to see the camera snout poking through a crack in the door.

"Shit," I say.

There's shuffling, and then Judy's head appears in the crack. "Great job, KB," she shouts. "Very natural. It's like you didn't even know we were rolling."

Now Mitch has a good reason to hate me.

Chapter 5

The twins thunder down the old staircase and into the living room, where half the neighborhood has gathered. We're going to watch an advance copy of *The Black Sheep* premiere, which will air in a few days. I'm surprised at how quickly Judy has managed to edit the episode. I've only been here six days, although it feels like more—and not in a good way.

"Pilot to bombardier," Matt shouts into a walkie-talkie. He zooms around the room with outstretched arms before raising the walkie to his lips again. "Prepare to lock in on target."

"Bombs away," Mason responds, hurling a hairbrush that resembles mine against the wall.

They are dressed as fighter pilots, in oversized leather jackets and swimming goggles. Matt is wearing white earmuffs strapped under this chin; Mason's are pink—and lacy.

"Boys!" Mona says sharply. "Are those Maya's bras?"

"Can't be," Meadow answers. "Maya's aren't padded."

All eyes—and cameras—turn to catch my reaction.

The flush rolls over me so fast it almost knocks me

down, but still I manage a feeble defense. "How do you know they're not Mona's?"

The crowd cracks up.

"Mona hasn't worn a bra since her mother's funeral in 1988," Max explains.

"And only then out of respect," Mona confirms.

Judy's smile stretches so far it threatens to decapitate her. Why isn't she bugged that the boys have confiscated the crew's walkie-talkies?

I snatch futilely at Mason while Matt targets his big brother, Mitch, who has appeared in the doorway. Raising his arms, Matt shouts, "Target locked in! Prepare for missile departure!" He loads a tampon, adorned by a tiny American flag, into my purple thong and launches it.

Time slows as the white projectile sails through the air. Heads turn to follow its trajectory. Three seconds later the tampon lands in Mitch's soda.

The twins high-five each other. "Splash down!"

Mitch sets his glass on a table and then reaches for my thong, now dangling from the snout of a ceramic otter. He offers it to me with a flourish and says, "Nice color."

Carrie's brother, Calvin, grabs the thong and twirls it over his head on one finger, whooping. In a frenzy, the twins leap for it until Max crosses the room and puts each boy in a headlock. Without waiting to retrieve my property, I bolt for the back door.

Bob and Chili are so intent on following me that they

collide in the doorway and curse at each other.

It's good to hear some profanity, even if it isn't my own.

The swing set in the backyard turns out to be a good refuge from the mayhem inside. Nothing in my past prepared me for this sort of behavior. In *my* home, people don't go out of their way to embarrass me. Yes, my parents are an embarrassment simply by virtue of being the dullest people on the planet. And yes, it kills me when they expose their weirdness to the public. Why two intelligent people can only make small talk about two subjects—the stock market and healthy living—is beyond me. But one thing I can say for them is that they don't *deliberately* embarrass me.

Another thing I can say for my parents is that they only slipped up on the birth control once. Obviously, I wasted too much of my youth wishing for brothers and sisters. Had our family been larger, my parents would have had breakdowns trying to draft enough *BLAH* legislation, yet it wouldn't have prevented sibling abuse.

I've never had the opportunity to develop a thick skin. Even at school I've mostly escaped ridicule by flying below the radar—far enough below that hardly anyone notices me, yet not so far that people single me out to bully me. It's a balancing act that's harder than it sounds.

With Bob's lens still trained on me from the deck, I push off on the swing. The movement seems to clear my mind, and it occurs to me that my mediocrity was genetically inevitable. When I was conceived, two sets of completely bland chromosomes combined not with a bang, but a whimper. It's not my fault that I am average. Ordinary. Unexceptional. Predictable. I find a synonym with every arc of the swing.

Then, as I soar up into the late afternoon sky, I realize that there is still hope. I took introductory biology, and I know that genes do not control everything. Environment plays a huge role in what we become. I didn't stand much of a chance of escaping the Banker Duplication Program in Manhattan, but now that I'm in Monterey, I might be able to work against my genes to become someone completely different from my parents. Someone with a personality. Someone outgoing. Someone interesting.

The Black Sheep could be my lucky break after all. Not because I want to be on television and expose my fight against mediocrity to a national audience, but because it gives me the chance to prove to myself that I am not a chip off the old block.

It won't be easy. I've got a long way to go and only a few weeks to get there.

Today I'm the type of person who retires to the swing set at the first sign of trouble. By the time I leave Monterey, I want to be a true Black Sheep. A Black Sheep doesn't crumble. A Black Sheep claims the padded bras as her own and laughs as the tampons fly. A Black Sheep tosses out her parents' rule book and invents her own.

The first rule of my new Black Sheep code arrives in my head fully formed: *A Black Sheep stands her ground.*

I leap off the swing at its highest point, psyched to face the enemy.

When my feet hit the ground, however, it is friend, not foe, that I face. "Judy sent me to get you," Carrie says. "She's cued up the show."

"Let's go to the mall instead," I suggest. It's not running away: a Black Sheep can stand her ground wherever she likes.

Carrie shakes her head. "Don't worry, Mona read everyone the riot act. Nobody is allowed to mention the tampon."

"Barbarians," I grumble, following her to the house. "They have no respect for privacy."

"That's what it's like in a big family," Carrie agrees.

"At least *your* brothers acknowledge you exist. Mitch has barely spoken to me since Judy secretly taped our conversation."

"She's hard not to hate, isn't she?"

I nod, pondering for a moment. "Do you think Judy put the twins up to that stunt? She wasn't even mad at them for taking her walkie-talkie."

The back door swings open and a Donkey smile appears. "Two minutes to curtain, girls. "

The beauty of rules, which I never recognized until today, is that they give you something to cling to in the midst of chaos. If I hadn't launched the Black Sheep code, I might be hysterical right now. Instead, I stand my ground as the show rolls even though Calvin is sitting behind me with the tampon tucked behind one ear. I stand my ground even though Mitch is snickering at the sight of my on-screen alter ego prancing around my parents' marble halls in pajamas. I stand my ground when the high-definition TV offers a shocking close-up of a blemish I didn't know I had. And I stand my ground when Judy asks on air if I have the runs, even though the rest of the audience convulses with laughter.

This is not my finest hour. I am coming across as totally obnoxious. Judy has edited out the scenes where I looked normal and kept only the ones where I'm picking up after the crew, wiping their fingerprints off shiny surfaces, rolling my eyes when they misidentify Mozart, and explaining the difference between a Monet and Matisse. The way she's cut this, I look like a snob. And a boring snob, at that.

"*I can't go to California,*" I tell the camera. "*I'm taking music theory class this summer. And economics. Plus I've got math camp.*"

Mitch snickers again. "Wow, life in the Big Apple is as exciting as everyone says."

"Hush," Mona says.

The show cuts to a close-up of Judy standing outside our brownstone. It must have been taped after she left, because she's holding a framed photo of me that she swiped from our mantel. *"This poor child hasn't been hugged in four years!"* she says.

"It's not like that," I say, but no one hears me because Calvin is pretending to sob gustily behind me.

Max reaches over to pat my back, but withdraws his hand abruptly when my father intones, *"Our daughter is not spending a month with beatniks."*

"We're not beatniks," Max protests.

"Sure we are, sweetie," Mona says. "And proud of it, too."

Back on screen, Judy asks me if I have any interests. I stare blankly at the camera for several long moments, twisting my ponytail before finally replying, *"I, uh, like to shop."*

"Grab your scuba gear," Mitch says. "That's pretty deep."

"Mitch," Mona says. "That's quite . . ."

Her voice trails off as her daughter's pretty face appears on-screen. The show's focus has finally shifted to Maya's last day in Monterey. But instead of skewering Maya's family as she did mine, Judy has featured a montage of scenes where the Mulligans are singing folk songs beside a campfire, frolicking in the backyard with the pets, and cooking a huge meal together. It's all glorious family harmony.

The show cuts to New York, where Maya's dark hair glistens under my parents' chandelier as they eat together at the dining room table we never use when I'm around.

"That's take-out food," I point out. "They dumped it

into my mother's Limoges china to make it look home-made."

"Maya looks wonderful," Max says, to no one in particular. "She looks happy."

Maya *does* look happy as she rearranges the furniture in my room and takes down my posters and spreads her cosmetics all over my bathroom counter. She looks even happier as she walks up Madison Avenue arm in arm with my best friend, Lucy, laughing at some private joke. And she looks happier still while contemplating Jan Gossaert's *Portrait of a Banker*, Mom's favorite painting, which is currently on loan to the Met.

My mother is obviously thrilled to be sharing this moment with Maya. At least it's obvious to me that she's thrilled. Mom doesn't have the full range of facial expressions normal people have, but her eyebrows are riding a little higher than usual.

"You call this *reality* TV?" I ask, looking over my shoulder at Judy. "There's nothing real about it. You made it look like *my* life sucks."

"I'm showing the truth as I see it," she says, shrugging. "Pictures don't lie."

I try to protest further, but a dozen people shush me because the show has cut back to Monterey, and the neighbors are excited to see themselves at the barbecue.

Carrie's image appears on screen, nodding her agreement with Meadow that Maya is a bitch. Carrie gasps in horror, but Meadow simply states, "Sometimes she is."

"That was a private conversation," Carrie says.

"Welcome to *The Black Sheep*, where nothing is sacred, thanks to your attention-craving friend," Mitch says, pointing to me.

He doesn't have time to say more before his own face appears on the screen. Make that his full physique, although the shots of our encounter in the bathroom have been blurred for prime-time viewing. The camera captures me sneaking covert looks below the waist.

Now it's my turn to gasp in horror. "I was just checking his—"

"Package?" Calvin interrupts, elbowing Mitch. "You called it, man. The shopaholic's a perv."

Carrie is halfway back to her house before the credits have finished rolling.

"Carrie, wait," I call after her. "Where are you going?"

"Home." She doesn't turn around.

"Mrs. Kowalchuk is hitting on Mitch. Don't you want to hang out and watch?"

She stops when she reaches her front stairs. "I just made a fool of myself on national TV. I practically said Maya's a bitch, and I *did* say that Mitch is hot."

"I know, but that's nothing compared to what I said," I offer consolingly. When she doesn't come back, I walk over to her porch.

"Yeah, but you made a *choice* to be on television," she says, starting up the stairs. "I'm an innocent bystander!"

I follow her to the door. "You didn't mind the cameras at the mall the other day. And remember, I asked Judy not to use what you said."

"Yeah, I know. I guess I'm not cut out for this kind of attention. Sorry, Kendra."

She steps inside and shuts the door in my face.

Bob and Chili are standing behind me when I turn around.

"Don't worry, kid," Bob says, reassuringly. "She'll come around."

I notice for the first time that Bob's *Black Sheep* T-shirt has been personalized with Magic Marker. Stretched across his paunch it says, YES, JUDY, I'M ZOOMING IN.

Chili isn't as confident. "I don't know. She totally slammed the door in Kendra's face. It was cold."

I head back to the Mulligan house with Bob and Chili trailing after me debating the status of my friendship with Carrie. "It doesn't matter," I say. "My life already sucks anyway."

My bags are packed by the time Mona finds me in the bedroom. I've decided to stand my ground back in Manhattan. If my parents haven't changed the locks, that is.

Judy tries to force entry into the bedroom, but she's no match for Mona, who's hiding more muscle under her tie-dyed tunic than I expected. Shoving a desk chair under the door handle, Mona tosses her floppy velvet hat over the camera mounted on the wall before cranking the radio to muffle our conversation. She probably learned these smooth moves during ecoterrorist operations.

Patting the bed beside her, she says, "It's just a TV show, Kendra. No one is going to take it seriously."

I sit down beside her. "My parents will. Millions of people are going to hear me say those terrible things about them when the show airs."

"Well, Maya's letter didn't paint the most flattering portrait of us, and I'm not fussed about it."

She should be. According to Judy, Maya's letter said her parents are immature and uncultured.

"Most children want the opposite of what their parents have chosen—at least until they have kids of their own," she continues. "I'm glad Maya is getting a chance to explore a different life."

"But what if she doesn't want to come back?"

"She will. She'll miss her family." Mona sighs before adding, "But she does seem to be enjoying herself."

"I highly doubt that," I say. "Judy's just twisted everything."

"Well, I guess that's how these shows work. They can take various bits and pieces and reassemble them to tell whatever story they want to tell."

"Aren't you worried about how you'll look?"

She shakes her head. "It is what it is. We're not ashamed."

"*I* am. I looked like a complete loser."

"That's not true. It was obvious that you're a clever girl." She chooses her words carefully. "You certainly know more about art than any of us."

"You mean I don't fit in here either."

She puts an arm around me. "You fit in just fine. Meadow thinks you're the best thing to happen to this house since Egg hatched."

It's only Meadow's opinion, but it makes me feel better anyway. "She does?"

"Didn't you notice that she's been styling her hair just like yours?"

I run a hand through my lank hair. "Maya's hair is way nicer."

"Don't be so hard on yourself, dear. You just need some time to spread your wings." She stands and beckons. "I've got just the thing to take your mind off your troubles.

"Let me guess: the aquarium?"

"Exactly."

Does every parent on the planet suffer from a compulsive need to educate?

Mona pulls me to my feet, and the ferret erupts from my suitcase holding his bottlebrush tail aloft. My startled squeal causes Judy to pound on the door, furious over missing the drama.

"Manhattan loves you so much he wants to go home with you," Mona says, opening the door abruptly so that Judy staggers into the room. "Isn't that sweet?"

Mona is so determined to see the glass as half full, you have to fight against seeing it that way yourself.

By the time Mona and I walk over to the aquarium, the rest of the clan has arrived by van and dispersed to their various tasks. There are so many Mulligans and friends-of-Mulligans volunteering here that Mona ought to get kickbacks.

Sensing that I could use some time alone, Mona sets me up with a video tape on otter conservation. It's a downer, as are most things educational. The species is making a slow comeback from near extinction, but one big oil slick could decimate the entire population.

I'd be totally bummed if I weren't so relieved to be officially off camera for the first time in over a week. Judy hasn't grown a conscience and decided to give me some space; otters bore the hell out of her, so she and the crew have gone in search of conflict at the oyster bar downstairs.

After the video ends, I track down Lisa's assistant, Kelly, who is sitting in front of the bank of monitors watching Otter Number 201, now known (to me, at least) as Maurice.

"He's looking a lot better today," I say as Maurice dives, spins, and glides around in his pool.

Kelly tells me he's being held for another week of

monitoring to ensure he's fit to swim, eat, and groom himself in the wild.

"Why does he circle constantly like that?" I ask.

"He's trying to find a way out," she says. "But look at him now." Maurice has rolled onto his back, covered his eyes with his paws, and gone to sleep. "He's gradually adapting, you see. But we don't want that to happen. He needs to keep up his fighting spirit so that he reintegrates after release."

I guess Maurice and I actually have something in common. I can totally relate to how hard it is to keep up your fighting spirit when you're living under a microscope.

I volunteer to watch Maurice so that Kelly can get something to eat. She hands me a chart and explains how to take notes about his behavior. As she leaves, I whisper, "Don't tell Judy you saw me," and she winks conspiratorially.

Black Sheep Rule Number Two: *Get the right people on your side.*

Maurice starts circling again and I find myself enthralled by him.

Too soon, however, Judy resurfaces. "Come on, KB, *do* something. There are no ratings in watching you watch seals."

I keep my eyes on Maurice. "When I finish up here, I'll raid Max's liquor cabinet and take the van out for a spin."

"Where did that attitude come from?" she asks irritably.

"It's not attitude, it's spunk. That's what you wanted, isn't it?"

"I changed my mind."

"Then how about finding someone else's life to ruin?"

Witness Black Sheep Rule Number Three in action: *Respect only the people who respect you.* Reality television is a dog-eat-dog world.

Lisa arrives at the door flanked by her assistant and a Darth Vader–clad flunky. Judy brightens and her head twitches in Bob's direction. He immediately raises his camera.

"What is *she* doing at the monitor?" Lisa asks her assistant.

"If you mean me, I'm monitoring Maurice," I say.

"She's not allowed to do that," Lisa says, continuing to ignore me. "She doesn't know the procedure."

"I know the procedure," I say, offering my paperwork. I didn't get through fifteen years in the Banker Duplication Program without being able to handle a simple chart. All I have to do is take notes about Maurice's activities including eating, sleeping, and playing. If he is favoring the wounded paw, I describe in detail.

Lisa flips through the chart and sniffs. "Well, I'm sure you'd rather be shopping. I hear that's more your thing."

I refer once again to Black Sheep Rule Number Three. "It's not illegal in California, is it?"

A toothy crescent appears spontaneously on Judy's face.

Spunk is clearly not a problem when it's directed at someone else.

"This isn't a joke for us," Lisa says. "We take our cause very seriously around here."

"I've been watching Maurice for an hour—"

"And a half," Judy supplies.

"—when I could have been at the beach. What does that tell you?"

"That you're a bored city girl in need of some meaning in her life?"

Ouch. She thinks she's so superior just because she's in graduate school. I'll have to talk to Bob about blurring her close-ups.

Darth removes his helmet to reveal Mitch.

"What's with the getup, cutie?" Judy asks him.

"It's to keep the otters from getting used to human contact," I explain. I've done my homework.

Mitch's expression is inscrutable. "Let her watch 201," he tells Lisa. "We need to introduce the new pup to the surrogate anyway."

"We have rules around here," Lisa says.

"I hear she's used to rules," Mitch replies, his eyes lighting on me for a nanosecond.

"I'm all about rules," I agree, although I'm not sure why I'm so eager to win this battle. Maurice is cute, but I can think of better ways of spending my time than staring at a monitor. I glance at Mitch, and his eyes dart away again. I hope I'm not becoming one of those girls who fake an interest in something just to impress a guy. That's not how a Black Sheep thinks.

Lisa gives in before I can back out. "All right," she says, "you can watch 201. But no contact with the animals—you're under eighteen."

"But Mitch—" I begin.

She raises her hand. "Mitch is an *exception*."

With that, she opens the door and leads Mitch out of the room, leaving me to shake my head over the fact that I actually volunteered for two more hours at this monitor.

"Mitch is an exception, all right," Judy says suggestively.

"What do you mean?" I ask.

Bob lowers his camera. "She's way too old for him."

"Absolutely," Chili agrees. "Lisa needs someone more mature. Someone with a steady job. Someone—"

"Like you?" Bob suggests, smirking.

Judy flops onto a couch and props her arms behind her head. "Mark Judy's words, people. That girl's thesis will be called *All About Mitch*."

My neck is stiff, my fingers are cramped from writing, and my eyes sting from staring, but still I resist when Mona comes to pull me away from the monitor. "I can't go now, it's feeding time! Do you see what he's doing? He's hiding food in the pouch under his paw for later." Who knew animals could be so fascinating? "Maurice is a genius!"

"Your genius will still be here tomorrow," Mona says. "And you need to eat, too."

I write "Maurice" on the front page of my report, alongside "Otter 201." To Lisa he may be just another otter, but to me he's special. Studying him didn't even feel like homework. It felt like it mattered.

Mona nudges me, and I turn to see Bob and Judy sprawled out on the sofa behind me, sound asleep. I gesture toward the door and we sneak out. I'll be back under the microscope soon enough.

Chapter 6

I am in that amazing place exactly halfway between waking and sleeping, where I can actually make myself believe I am at home in New York, curled up in my queen-size bed.

"Did you know that you drool?" a voice asks.

I ignore this and focus instead on how my own comforter at home would feel.

"It's disgusting," the voice continues. "I guess with your lip sagging like that you probably can't help it. It's like how my granddad's used to be after his stroke."

If I count backward from a hundred, I might be able to drop off again. Ninety-nine, ninety-eight, ninety-seven . . .

"And you snore, too," the voice adds. "No wonder you can't get a boyfriend."

"Bug off, Meadow," I say, keeping my eyes closed. There's a tickling sensation behind my ear, and I jerk my head away. "Quit it. I need to sleep."

A tongue licks my neck, and I open my eyes instantly, only to see something red blinking at me. Sitting up so suddenly that Manhattan flies off the bed, I snatch the camcorder out of Meadow's hands.

"Hey, you ruined my shot!" she says.

"What the hell are you doing? There's already a camera on the wall, do you have to stick one in my face, too? Wait, did Judy ask you to get a close-up?" I grab her arm and give it a little twist. "Tell me."

"Ow! Stop it."

"I can't believe you'd invade my privacy like this."

Meadow's face puckers. "I was just trying to get a shot of you and Manhattan. He was curled up in your hair, and it was so cute." She sounds as if she's fighting the urge to cry. "It wasn't for Judy, it was for me—so that I can remember you when you go home."

And the Turd of the Year Award goes to . . . Kendra Bishop!

I sink back on the pillow, wondering if I'll ever get the hang of having siblings. "Sorry, Meadow. When I saw the camera, I assumed Judy was behind it. You know what she's like."

Meadow nods. "She shoved me into the wall yesterday to get a clear shot of you when you broke Mom's one-of-a-kind otter platter."

"Another great moment of my life captured for posterity," I say, patting the bed.

Meadow crawls in beside me. "I hated that platter anyway. The otter looked like a squirrel." She accepts the camcorder back with a smile. "This is Mitch's, but I borrowed it to make my own home movie."

"Does he know about that?"

She sidesteps the question. "I'm calling it *The Making of Black Sheep*. What do you think?"

"I think there are more interesting stories to tell."

She yanks all the covers off me. "Not in my life. At least, not so far."

The doorbell rings downstairs, and a few moments later Mona calls, "Kendra, Carrie's here to see you."

I leap over Meadow and start pulling on my clothes.

"I thought Carrie blew you off," she says.

I haven't heard from Carrie since the screening four days ago, but I'm not about to admit that to Meadow. "We're both busy, that's all."

Carrie is already standing outside the bedroom door when I open it. She pushes past me into the room and closes the door behind her. "I told Judy I needed to use the bathroom," she whispers, "so we've only got about three minutes of privacy before she comes looking." She stares pointedly at Meadow. "Do you mind?"

Meadow directs the camcorder at her. "Yeah, I mind. I need to capture your apology to Kendra for my movie."

I assist Meadow out of my bed and out the door. "I can take it from here."

When she's gone, I toss a T-shirt over the camera in the corner. Carrie whispers an apology for overreacting about *The Black Sheep* footage and asks if I'm still coming to

Aaron's party tonight, telling me I'll be missed if I don't.

"Reunited and it feels so good . . ." someone sings tune-lessly from the hall. The door bursts open to reveal Judy, shoulders squared for a showdown. She's packing a mini-DVD camera where her pistol would be. "That was all very touching, Carrie, but it's not nice to lie to Judy. Someone might get hurt."

"Move it, KB!" Judy hollers from the Black Sheep van driving alongside my bike. She's leaning over Chili and Bob, who are filming out the open side door.

My lungs are burning and my thighs are shaking, but I force myself to step it up. "I'm going—as fast—as I can," I pant.

We were halfway to the aquarium when Judy decided she needed some generic bike shots. She picked a couple of streets across town, and I've been riding up steep hills ever since. I assume this is a punishment for insisting on going to the aquarium this morning when we could be doing something more ratings-friendly.

Judy waves her decaf, double-shot, no-foam, extra-hot Starbucks latte in my general direction. "Judy isn't happy, KB. Last week you complained all the way over to that giant splash pool, and now I can't keep you away from there."

"Maurice—won't be around—much longer," I manage to get out. I want to spend time with him." He's the closest thing to a pet I've ever had.

"If you could teach him how to talk, I'd be all for it. But it's dull, KB. You're as dull here as you were in New York."

That's probably true, but after Maurice's release, I'll still have a few weeks to turn my life from dull to dazzling. "Well, you picked me for the show because I'm boring, remember?"

"But Judy wants to help you change all that," she says.

Her van hits a bump, causing the latte to fly out of her hand. It hits Chili in the head and explodes all over the camera. Amid all the hysteria, no one notices I'm riding back downhill toward the aquarium.

My "pace van" catches up to me at Cannery Row. Judy has refueled at Starbucks, but her smile has disappeared.

Bob, Chili, and various other crew members hop out to capture my progress on foot, knowing that the rest of my journey is going to be a series of interruptions. These days, all the shopkeepers want my autograph or a photo—and free publicity. Apparently I am the only one (other than my parents, I presume) who hated the first episode of *The Black Sheep*. Whether I like it or not, I'm becoming a bit of a celebrity in this town.

On the upside, there are the freebies. Today's haul includes aromatherapy candles, a bag of saltwater taffy, a stack of comic books, and a magic wand that I intend to test on Judy later. Yesterday's haul featured a certificate for ten complimentary video games, a jar of Hellfire Salsa, a California flag, and a bottle of champagne that Judy immediately confiscated.

On the downside, it takes twice as long to get anywhere.

I'm almost late for my shift of monitoring Maurice, and Lisa starts in on the lecture without delay. "I expect you to be on time and act professionally," she says.

You'd almost think there was a paycheck involved. But if I argue, it will only bring on more reminders about how it's hard work and discipline that got her into graduate school. Far be it from me to give her a chance to brag.

I grab a chart and get down to business, with Lisa hovering over my shoulder and explaining the procedure as if I'm not already a pro at it. Mitch's arrival saves me from pointing this out. He asks Lisa for help with an otter, and she takes off so fast that I feel the after-burn on my neck. Judy winks at me before pursuing them with the crew.

There's no way Lisa and Mitch are an item. Sure, he's hot, but he has a black hole where his personality should be. Plus, he's barely out of high school. Lisa would have to be really immature for her age to go for Mitch. But then, guys her own age probably get turned off by nonstop lecturing.

My time with Maurice is running out. If all goes well, Lisa expects to release him in just a few days. Even though I know that's exactly how it should be, I can't help worrying. Here, he is safe and well cared for. Out there in the big bad ocean, it's every otter for himself, and Maurice looks awfully thin. Lisa is pretty stingy with the fish, if you ask me. If she weren't so focused on Mitch, she'd notice that Maurice is hungry.

Fortunately, someone is more attentive to his needs. That would be me, his new best friend. A friend doesn't let another friend starve just because the boss is busy chasing younger men. So, at the end of my shift, I drop my report on Lisa's desk and head for the food preparation room, where people are assembling buckets of crab and mussels for the various residents.

I've watched otter feedings many times on the monitors. Lisa would have me believe that it's a mysterious, compli-cated ritual, but there doesn't appear to be much skill involved. Any ten-year-old could do it.

Besides, this Black Sheep no longer follows the flock unquestioningly. My new code continues to evolve. It's not just a series of rules anymore; it's a whole school of thought. Black Sheepism is simple yet edgy; scholarly yet enlight-ened; structured yet flexible. As a Black Sheepist, I reject the philosophies of the current regime and forge ahead with my own.

It's not easy developing your own movement, though, and as mine matures, I've had to reorder my rules on the fly. Black Sheep Rule Number One, for example, has just now become what it always should have been: *Rules are made to be broken.*

The food prep volunteers are so deep into their discussion

about porifera (which sounds exotic but turns out to be the sea sponge) that they don't even notice when I help myself to a bucket of fish scraps and sneak out of the kitchen with it. My luck holds in the supply room, where I liberate a welder's mask and poncho and slip into them unnoticed.

If I'd known breaking the rules was this easy, I'd have started years ago.

Things get tougher when I arrive on the deck of Maurice's pool to find a volunteer in identical Darth Vader garb scrubbing down the tiles.

"I thought he'd already been fed," the other Darth says.

The voice sounds too low for Lisa's and too high for Mitch's, so I bluff. "Lisa ordered an extra feeding to build up his strength before he's released."

The volunteer nods as if this makes perfect sense, collects his or her gear, and leaves.

Who knew I was such a good actor? Maybe I belong in television after all.

I walk backward to the edge of the pool, just as I've seen Lisa do it, and Maurice starts barking excitedly behind me. Following the standard routine, I scoop a handful of slimy fish and toss it over my head. There's a series of splashes, followed by loud crunching. It would be disgusting if it weren't Maurice. As his new best friend, I'm willing to overlook bad table manners.

If Judy had any sense at all, she'd focus the whole show

on my remarkable interspecies connection with Maurice. The audience would sob uncontrollably as we face the ultimate separation, but I will be strong. I understand that he has to go back. He probably has a family out there that misses him, maybe a fuzzy-faced otter wife who doesn't mind his crunching.

I have turned to gaze at my little pal when a sound makes me jump.

"What the hell are you doing?" someone says in a low hiss.

The empty bucket flies out of my hand and hits the deck with a clatter. Maurice dives to the bottom of the pool and stays there.

I fooled the first volunteer, so I'm sure I can fool the second. "Lisa ordered an extra feeding to prep him for release." I'm impressed by the way the lies are rolling off my tongue today. Usually I babble nervously under pressure, but as a newly indoctrinated Black Sheep, I'm one slick customer.

"Oh, did I?" the new Darth says. "Why don't I remember that?"

Oops. My only hope now is that Lisa doesn't recognize my voice.

"Get in my office right now, Kendra."

Okay, so I won't be collecting the People's Choice Award just yet.

* * *

The light of Chili's camera burns like an interrogation lamp. In the shadows behind him, Mitch is slumped in his chair. Judy, on the other hand, is perched on the edge of hers as if life at the splash pool just got a lot more interesting.

I hook my elbow casually over the back of my chair, following Black Sheep Rule Number Five: *Never let them see you sweat.*

"Why do you think you're an exception to the rules around here?" Lisa demands. She's asked the same question several times in the past ten minutes and it's taught me a valuable lesson: people can ask any question they want, and I can answer it any way I want. A Black Sheep doesn't just tell them what they want to hear; a Black Sheep stays on message.

"Like I said, Maurice looked hungry," I repeat. "I was worried he wouldn't be strong enough for release in two days."

"He looked hungry to your expert eye?"

"That's right."

"And you could tell that *how?*"

"I've been watching him for days. We have a connection."

Judy laughs. Lisa and Mitch don't.

"I really don't know what to say to that," Lisa says.

"Okay, then," I say, half rising. "If we're done here . . ."

"We're not."

I sink back into my seat and glance at my watch. Carrie and I are supposed to meet shortly to get ready for the party. I could wrap this up quickly by telling Lisa what she wants to hear: that I lost my head to fame; that Judy is pressuring me to do the wrong thing; and last, that I am very sorry for breaking the rules. Unfortunately, my mouth has other plans. "I don't see why you're making such a big deal about this, Lisa. It was just a bucket of fish."

"It was not just a bucket of fish. The rules exist for a reason."

"Just think of me as an exception to the rules—like you think of Mitch."

Lisa scowls, but doesn't respond.

"Tell me, Lisa," Judy says, "will Kendra's behavior derail your plans to *Free Willy*?"

My bravado evaporates instantly. It never occurred to me that sliding Maurice an extra snack could ruin his chance at freedom. "Why would that matter?"

"You gave him the wrong mix," Lisa says. "If he gets sick, we can't release him."

Judy's head twitches toward Chili, but he is too riveted by Lisa to notice. At least, he is until Mitch nudges him helpfully. "Judy wants you to get a shot of Kendra's expression," he says. "She looks like she's going to faint."

"Shut up, Mitch," I say. How can he make fun of me when there's so much at stake for Maurice? "Do you think he'll be okay, Lisa?"

She pauses long enough to make sure I really get the point before letting me off the hook. "Probably."

I'm so relieved that it takes me a while to tune in to the lecture again.

"I won't tolerate your recklessness," Lisa is saying. "I'm sure you get away with acting like a spoiled child in New York, but around here, the animals are the priority."

"Maurice is a priority for me, too," I tell her.

"If you want a pet, get a goldfish. The rest of us are here to study, and you're disrupting our work. Since you can't be trusted, I don't want you here unless you're supervised."

I gesture at the crew. "I'm supervised constantly."

Lisa turns to Mitch. "Your family brought her in here, *you* keep an eye on her."

Judy jumps in before Mitch can protest. "Good idea. Mitch is used to babysitting."

Black Sheep Rule Number Six: *It isn't murder when you're doing the world a favor.*

Carrie rolls her eyes as Mitch stalks ahead of us up the street. "I know Mona asked him to chaperone tonight, but it's not like she's around to know whether he actually does."

"He would know," I say, projecting my voice. "Perfect, responsible, *exceptional* Mitch would never ignore a commitment."

Mitch speeds up until he's nearly out of sight. Not that

I care. I couldn't be happier that he refused to walk with us. Since the crew went ahead to set up, Carrie and I have a rare opportunity to chat privately. We've already managed to share stories from our past, and our hopes and dreams for the future. Finally, I have the chance to ask the question that's been on my mind for days: "Do you think that hot guy from the mall will be at the party?"

"Jordan? Absolutely. He's Aaron's best friend."

We turn down Aaron's street and I'm suddenly wracked with insecurity about my hair, my makeup, my outfit, and my personality—or lack thereof.

"You'll be fine," Carrie reassures me. "That skirt and tank top are all you need. It's casual and sexy all rolled into one."

At the end of the driveway, we hear someone shout, "They're here," and the bright lights of several cameras flick on. Although I've become more accustomed to being in the spotlight lately, it's still intimidating. I stop in the middle of the road and rummage through my purse.

"Quit stalling," Carrie says. "You're practically the guest of honor."

"Please."

"I'm serious," she says. "You're famous around this town. I've had calls from people I don't even know asking if they can hang with you."

"That's ridiculous," I say. Although I owe a lot of my newfound popularity to the cameras I can take credit for some of it. While I'm not cool myself, I do come from a cool place. I'm practically an ambassador.

Clicking my purse shut, I throw my shoulders back and lead Carrie up the front stairs with a new attitude—a Black Sheep attitude. There's a crowd on the front porch, Judy among them. She takes a long drag from her cigarette as I approach.

"You made it," she says, exhaling a stream of smoke in my face. She's wearing a low-cut sundress, high-heeled mules, and bright blue contact lenses. For a moment I dare to hope she's off duty, but she snaps her fingers at me to follow her into the house.

Chili turns his lens on me, and within seconds I am surrounded by a circle of strangers. A very well-dressed circle of strangers. It's only a house party, but everyone has gone all out. In fact, I'm underdressed. I turn to Carrie to complain, but the bright lights have already driven her out the back door.

Aaron welcomes me with a kiss on the cheek and introduces Jordan, who promptly offers me a beer.

I hesitate. I haven't explored Black Sheepism enough to know whether underage drinking is part of the movement—especially underage drinking on national television. However, a Black Sheep cannot be a wimp. These people think I'm an urban sophisticate—a cultural trailblazer. They might even believe my life is one long string of concerts, parties, and gallery openings.

Black Sheep Rule Number Seven: *Give the public what they want.*

"I prefer martinis," I say, waving the bottle away.

Aaron and Jordan glance at each other quickly, probably impressed by my worldliness.

"I'll see what I can do," Aaron says, "although my parents locked the bar."

Tia, who has joined us, says, "According to *In Style*, martinis are the hip drink in New York clubs right now. Are you into the club scene?"

I'd say yes but I doubt she's referring to the Algebra Club. "I'm, uh, more into the gallery scene. There's a phenomenal retrospective at the Guggenheim right now." At least, Mom said it's phenomenal. I was sulking too much over giving up an afternoon of discount shopping with Lucy to get anything out of it. "It's on modern art of the 1920s."

"How can art that's eighty years old be called 'modern'?" Aaron asks.

"Modernism actually dates back to the late nineteenth century," I explain, happy to share my knowledge, as a good ambassador must. Mom covered the modern art movement so extensively during our après-gallery quiz that I almost passed out over my tea and scones. "The movement got its name because artists were rejecting the past as a model for the present." Much like Black Sheepism, in fact.

"That's cool," Tia says. She sounds serious, but a couple of the other kids snicker and start edging away, revealing

Mitch leaning against the living room mantel. He's smirking.

Okay, so I overestimated my audience's appetite for culture, but maybe I can recapture their interest by exploring common ground.

"I haven't missed the art scene, though," I say. "Your aquarium is more interesting than any gallery."

Aaron shrugs indifferently. "Never been."

"Me either," Jordan says.

"I went on a school trip once," Tia says. "There are fish, right?"

"More than fish," I say, trying not to look surprised that they know so little about a local landmark. After all, plenty of New Yorkers haven't been to the Empire State Building. "There are penguins and turtles, and a pool where you can touch a stingray."

"Is there a pool where you can touch a beaver?" another guy asks, and Tia punches him in the arm.

An ambassador has class, so I ignore him and carry on. "It's worth a visit for the sea otters alone. They're so much fun to watch."

Tia tries to feign interest. "Really?"

"Really," I say. Maybe I could win back unsupervised aquarium visits if I manage to recruit some new volunteers. Surely they'd want to get involved if they knew all the facts. "Otters are so smart you wouldn't believe it. Unfortunately, they're endangered. People used to kill them for their pelts."

"Uh-huh?" Tia gives up all pretense and turns a full-watt smile on Chili.

"The aquarium's always looking for people to help out," I continue. "Especially with raising public awareness."

Judy slices a hand across her throat. "Save your battery for something interesting, Chili. Let's set up in the backyard and get some B-roll of the party."

They head outside, and most of the party stampedes after them. Only Aaron and Jordan seem to be immune to the call of the camera. But what do I do now? Obviously my shtick isn't working, and I haven't had much practice dazzling guys with my sparkling conversation.

"I guess environmental activism isn't for everyone," I say, running a hand through my hair and smiling nervously at the guys.

"I guess not," Aaron says, returning my smile and running a hand through his own hair.

I remember reading an article in *Cosmo Girl* that said mimicking gestures is one of the "Five Surefire Signs" that a guy is into you. Well, Jordan is cuter, but Aaron is still pretty hot. And a Black Sheep always has a backup plan.

"You guys should think about getting involved," I continue. "I could introduce you to the director of volunteers."

Aaron suddenly leans toward me, as if he is going to kiss me. As much as I'd like to be Black Sheep–casual about it, I lean away from him. It's not so much that I object to kissing a guy I've met only once before; it's that it would be weird in front of Jordan. Monterey is a little too laid back in some respects, if you ask me.

Far from being discouraged, Aaron leans closer still and parts his lips in an exaggerated smile. "Are my teeth okay?" he asks. "I forgot to brush after dinner."

Cosmo didn't cover this turn of events. "Yeah, you're all clear."

"Then I'm ready for my close-up," he says, letting out a loud belch that engulfs me in lager fumes.

Jordan shakes his head as his friend leaves. "The guy's a pig. Sorry about that."

"It's okay." I glance around and see we're entirely alone. Obviously the real guests of honor here are the film crew, but I think I can cope with the disappointment. Who needs a crowd when you've got one cute guy?

"I hear you're like a celebrity at Cannery Row," he says.

"Oh, not really." A Black Sheep is always modest.

"You're getting all kinds of free stuff, right?"

"Nothing too exciting."

"But the arcade manager said he gave you free game coupons."

Okay, so our definition of exciting differs, but I see what he's doing: he's hinting around for a date. Fortunately, *Cosmo* was clear about my next step. I must encourage him. "That's right, and I haven't used them yet because I'm not that good at video games. Maybe you could—"

"Take them off your hands?" he interrupts. "That's what I was hoping you'd say. There's this girl I want to ask out, but I'm low on funds. You know how it is."

My diaphragm takes so long to expand after the sucker punch that I fear it's down for good. Eventually I get enough breath to say, "Sorry, I promised them to Mitch."

"Mulligan?" he asks, crestfallen. "He sucks at video games. Are you sure?"

"I'm sure. But I have a jar of free salsa if you want it."

He doesn't even bother to answer before bolting out the back door.

Now I'm really alone, and this is officially the worst night of my life.

Mitch appears in the kitchen doorway. "He's right. I do suck at video games." He waits a beat before adding, "But I'll take the free salsa if you're offering."

"It's all yours," I say. My voice sounds faint and faraway, because it's traveling all the way up from deepest mortification.

He must know this, because he says, "They're both jerks."

I swallow hard as this sinks in. "You were listening the whole time?"

"Pretty much. It's not like I could face going outside. But look on the bright side: I didn't film your conversation for the rest of America."

"How many times do I have to tell you that Judy lied to

me about that? Can't you give it up now?"

"Okay, but only because I can see you're overwrought that it didn't work out with the jerks."

"Shut up."

"Uh-uh, you've used that one today. Maybe someone will offer you some free comebacks down at Cannery Row."

I throw myself onto the couch, exasperated. "Just leave me alone."

"Can't. Chaperoning. I'm exceptional at it, remember?"

"Then let's go home."

"But you haven't even had a martini yet."

I close my eyes, defeated. When I open them again, he is standing over me, pouring Sprite into a plastic martini glass.

I accept the glass with a sigh. "I just drove thirty people outside with my conversational skills. It's the first time I've ever really understood how my parents feel."

"I'll let you in on a little secret: jerks find beer more interesting than art."

I laugh. Obviously the faux martini is loosening me up.

"You shouldn't care what they think," he says, pulling back the curtain to reveal thirty teens trying desperately to attract the crew's attention by bellowing several different songs at the same time.

"It's like they're auditioning for *American Idol*," I say.

Mitch offers a rare smile. "More like *American Idiot*." He stares out into the backyard for a while before speaking again. "If you're really interested in otters, you should see them in their own environment."

"You mean the ocean?"

"No, I mean the Del Monte Center. They've taken over the food court. Some poor old lady got swarmed for tuna salad last week."

"That's why I always go for the mock egg," I say. "I hear they hate tofu."

Mitch's smile widens. "If you promise not to tip Judy off, I'll take you to see them tomorrow."

Okay, so maybe this isn't the worst night of my life, after all.

Manhattan leaps into the open dresser drawer and attacks the orange circle of light that is tracking across my clothes.

"You'll need to wear a bathing suit," Meadow whispers.

"A bathing suit?" I whisper back. "Why?"

She peers up at me, and the beam of her tiger head flashlight hits the ceiling. "Because you'll be tracking otters."

I had to tell Meadow about my plans to sneak out early with Mitch. I was afraid she'd make such a commotion when she found me gone that the overnight crew stationed outside in the van would alert Judy.

"He said 'seeing' otters, not tracking them," I say. "I don't even own a bathing suit." If I did, I certainly wouldn't be wearing it on a date, even if it's only a date to see otters.

"How can you not own a bathing suit? Everyone owns a bathing suit."

"Why would I need one? There are no pools in New York City." Okay, they exist, I've just never been in one of them. Bankers don't need to swim, so my parents don't waste time on water. In fact, I only know how to dog paddle because Lucy's family took me to Florida to visit Nana Russell and she taught me the basics.

Meadow is so thrown by this news that she has to turn to Logan for support. As in Logan Waters, the pop star for whom she recently erected a shrine in the corner, featuring posters, CDs, magazines, and other groupie paraphernalia. I think she's hoping he'll watch the show, see the shrine, and come to take her away from all this.

The flashlight hits Logan's smile and gives her strength to carry on. "You're such a freak," she says.

"This from the girl who went through my magazines and drew devil horns on the model Logan is dating."

Meadow grins, as unfazed by her freakish behavior as I am by mine. So what if I don't have the right otter-watching gear? When a Black Sheep runs into a situation for which she isn't prepared, she simply creates a new rule, in this case: *Adapt, Adjust, and Ad-lib.*

"Either keep the light steady or give it to me and go back to bed," I say.

She trains the beam on my drawer once more, and I ease a pair of shorts and a T-shirt out from under the ferret. It's just the right outfit for a sunrise walk along the shore.

Meadow shines her light on my face so that I can see my reflection in the mirror while I apply eyeliner and mascara. Then I twist my hair into a casual updo and pull out a few tendrils. It may be a quarter to five in the morning, but if there's even a slight possibility that Mitch considers this a real date, I can't go with flat hair, and eyes that look lashless when no one is aiming a flashlight at me.

"You're going to a lot of trouble for some otters," Meadow observes from her perch on the bed.

"We're going on to the aquarium later. Maurice likes me to look my best."

"Did you know otters are in the same family as weasels and ferrets?"

"Maurice is not a ferret, and I want you to apologize to him later for saying so."

She snorts. "You're awfully calm for someone who doesn't like water."

"It's no big deal." Why would it be? I've been watching otters for weeks and today I'll see them in a different setting, that's all. Even a confirmed New Yorker likes to feel the sand beneath her feet once in a while.

Frankly, I'm more nervous about trying to get along with Mitch. We've never lasted more than an hour together without a fight. Plus, I'm worried that he'll pull some stunt like taking me on a really tough hiking trail just to prove his manhood. Lucy says guys do stuff like that all the time. But if Mitch does get all macho, I will cope. A Black Sheep takes it as it comes.

Meadow directs her light out the window and onto the driveway. "You'd better hurry. Mitch is loaded up and ready to go."

Over her shoulder, I see Mitch standing in the circle of light beside the van. He cuts a finger across his throat to signal that we should turn off the light. "What was that on the roof of the van?" I ask, as the light goes out. "A boat?" Meadow snickers. "Oh my God, you're even more of a freak than I thought."

Black Sheepism has been progressing in leaps and bounds lately, but it's desperately short on information in the relationship department. Last night's fiasco with Aaron and Jordan didn't give me much faith in what I've picked up from *Cosmo* either. Especially since they were relatively normal guys and Mitch is far from that. He is the freak in this equation, not me. Who would invite someone on a date without specifying it's on the high seas? When he said he'd take me to see otters "in their own environment," I assumed we'd be staying in *ours* to do it.

The least he could do is try to make polite conversation. I've been doing all the work en route to Nature-ville, and it hasn't gone well. Clearly, he's not a morning person. I started out all bright and chipper, asking questions and generally being dateable. All I got in return were grunts. I asked why he's bringing a boat along, and he said, "It's a kayak." So then I asked if he does this often and he said, "Yes." Running out of steam, I asked if the otters would be up by the time we got there.

"As long as they set their alarm," he said. "I called ahead to say we're coming."

Okay, it was a stupid question, but at least I'm trying. It's rude to invite someone out and then ridicule her, if you ask me. But I can be as silent as he is, if not more so. A Black Sheep enjoys spending time with her own thoughts.

The sky is lighter by the time we pull onto the shoulder and get out of the van. Mitch unhooks the red kayak and takes it off the roof. There's a yellow one strapped beside it.

Uh-oh.

"This one's Maya's," he says. "Can you carry it?"

Of course I can carry it. If Maya can, I can. Technically, it's not that heavy, just long and cumbersome. I keep losing my grip and smashing it into things. Each time, Mitch flinches. There's enough light now to see that.

As I follow him down the winding path to the shore, I make up my mind that this is definitely not a date. Maybe it's some kind of test to see if I warrant a real date. Or maybe he's going to bump me off to end the TV show. I should have brought Meadow along as protection.

If it's a test, I fail miserably ten minutes into the walk, when I trip over a rock and fall under the kayak. Mitch puts his down and pulls mine off me. "Just leave it here," he says. "I'll come back for it."

I trail after him empty-handed, trying to plot my escape. I know that Mitch is a pro at kayaking, but he won't be in the boat with me and he isn't much of a talker. If I have to figure out how to drive the thing on my own, I'm in big trouble.

"Are there sharks out there?" I call after him.

"It is the ocean," he says.

Mitch, too, has mastered the art of answering questions any way he wants.

"Have you seen any around here?" I ask.

"Not *right* around here. How close do you mean?"

"You're trying to scare me."

"No, *you're* trying to scare you. I'm just helping out."

I see there's a price to be paid for hanging out with smart, hot guys. They toy with you like sharks tossing a surfer's severed limb. "Do sharks eat otters?"

"As appetizers," he says. "Kayaks are the main course." He turns, and I see his teeth glinting in the gloom.

It was actually better when he wasn't speaking. Then I could almost imagine that we were destined for each other.

Dawn is breaking by the time we finally reach the shore. Mitch sets his kayak on the ground and says he's going back for Maya's.

"I've got a better idea," I say. "Why don't I watch you from the shore?" A Black Sheep cannot grab life by the tail if a shark grabs her first.

"You're coming with me, City Girl. The otters got up early just for you."

* * *

Mitch sets the second kayak beside the first one and opens his knapsack. "First things first," he says as he tosses something dark at me. "Put on your skirt."

My skirt? What's he doing carrying a skirt? Is it something kinky? If so, he's in for a disappointment. I whip the fabric back at him. "I'll be more comfortable in shorts, thank you."

Mitch shakes his head, bemused. "Most people wear it *over* their shorts." He wraps the fabric around his waist to demonstrate and pulls the attached suspenders over his shoulders. "It snaps onto the cockpit to keep you dry."

I watch as he trades his running shoes for a pair of neoprene booties and straps on a life vest. Anyone else would look like a total nerd in that getup, but the fact that he is entirely unselfconscious about it somehow makes him hotter than ever.

"Hurry up and dress, Cinderella," he says, hauling Maya's yellow kayak down to the water. "Your pumpkin awaits."

I sullenly pull on my kayaking gear, knowing that I will not look hotter in it because I'm uncool in the first place.

My nylon tutu sways as I pick my way down to the shore in rubber booties. Mitch is standing knee-deep in the surf, holding the kayak steady for me. There's a tiny opening that I'm apparently supposed to jam myself into without tipping. I stare at the boat, gripped with fear—not of drowning but of something far worse: humiliation. The Black Sheep rules swirl in my head, but I can't catch hold of one that might help me make the first move.

"You'll be fine," Mitch says, sounding a little nicer. "It's awkward, but the water is shallow and I'm here to keep her steady."

The correct rule finally lands: *Suck it up*. At this point, what else am I going to do? Sit in the van and wait for him?

Mitch explains how I'm supposed to get into the boat using my paddle for support. He walks me through it step-by-step, making it sound like any reasonably coordinated person could do it.

Twenty minutes later, I accept that I am uncoordinated as well as uncool. Playing twister on a waterbed would be easier than this. I am soaked to the armpits and I still haven't managed to get into the kayak.

"One more try," I gasp. This time, my sodden shorts sink to my ankles. Mitch is still leaning over the boat, so he gets a close-up of my panties—the ones with the dollar signs all over them that Lucy gave me last year as a joke.

"Ka-ching," he says, grinning.

"Don't look!" I yank up my shorts and anchor them in place with one hand.

"Then get on with it already," he says. "The otters are already breaking for lunch."

With a valiant effort, I swing one leg aboard. Mitch tells me how to use the paddle for balance, but I can't bring myself to lift my other foot off the ground.

Exasperated, he grabs my leg and stuffs it into the boat. The kayak rolls perilously, but he steadies it and attaches the spray skirt. "Don't move," he says, letting go to climb into his own kayak.

A couple of gentle waves lift the kayak and drop it again. Miraculously, I don't tip. "Hey, this isn't so bad," I say, turning to look at Mitch. The movement causes my kayak to list sharply to the right.

"Use your paddle!" he calls. "Lean to the left!"

I dig my paddle into the ocean floor and throw my weight over to the other side.

"Not so hard!"

I rock to the right, and am about to flip, when Mitch manages to line his kayak up alongside mine and grabs it.

"Keep your movements slow and gentle," he says. "Imagine yourself standing on the arm of a seesaw and try to find your balance."

I've never stood on the arm of a seesaw. *The BLAH* was quite specific about misuse of playground equipment. Still, I can imagine it. Balance is a series of constant tiny adjustments. It's a state of mind.

When I've achieved a Zenlike calm, I begin to follow Mitch's directions for paddling. Just a dip to the right and another to the left and we're off. Slowly but surely, I get a feel for it. Soon I am so focused that Mitch's voice startles me.

"Faster," he says. And then, "Too fast. Just try to—"

"I'm finding my rhythm," I interrupt. "You just keep your eyes open for sharks."

He leads the way out toward a point of land that juts into the ocean. The water gets a little rougher, but with constant recalibration, I manage to make it into the quiet inlet without capsizing. Here, thick forests of kelp spread for about two hundred yards offshore. In the distance, there's a long white beach with windswept cypress trees clinging to the rocky cliffs above it. The pale blue sky above and the deeper blue of the water below make it a breathtaking sight.

I set my paddle down and stare. "This is incredible."

Mitch actually smiles right at me. "I know, and no one ever sees it, because there's no road access. It's my secret cove."

He's sharing his secret cove with me! That can only mean one thing: it *is* a real date. For all I know, Mitch may even—

"I was sure you'd blow it with Judy," he says.

Okay, so he doesn't exactly love me. "Thanks a lot."

"Can you blame me? Every time I turn around, there's a camera in my face."

"Tell me about it." He opens his mouth to speak, and I hold up my hand. "I know, I know, it's my own fault."

"Well, I don't want to see cameras here. Judy would suck the magic out of this place in three seconds flat."

"And then ask for a re-shoot," I say.

He gives me another smile before unsnapping his skirt

and pulling out his knapsack. Then he maneuvers his kayak next to mine and passes me a banana, a juice box, and a bag of trail mix. Setting our paddles across our boats, we drift along eating our breakfast. Every so often he reaches out to grab my kayak to keep it close by.

It's a perfect moment—maybe the best of my life so far. At first it's hard for me not to start up a little chitchat about the scenery or the kelp or just about anything else to break the silence. But I sneak a sideways glance at him and decide to keep a lid on it. He looks happy enough. Maybe he's the type of guy who doesn't expect to be entertained on a date.

Eventually, I stop obsessing over the fact that I am on the most exciting, most uncomfortable date anyone ever had, and start enjoying the sound of the water slapping quietly against the boats, and the seabirds calling to each other as they circle above.

The sun has climbed over the ridge behind us and is glistening on the water like a million silver sequins.

"It's like Fifth Avenue," I say wonderingly.

Mitch looks at me as if I've lost my mind.

"The water," I explain. "There's something in the pavement on Fifth Avenue that sparkles just like this on a sunny day."

"Don't you ever get sick of all that concrete?" he asks. "And all the buildings? I bet you can't even see the stars at night."

"Maybe not the ones in the sky, but there are millions of

lights in New York City. It's a constellation all on its own."

He watches me curiously. "Homesick?"

I think for a moment before answering. "Sometimes. This has been a lot harder than I expected."

He collects the remains of my breakfast and stows the bag under his skirt. "You expected moving alone to a strange city to be easy? You're more intrepid than I am."

Intrepid? I love that! Intrepid screams Black Sheep. Talk about evolving! They'll never let me back into the primordial ooze at this rate. I, Kendra Bishop, am an intrepid person.

Except that I'm not, really, and there's no use pretending. "More like stupid. If I could take back that letter I wrote to Judy . . ." I shudder. "It was awful."

"Do you wish you hadn't come?"

He's scanning for otters, so I can't tell if he cares one way or another. "Not exactly. But I wish I weren't part of this show. I wish I hadn't exposed my family's weirdness to the whole world."

"Not the whole world—just North America."

"That's comforting."

After a pause, he says, "They don't seem that weird to me."

"Oh, they are. You're only seeing the tip of the iceberg. And Judy's slanting the story."

"What did your parents do to make you write the letter?"

125

I consider telling him about Rosa but decide against it. The sun and the waves have lowered my defenses, but I still know he could use that against me. "I can't really talk about it."

"No problem," he says, letting me off the hook.

If the situation were reversed, I'd be trying to pry the story out of him just to see what makes him tick. "Things just weren't good at home, that's all. My parents are trying to mold me into a banker against my will, and it's a painful process." I turn the tables before he can ask anything more. "I think it's cool that you're doing exactly what you want to do with your life. By studying marine biology, I mean."

He shrugs this off. "It happens to be exactly what my parents would want, so I got lucky, I guess. I've been involved in environmental causes my whole life."

"I don't know very much about environmentalism." That's an understatement.

"I guessed that from the dollar signs on your underwear," he says.

"That's a joke. I'm not as shallow as you think."

He gives me a little splash with his paddle. "I'm kidding. Environmentalism just means being aware of how our behavior affects the planet. Even making small changes can help to leave the world a little better than when we found it."

I'm not so enthralled by him that I don't recognize a lecture when I hear it, but it's more tolerable when I can look into those blue eyes as I listen. There's something sexy about a guy with a cause.

Suddenly I hear a familiar grunting sound and spin around so fast I almost tip the kayak again. Mitch steadies it with his paddle and pulls out his binoculars. Ahead of us in the kelp a dozen brown heads bob up and down. Mitch puts a finger to his lips and we paddle toward them. Every whiskered face turns curiously to watch our approach. I want to see how close we can get, but Mitch stops well back from them and lifts his binoculars.

"Hey, it's Dory," he says, his voice more animated than I've ever heard it. He hands me the binoculars. "The one with the scar on her head. She's Number 505—the first otter I ever tracked."

Dory is floating on her back, calmly grooming herself.

Mitch's smile is so bright it competes with the sparkle of the waves. "She's doing great. I lost track of her a couple of years ago and wasn't sure she made it."

I hand him the binoculars so he can watch a little longer. When I figure he's spent enough time mooning over his old girlfriend, I take them back and ask, "So you're a fan of *Finding Nemo*?"

He raises his eyebrows. "What do you mean?"

"Don't be embarrassed. Lots of wilderness-loving tough guys love Disney."

"Well, not this one."

I can tell he's lying. "Meadow says you own the DVD—and that you've watched it a hundred times."

His mouth drops. "She's dead."

"Ha. Busted. She never said a word."

He grins sheepishly. "For the record, it's no more than twenty times."

"I won't tell anyone—as long as you agree to keep quiet about my Material Girl underwear."

He reaches out and pulls my kayak right next to his. "Deal."

Something about the way he's looking at me gives me goose bumps, although it may just be the cool breeze on my wet clothes. Whatever he is thinking, I don't think he hates me anymore. Obviously the rules of kayaking apply equally to relationships. If you make any sudden moves, you're tipping all over the place. Once you slow down and find the balance, it sorts itself out.

Mitch cocks his head to listen. "Do you hear that?"

For a moment, all I can hear is the water and gulls. Then I catch a distant hum.

"It sounds like a boat," I say. "I thought you said no one ever comes here."

"Not till today," he says. His brow furrows and I know the spell between us is broken.

A boat appears around the jut of land. I can make out three passengers, and as I watch, the smallest one raises a hand to her lips as if she's drinking something. My heart sinks. I can almost smell the decaf double-shot, no-foam, extra-hot latte from here.

"Oh, no." I raise the binoculars to see Chili at the back of the boat, steering, while Bob films from the middle seat. Judy is at the bow, Starbucks cup in one hand. She raises the other and waves.

"Tell me this isn't happening," Mitch says.

I look at him helplessly. "I'm sorry."

His eyes become blue lasers. "This is *my* place. You promised."

"Mitch, honestly, I didn't tell her."

"Then how would she know?"

He shoves my kayak away and I fight to steady it.

"They're heading straight for the kelp," he says. Raising his voice, he shouts, "Cut your engine!" The otters are startled at the commotion and dive.

In the other boat, Judy waves her coffee cup and calls, "Stay right where you are. We'll be right there."

They can't hear Mitch over the sputter of their motor, and when they reach the kelp, the motor makes a horrible screech as its blades get snarled in the plant's rubbery tentacles. The boat jerks to a stop, sending a rush of waves our way. I hastily loop the binoculars around my neck and pick up my paddle, but it's too late. The wave catches the side of my kayak and flips it.

Hanging upside down in the water, I fight to free myself from the spray skirt, tearing at it with both hands. Finally someone else's hands tear it away for me and pull me to the surface.

"Are you okay?" Mitch asks, releasing me.

Gasping, I tread water, just as Nana Russell taught me. "I'm fine." Then a horrible thought strikes me. "The otters . . . ?"

"None injured—no thanks to you."

Just as fast as I fell into the water, the old Mitch has returned. "I didn't—"

"Save your breath, you're going to need it," he says.

He hauls himself out of the water and flops across his kayak. His wet shorts cling to his butt, and I have to admit, if I weren't in the process of drowning, I'd enjoy the view.

"Heads up, KB!" Judy shouts as Chili rows toward us. "Look this way."

Mitch rights himself in his kayak and collects his paddle. "You owe me a set of binoculars."

"Stop all that splashing. Bob needs a tight shot," Judy says, now much closer. "Okay, kick it up again—make it big. Where are the seals, KB? I want a shot of you swimming with the seals."

Mitch snorts in disgust and starts paddling away.

"Where are you going?" I call after him. "What about me? I can't get back into the boat on my own!"

"Your friends will give you a hand," he calls back over his shoulder.

"I could drown before they get here!"

I'm exhausted and I can't tread water for much longer. Now that it's too late, I can see that an occasional jog with the folks would have helped my lung capacity.

Mitch is almost out of the inlet when I gather what's left of my breath to bellow, "If I die, it's on your head! You'll rot in jail for the rest of your life, and then how are you going to save the world, Superman?"

He shouts back, "Go home, City Girl."

"You may love the planet, but you don't give a shit about people!" Oops. I hope Bob's mike didn't pick that up. On the other hand, if Bob is getting this, I want America to know what a monster Mitch Mulligan is. And what a wonderful person I am. "Tell my parents I forgive them!"

I don't need Judy to point out that this is good TV. I wonder if they give out Emmys posthumously.

"Tell them yourself, drama queen," Mitch calls. "You've thrashed your way into shallow water. Stand up."

It's just as well I didn't drown this afternoon, because my parents are too busy bonding with Maya to plan my funeral.

With Bob's camera in my face, I struggle to keep my expression neutral as I watch Maya and Dad touring his office; Maya and Mom having an animated discussion at the Whitney; Maya and Lucy laughing their asses off at a Broadway play. It's not like I care that much, but would it kill them to pretend they miss me a little?

There's no escape from the images, however, because Judy read me the riot act after Bob and Chili pulled me out of the water earlier. Belching coffee fumes into my face, she ranted about how she'll sue me for breach of contract if I run off again, and how it's her right to document every aspect of my life because she "owns me."

It was enough to make this little black sheep feel cheap.

Chapter 8

Today there's a production assistant on security detail in the upstairs hallway as I leave the bedroom. Judy usually keeps the crew "lean and mean," but she's obviously brought in reinforcements.

"The lamb's on the move," the PA says into her walkie-talkie. "Kitchen ETA, sixty seconds."

"Got it," Judy's voice crackles back. "Keep a close eye on her."

How I'd manage to escape between bedroom and kitchen is beyond me, unless that magic wand I got at Cannery Row last week actually works. Still, the PA follows me so closely that when I turn at the bottom of the stairs, she runs into me.

She presses her walkie button again. "Incoming."

I shake my head in disgust. Since my ill-fated trip to otter country with Mitch, *The Black Sheep* crew has been out in full force. Things had been a bit more relaxed lately, with occasional moments of privacy, but no more. Judy has stepped up surveillance, and a camera follows me wherever I go, with the exception of the bathroom.

The kitchen is abuzz with activity when I enter. Bob is at the stove beside Mona, stirring a vat of scrambled eggs.

Chili is standing behind him playing backseat cook. "Add a dash of cream."

"Water makes a fluffier egg," Bob counters.

Judy picks up a camera and shoves it at Chili. "How about doing your job—while you still have one?"

He tracks me to the kitchen counter, where I stand by to grab the next two slices of bread as they pop out of the toaster.

Meadow looks up from the toast she is buttering, and I see she is wearing full makeup applied with a very heavy hand.

"Is that my purple eye shadow?" I ask.

She shrugs. "I found it on the dresser."

"You mean in my makeup bag."

"I can't remember the details. I've got a lot going on, you know."

I start spreading peanut butter on my toast. "How about asking first? Maybe I don't want your eye cooties."

"Then I'll keep it. It suits me better anyway."

"You think? Let's check with Kieran on that."

Her hand spasms midair while reaching for the strawberry jam. "Who?"

"That guy from your class we ran into at the drugstore last week. You know, the one who asked for your autograph. Maybe he'd like to weigh in on the eye shadow."

134

Her face matches the jam. "You think you're so smart. *Mom!*"

Mona turns from the stove, where she's frying a couple of pounds of turkey bacon. "What, honey?" Seeing me, she says, "Oh! You're here."

Of course I'm here. Where else would I be?

Max comes in from the backyard with the twins. "Kendra! What are you still doing here?"

"I'm supposed to stay another two weeks," I say. "If I've been fired, no one's told me yet."

Max laughs. "No such luck, kid. I just thought you'd be in Big Sur with Mitch."

Fat chance of that. Mitch and I haven't spoken a word to each other since he left me to drown. In fact, he's spent the last two days next door at the Watsons. I know that because I've seen him from the bathroom window coming and going with Calvin. Not that I'm spying or anything. I just spend as much time in the bathroom as Judy and the family roster allow because it's the only place I can be alone.

"Kayaking isn't really my thing," I tell them. Actually, I kind of liked it, except for the drowning part, but I can't be straight with them. They're nice people and they don't need to know their son is a moron—a moron who had the nerve to call me a drama queen.

"They're releasing an otter this morning," Mona says. "The one you've been monitoring. We figured you'd go to watch."

"Maurice?" I drop my knife on the floor with a clatter. "They're releasing Maurice?" Egg starts to whimper in his high chair.

Judy twitches, and Bob immediately abandons the eggs to seize his camera. Chili hustles around the counter to get a clear shot.

The cameras don't inhibit my reaction today. "Why didn't someone tell me?"

Mona goes over to soothe Egg. "I'm sorry, dear. We thought you knew."

I can understand why Lisa wouldn't tell me—she's still mad that I broke the rules. But Mitch is another story. He knows how much Maurice means to me. "I didn't even get to say good-bye."

I race for the front door, followed by the entire entourage. On the porch, I toss my toast into the bushes and grab Maya's bicycle.

"Honey, you can't ride," Max says. "It would take hours to get to Big Sur on a bike."

"Can you drive me?" I plead. "It's really important."

"I would if I could, but the van broke down again."

Mona turns to Judy. "*You* drive her."

"Mona, sweetie," Judy says, "I don't think you understand my role here. I'm supposed to document events as they unfold. If I started chauffeuring KB around, I'd be influencing the outcome of those events, thereby destroying the authenticity of the show." She leans in a little and adds slowly, "I'm an observer, not a participant."

Mona flips her long gray braid over her shoulder and gives Judy a look that would turn anyone who had a heart to stone. "That's the biggest load of crap you've delivered so far." She holds one hand in front of Chili, palm up. "Give me the keys to your van."

Chili lowers his camera. "Huh?"

Judy shakes her head. "Don't, Chili. Insurance . . ."

"If you know what's good for you, young man, you'll hand them over," Mona says, crowding Chili a little. He surrenders them without delay.

Max looks on in obvious pride as my guardian angel in purple Birkenstocks leads the parade down the driveway.

"This is highly unorthodox," Judy calls from the rear of the van, where she's sitting on camera cases with Bob and Chili.

Meadow and I are sharing the passenger seat, and we have to brace ourselves as Mona takes a hard right. Equipment slides across the floor of the van, and something collides with Judy's flip-flops.

When Judy stops screaming, Mona glances in the rearview mirror and asks, "Shouldn't you be wearing safer footwear?"

Judy mutters something unintelligible.

"There are children present," Mona says.

"One child," I point out. "Although she's made up to look thirty."

Meadow pinches me savagely.

"I could have you charged with stealing," Judy continues.

Mona chuckles. "Add it to my record."

"What record?" Meadow asks.

"Never mind," her mother says.

Meadow starts dancing in her seat when we get close to the beach. "I can see them launching the Zodiac!" We hang on to the dash as the van careens down the gravel road toward the ocean. "Faster, Mom! We're going to miss it!"

Mona guns the engine and people on the beach turn to watch as we streak toward them. When we reach the end of the road, Mona slams on the brakes and the van skids to a stop in a spray of gravel and sand. We miss a jeep by inches.

I scramble out before everyone else and run to the shore. Mitch is standing with a group of people, watching the Zodiac as it approaches a small raft of otters. That he doesn't show the slightest recognition when he sees me infuriates me even more. In fact, the only time I remember feeling this angry is when my parents fired Rosa.

I waste no time in getting to the point. "I hate you."

Mitch makes a show of looking over both shoulders to see who's with me. "Save the drama for the cameras."

He's trying to throw me off, but I'm not falling for it. "Why didn't you tell me this was happening today?"

Mitch shrugs. "I didn't think you'd care."

"You knew I'd care."

Noticing that Bob and Chili have sidled up behind us, Mitch says, "You're right, I did know you'd care about missing a good photo op. It was horrible of me. I'm so sorry."

"Thank God your parents are nicer than you are. Mona hijacked the show's van and nearly killed us all to get here in time."

He points to Judy, who's limping across the beach on her injured foot, and says, "She should have tried a little harder." Then he turns to another aquarium volunteer and says, "Can I borrow your binoculars? Someone dropped mine in the ocean and hasn't bothered to replace them."

The Black Sheep code is quite precise on matters of this kind: *Life is too short to waste it on losers.*

Mona is on a rocky outcropping above the crowd when I find her. How she made it up there in a skirt and Birkies I don't know, because it's pretty tough going in jeans and sneakers. Judy and crew gather at the bottom to fight over who should haul the equipment up after me.

"Are you all right, dear?" Mona asks, patting the rock beside her.

I shake my head. "I'm worried about Maurice. What if the other otters don't accept him? This isn't his family, you know."

"Actually, it might be," she says. "We're very close to where he was recovered. But if not, he'll find a way to integrate. Didn't you tell me he's a genius?"

I smile in spite of myself. "He is. But what if he isn't ready?"

"He's ready," she reassures me.

"What if he gets into trouble out there on his own?"

"Then they'll bring him back in." She points to the electronic equipment the aquarium staff have set up. "They'll be tracking him with a transmitter, and volunteers will be keeping an eye on him from a distance."

This makes me feel better. "He can really come back? I mean, if it doesn't work out in the wild?"

"Absolutely," she says, giving me a one-armed hug. "We're his surrogate family, and the door is always open to him."

She passes me her binoculars. Three people in Darth Vader costumes are aboard the Zodiac, which is floating a few hundred yards from the otters. I can tell which one is Lisa by her bossy gestures. After surveying the scene for what seems like hours, she finally moves Maurice's cage to the edge of the boat and tips it. He slides into the ocean with a little splash.

I hold my breath until his auburn face breaks the surface of the water. He swivels to take in his surroundings before diving. When he comes up again, about thirty yards from the boat, he turns toward the shore, and for a split second, it seems that he is looking right at me. Then he begins a slow approach to the other otters until he is ultimately absorbed into the mass of kelp and bobbing heads.

And that's it. He's gone.

"Don't cry," Meadow says. "Your makeup will run."

I turn and see that hers is already running, and because there's so much of it, the effect is frightening.

"I'm not crying," I say. The Bishops don't cry. Our tear ducts are sealed off at birth.

Meadow isn't the only one who clambered up the rock while I was distracted. Chili is there, and even injured Judy, who is clearly willing to suffer for her art.

Mona stands and pulls Meadow away. "Let's give Kendra a moment to say good-bye to her friend."

I scan the surface of the water with Mona's binoculars. If all goes as it should, I will never see Maurice again.

"Now that's the stuff ratings are made of," Judy booms in my ear. "Well done, KB." She grabs my shoulder and gives it a squeeze.

"Leave me alone."

"No can do. Chili's battery died in the middle of it all," she says. "We missed the emotional blah blah, so I need to get Mona back here and you're going to run that conversation again, okay?"

"I can't just—"

"Sure you can, sweetie. And if you could make the crying bigger, it would help sell the wide shot." After pointing at Bob, who's shooting us from the beach, she demonstrates a mock sob. "You know, put a little shoulder into it."

"I am not crying," I repeat. "The wind is making my eyes run, that's all."

"It's all the same to me." She turns and calls, "Mona! Be a doll and climb back up here, would you?"

I raise the binoculars once more. "I need to make sure Maurice is all right."

"Your seal is fine. He's free, isn't he?" She yanks the binoculars away from my face. "Now, let's get this shot while the Zodiac is still in the background."

I try to resist, but Judy has a vise grip on my shoulder, and the cord of the binoculars is strangling me.

"Let go of her," someone says.

Judy stops bullying me and turns to glare at Mitch. "Well, well, if it isn't the knight in the shiny red kayak. As I recall, you took off when KB really needed rescuing. I was the one who brought our girl home safely."

"Yeah," he says, "you're a real humanitarian." He turns to Chili and holds one hand up in front of the lens. "Just give her a minute, man."

Chili lowers his camera. Mitch looks at me for a second and I hastily wipe my face with my sleeve. Maybe he will think my eyes are just tearing from the strangling.

Judy slaps Chili's arm. "What the hell is wrong with you? Save the male bonding for the locker room. I pay you to get the damn shot."

They're still bickering as I hold up the binoculars to watch for an auburn head to emerge from the kelp one last time.

* * *

142

Judy's face is pressed up against the glass windowpane in the door to Lisa's office, watching us. Lisa may be a thorn in my side, but my admiration for her has grown since she barred Judy from the administrative offices. I've heard differing reports about what happened, but from what I can piece together, Judy spilled a venti latte over some reports on Lisa's desk and refused to apologize.

"Come on, Lisa," I plead as she sorts through a stack of papers on her desk. "I promise I'll do a good job."

She shakes her head. "I don't want you near the otters. You get too emotionally involved and it affects your judgment."

"I am not emotional," I protest. I may be somewhat more in touch with my feelings than my parents, but that's as far as it goes. "And if you let me track Maurice, there'd be an ocean between us."

Lisa walks over to the office door and pulls the blind down on Judy's face. "As I understand it, you can't even swim. That's a prerequisite for ocean work."

Fine. Be picky. "Can't I be involved in the otter rehabilitation at least?" That way, I'd still be able to hear news about Maurice's progress. "I could help with—"

Lisa holds up a hand as the phone rings. Crossing back to her desk, she picks it up. "They're *what?*" she says. "They can't." She starts throwing around terms like, "chemical pollutants," "damage at the cellular level," and "heavy metal body burden." To finish, she barks, "We are not putting up with any crap from that golf course."

She slams the phone down and rifles through the papers on her desk, oblivious to me. Finally she looks up. "Why are you still here?"

Someone should tell her that getting into a Master's program doesn't give her the right to be rude and condescending. I'd tell her myself if she hadn't just baffled me with scientific jargon.

"I'm waiting for you to tell me how I can help out around here," I say.

She glances at the door, where the outline of Judy's face is still visible. "Why are you so interested, anyway?"

I see where she's going, here. She thinks I have an ulterior motive—that I'm incapable of being selfless. Well, I can put the welfare of marine life above my own concerns. Black Sheepism is about taking a stand. If it happens that I can do that while Mitch Mulligan is supervising me, all the better. He will soon see that I am deeper than a tide pool.

I gather my strength to say what she is probably waiting to hear: "I just think I could learn a lot from you, that's all."

She passes me a stack of files. "Put these in alphabetical order. If you can handle that, we'll move on to bigger learning opportunities."

I'm still scrubbing kennels two hours after Judy discovers a convenient allergy to chlorine and disappears with the crew. Unfortunately, Mitch hasn't witnessed my selfless dedication, having flouted Lisa's order to supervise me.

A sudden noise makes me look up, to see a man I don't recognize standing in the doorway. He's holding a bundle wrapped in a blanket.

"Do you work here?" he asks.

Nodding, I push my hair back with one rubber-gloved hand. "Can I help you?"

"Yeah, you can take this."

Something tells me to hold off. "What is it?"

"An otter pup. I found it on the beach and I think it's sick."

He tries to pass the animal to me, but I step back. "If you'll just wait one second, I'll get someone in here."

I consider telling him that people are supposed to call the aquarium when they find an animal in trouble rather than capturing it themselves, but I decide to leave the preaching to the expert. Picking up the phone, I ask the receptionist to page Lisa.

"Are you going to take this damn thing or not?" the man asks.

"I'm not qualified, sir, but Lisa Langdon is on the way. She's in charge of otter rescue."

"Well, *you* might have all the time in the world, but I have to get back to Carmel. I have an art gallery to run." He thrusts the bundle into my arms and heads for the door.

Holding the otter pup at arm's length, I call after him, "Wait! We need more information."

He disappears down the long corridor.

Before I can figure out what to do with the bundle in my arms, Lisa arrives. "What's that?" she asks.

"It's an otter."

Her eyes widen until I can see the whites all around. "Are you out of your mind?" she says. "That is not a baby."

"I know that, believe me. Take it before it goes for my face."

Her voice gets higher and tighter. "You can't hold an otter in a blanket."

"Can you postpone the lecture? One of us is already traumatized and the other one is going to be, and I don't want to be holding it when that happens."

She zooms into action, grabbing a pair of elbow-length gloves from the supply cupboard and taking the otter out of my arms. Sliding it into one of the clean kennels, she pulls the blanket away quickly.

"*Never* wrap an otter in a blanket," she continues, as if I were likely to get into the habit. "Their fur is so thick they could overheat."

"I didn't do it," I point out. "Someone else did."

Lisa is on a tear that prevents her from hearing. "There's a reason I want you to stay away from the animals, Kendra. You don't have a clue how to handle them. I barely get finished telling you not to get emotionally involved, and the next thing I know, you're rocking one in your arms. There are enough threats to the otter population around here. Do I have to add *you* to the list?"

"Come on, you're not even listening to me."

She stalks over to the door. "You've been nothing but trouble since the day you arrived," she says. "You're a hazard to the animals and a hazard to yourself. Consider yourself banned from this aquarium."

Chapter 9

"Have you tried calling?" Carrie asks, offering me tissues. "It's been a couple of days."

I take a handful of tissues and press them to my face. "What's the point? Lisa won't change her mind."

Judy snatches the tissue from me. "Watch the makeup! And for the love of Judy, find something else to talk about. Getting kicked out of the aquarium is the best thing that ever happened to you, KB. You said you wanted adventure in your life, and I can guarantee you're not going to find it at the bottom of a fishbowl."

She's missing the point, which is that I've never been kicked out of anything in my entire life. Bishops do not get fired.

Judy checks her watch and pulls up my hood. "Fix your face, KB. The press will be here any minute."

A *Black Sheep* crew member strolls by, and Judy follows him, calling, "Where the hell is my latte?"

When she's out of earshot, Carrie says, "Maybe Mitch could talk to Lisa. After all, he stood up for you in Big Sur."

"That was about sticking it to Judy, not about helping me." I take more tissues to mop up the sweat that's dripping into my eyes. "Anyway, my being banned from the aquarium won't matter after I've died of heat stroke." I scratch the top of my head through the fabric. "God, could this costume be any itchier?"

Carrie grins. "Now, now, little black sheep. Watch that baaaaaa-d attitude!"

I toss the hood off, sulking, but I don't blame Carrie for having a laugh at my expense. When Judy told me that I'd be cutting the ribbon at a local restaurant opening, she neglected to mention that I'd be doing so in a sheep costume. It's eighty degrees in the shade, and I'm wearing curly black faux fur from head to toe, and a rubber snout.

"Hood up, KB!" Judy hollers across the parking lot. "Get into position—and put on your damn sombrero!"

I pick up the enormous sombrero with my "hooves," and Carrie helps jam it over long, floppy ears. Then I take my place beside a sign that reads, EVEN A BLACK SHEEP LOVES PACO'S TACOS.

"I don't understand why Mitch is being such a jerk," Carrie says, resuming our favorite subject, as if there's a single nuance left unexplored from our many discussions over the past few days. "I mean, one minute he's groping your kayak—"

"He was trying to keep me upright," I interrupt.

"He was flirting and you know it."

"I thought he was, but obviously I was wrong."

"You weren't wrong," she asserts. "A girl knows when a guy is flirting with her. It's animal instinct."

"Don't talk to me about animal instinct right now. I might start grazing on the shrubbery."

She giggles. "By the way, I caught last night's episode. I feel I should tell you that underwear isn't standard kayaking attire around here."

"My shorts fell off when Bob pulled me into the boat, and Judy insisted the shot was integral to the story line. She didn't even have the decency to fuzz it up the way she did when Mitch was naked."

"Kendra, you've got to expect the unexpected with Judy around. We're going shopping for a bathing suit."

"I'm always game to shop," I say. "But for the record, I'm getting used to constant humiliation. A Black Sheep's pride must be practically bulletproof."

Carrie looks over my shoulder. "I'm glad to hear you say that."

I turn to see Judy leading a donkey toward us.

"Isn't he cute, KB?" she asks, scratching the animal's ears. Only one donkey is smiling. "You're such an animal lover I'd knew you'd be all for this."

"You've got to be kidding," I say. "There is no way a sheep would be riding a donkey. It's physically impossible."

"Television breaks the laws of physics all the time. So saddle up, senorita. Mary's little lamb wants a taco."

* * *

The sun beats down on the concrete parking lot as Paco Gonzales stands before the small crowd, sharing credit for the launch of his new franchise with everyone from his mother to his podiatrist. Just as I start to think I might faint and fall off the donkey, Paco grabs the reins and tows me over to the red ribbon that hangs across the restaurant's entrance.

"It is my honor to present Senorita Kendra Bishop, from the hit television show *The Black Sheep*," he announces. "After officially opening Paco's Tacos, she will be signing autographs at the party inside."

I take the scissors Paco hands me, grateful that my hooves, unlike the real thing, have opposable thumbs. As per instructions from Judy, I hold the scissors near the ribbon and pause for the local press. Photographers from the *Monterey County Herald* and the *Carmel Pinecone* call, "Over here, Kendra!"

Behind them, a child cheers and waves a helium-filled balloon shaped like an avocado. This type of event would be ludicrous in New York, but it's obviously a bigger deal here, and it wouldn't be fair of me to project my big-city snobbery onto them. Straightening my sombrero, I sit tall in the saddle and give the photographers my brightest smile.

A group of boys in the back row suddenly whoops with laughter, and a voice rises above the rest, "Which one is taking the dump—the donkey or the sheep?"

* * *

I flop onto a bench and toss back my hood. Air-conditioning has never felt so good.

"Uh-uh-uh," Judy admonishes. "You're still working, young lady. Besides, that hair is just . . ." She waves her hand in front of her face to fan away the imaginary stench.

Carrie arrives carrying two plates of Paco's finest Mexican fare and says, "You'll never guess who I met at the buffet: Aaron and Jordan."

I pull off my hooves to eat a burrito. It's a challenge with the rubber snout, but when there's food involved, a Black Sheep perseveres. "What are they doing here?"

"I invited them," Judy says, plucking a couple of nacho chips off my plate. "I thought it would be nice for you to have some of your new friends around."

She tells me to pull myself together and takes off to find the guys. Knowing it's useless to argue, I replace the hooves and hood and roll my eyes at Carrie. "Have I not suffered enough today?"

"A Black Sheep's pride is bulletproof," she reminds me. "Just remember, no matter what happened at the party, Aaron and Jordan want to be on TV. And for that, my furry friend, they need you. Who's the star?"

"I am," I say.

"I can't hear you."

"*I'm* the star."

"And a black sheep is . . . ?"

"Bulletproof," I supply. Thanks to Carrie, I'm starting to feel it again. "I don't give a pile of donkey dung what people think of me."

"Atta girl," Carrie says, passing me a stack of napkins.

"What's this for?"

"There's salsa on your snout."

"If it isn't the girl with the peso panties," Aaron says, smirking. "Are you wearing them today, or do sheep go commando?"

"Sheep prefer not to talk to asses," I say, holding my hooded head high.

"I notice they don't have any problem riding them, though."

Judy intervenes before the situation escalates. "Aaron and Jordan are going into San Francisco to see Sand on the Beach."

"Isn't there enough of that around here?" I ask.

"It's a band," Aaron says.

Without Lucy to protect me, I suppose it was only a matter of time before my ignorance about pop culture became public knowledge. But a Black Sheep doesn't hesitate to bluff. "I knew that."

"Sure you did," Aaron scoffs.

We lose Judy again as the cute photographer from the *Carmel Pinecone* walks by. Bob powers down his camera, and when the red light disappears, so does Aaron.

"I'm sorry about what happened at the party," Jordan

says, hanging back. "You know, about asking for the gift certificates and all."

A Black Sheep doesn't hesitate to play dumb, either. "What gift certificates?"

"For the arcade, remember? I wanted to take that girl, but it turns out she wasn't into me anyway."

I smile. "Gee, that's too bad."

"Do you still have them?"

A Black Sheep never gets burned by the same guy twice. "Nope."

"Okay, well, keep me in mind if you get any more."

"Excuse me?"

He has the decency to become flustered. "I meant we could use them *together*. You know, like a date."

When I came to Monterey, I'd hoped a cute guy would ask me out, but I never imagined it happening when I was dressed as a sheep. If I thought there was any chance of making Mitch jealous, I might go for it. As I don't, I stick to my principles. "I don't think so, Jordan."

"Would it make a difference if I apologized *on camera?*"

"It looks like I haven't washed my hair in a month," I moan, catching a glimpse of my reflection in the bowl of the Watsons' stainless steel Mixmaster.

"Untrue," Carrie says, pulling a tray of brownies out of the oven. "Although it has been through a lot today."

She sets the brownies on a tray to cool and inspects

them closely. Baking has been Carrie's passion since she received an Easy-Bake oven at age six. Her goal is to attend the Culinary Institute of America one day and become a pastry chef.

Carrie's dad comes in from the garage carrying his golf clubs. "Ah, the sweet smell of brownies," he says, picking up a fork to attack the tray.

Carrie fends him off with her spatula. "I can't believe Mom let you out of the house in those pants," she says, eyeing his turquoise plaid.

He strikes a pose for our benefit. "They almost distracted people from my golf score. What do you think, Kendra?"

"I think you're lucky Judy and her crew are still down at Paco's," I say.

"I'll have to get used to the spotlight, what with you practically living here these days."

He's exaggerating. I have been over more often lately, but that's only because Carrie and I have a lot to talk about. It's not like I'm hoping to run into anyone I couldn't run into at the Mulligans, if he stayed where he belonged.

Carrie swats her father with the spatula. "Dad."

"What?" he says. "Who wouldn't want a camera crew underfoot all the time?"

Calvin slides into the kitchen in dirty sweat socks. "Brownies!"

"For our guest," Carrie says, moving them out of his reach. "Not for you."

"Kendra's not a guest, she's here all the time," Calvin says, doing a double take at the sight of my hair. "Yow! What's with the lid?"

Horrified, Carrie applies the spatula to her brother as well. But the teasing doesn't faze me like it used to. The Mulligans are building my tolerance, whether I like it or not.

Calvin pulls a bag of cookies and some chips out of the pantry. "You look like Cruella De Vil on a bad day."

"Now, son," Mr. Watson says, as Calvin moves on to unload the refrigerator. "You just keep your mind on eating me into the poorhouse."

"There's two of us," Calvin says. "I'm fixing Mitch's laptop." Tucking a couple of sodas under his chin, he backs away. "How was your company tournament?"

"Embarrassed myself as usual," Mr. Watson says. "We have one of the finest courses in the world right next door in Carmel, and it's wasted on me."

"Don't tell Mitch you golfed Boulder Beach," Calvin says.

"Why would he care?" Carrie asks.

Calvin shrugs as he leaves the kitchen. "Something to do with otters. What else is new?"

I tell Carrie about how angry Lisa got the other day during a phone call that somehow related to golf. "She banned me not long after that."

"Well, if you want back into that aquarium, I know someone who can help."

Carrie knocks on Calvin's door.

"What?" he shouts.

"Kendra and I want to talk to Mitch."

Silence. Whispering. Fragments reach our ears.

". . . climb out the window."

". . . not worth a broken arm, man."

". . . closet . . . ?"

". . . hockey gear . . . I could suffocate."

Carrie pounds on the door. "We can hear you, losers."

"Can't it wait?" Calvin calls. "We're still fixing the laptop."

"Sure," Carrie says, "But I have brownies."

Calvin opens the door and tries to snatch the plate, but Carrie shoulders her way in. I follow, stopping dead in my tracks when I see the condition of Calvin's room. It's a hellhole. The bunk beds are unmade, and clothes, books, and electronic equipment are strewn everywhere. Calvin has to shove a half-eaten pizza aside with one foot to make room to stretch out on the floor. The entire room is like a scratch-and-sniff version of one of Jackson Pollock's busy, paint-splattered canvases.

"You prefer *this* to your own home?" I ask Mitch. His bedroom at the Mulligans' is off limits to everyone, but I caught a glimpse of it once, and from what I could see, he's a neat freak.

"There are no cameras here," Mitch says, glaring at me.

"At least, there weren't until you started stalking me."

Stalking him! I turn to leave, but Carrie grabs my wrist. "Mitch, Kendra wants you to talk to Lisa about lifting her ban at the aquarium."

Mitch pops an entire brownie into his mouth before asking almost unintelligibly, "Why doesn't Kendra ask me that herself?"

I consider swatting him in the head with Calvin's plastic light saber, but I know I'm going to have to suck it up. "Will you talk to Lisa for me?"

He gives Calvin a chocolately grin. "Did you hear the magic word?"

"I don't think I did," Calvin says, helping himself to a second brownie.

I grit my teeth. "Please?"

Mitch stalls a bit longer before saying, "I guess I could try. Lisa and I have plans tomorrow anyway."

I wonder if he means a date, but he starts to explain—to Calvin, not me—that Lisa is collecting water and marine vegetation samples from locations along the coast as part of her graduate fieldwork. So far, she's found that toxin levels are higher the closer you get to the Boulder Beach Golf Club. Her theory is that this is caused by runoff from the pesticides and fertilizers used to keep the club's fairways green.

A few days ago, Lisa learned that Boulder Beach has bought a tract of prime oceanfront property and plans to move its fourteenth hole to this new location. Because it will sit above a partially enclosed cove, she believes the "chemical soup" will be concentrated enough to poison the food chain larger marine mammals depend upon. What's more, the fertilizer runoff may foster kelp growth, which will attract more otters to the area.

"Will otters die from eating the tainted food?" Carrie asks.

"It's possible," Mitch says. "And the toxins could also affect their ability to reproduce. Either way, it won't help build their population."

"I'm sure the club's owners wouldn't move the hole if they knew it would cause so much damage," I say.

Mitch rolls his eyes. "The club spent millions on that land. They're not going to care about a few otters more or less."

"Can't Lisa at least call the owners and talk about it?" I ask.

"She has her own plan," he says. "She's going to collect evidence and then approach the Ocean Conservancy to lobby the state to shut down the fourteenth hole."

"But won't that take years?"

He nods.

"Then forget science. Why doesn't she start up a protest group instead?"

"Because she's an academic, not an activist."

"Maybe we could do it."

"We?" Calvin asks.

Mitch doesn't say anything, so I keep talking. "Yeah. Maybe we can find a way to make them care. We can't give in to some rich guy swinging an eighteen-carat gold club."

"Gold clubs would bend," Mitch says.

Why do guys take everything so literally? "My point is that animals don't have a voice. We need to raise ours for them." I'm really starting to warm up to the idea now.

He isn't convinced. "I've watched my parents take on the establishment, and I know a battle like that can take years, too. Science might actually be faster."

"That sounds pretty cynical coming from someone who said he wants to leave this planet a little better for the next guy," I say.

He stares over my shoulder, lost in thought. Finally he says, "I guess it wouldn't hurt to try."

Carrie points to the brownie in his hand. "He's not eating. That means he thinks it's a great idea."

He bites into the brownie. "It means it's worth exploring."

"In other words," Carrie translates, "Kendra, you're brilliant."

Mitch starts packing up his computer. "I'll run it by Lisa."

"Why look, your laptop is suddenly fixed," I say. "It's like magic. If you'd prefer to climb out the window, I can carry it home for you."

"You're funny," he says, leading me into the hall.

"And also brilliant," Carrie yells after us.

"Get out of my room," Calvin tells her. "We were having a good time until you showed up."

Mitch stands behind me, watching with his arms crossed as I tape a flyer to a lamppost on Alvarado Street.

"Add more tape," he says. "Gale force winds can spring up out of nowhere."

He's being sarcastic, but I wrap another yard of clear packing tape around the post anyway. "I'm not taking any chances. We want a good turnout."

The flyers are advertising the first meeting of our new protest group, Team 14.

By "our," I really mean Lisa's. And by "protest," I really mean "public education."

Lisa initially dismissed the idea, probably because Mitch told her it was mine. Once she recognized the endless opportunities it would give her to stun people with her knowledge and credentials, however, she was on it like an otter on a pound of squid. She even gave in when Mitch pressured her to let me come back to the aquarium, but only after reminding him that he's supposed to supervise me.

This time he's taking that order more seriously, because he volunteered to come with me to put up posters today. Bob and Chili are shadowing us, but Judy is sleeping off the margaritas she enjoyed at Paco's grand opening.

I twist the tape gun to the side and try to slice the thick

tape against the sharp edge. The tape pops out of its dispenser, uncoiling as it hits the ground. I gather it up until it's wadded together in a filthy ball.

"May I?" Mitch asks.

"No," I say, wrestling with the tape a bit longer. "I can handle it."

"Obviously," he says, whipping out a pocketknife and cutting the tape. "But fortunately you don't have to do it alone, because I, Mitch Mulligan, am a postering expert, and I'm willing to share my techniques with you at no cost."

"Zoom in, Bob," I say. "This is going to be gripping."

Mitch holds a poster against the window of a diner. "First, select a good location and place the poster at eye level. Then take out your *properly loaded* tape gun, which makes dispensing a breeze. When *im*properly loaded . . . well, you saw what happened." With a deft movement, he secures a corner of the flyer to the window with a small piece of tape. "It's all in the angle and the wrist."

While Mitch is addressing the camera, a man in a white apron comes up to the window inside the diner and raps sharply on the glass. Mitch jumps, sending his tape gun crashing to the sidewalk.

The man opens the door. "What are you doing to my window?"

Mitch offers the man a flyer. "We're promoting—"

"I don't want to hear it," the man says. "You're defacing private property. I'm calling the cops."

"No need, sir," I interject. "We'll take it down."

The man glances from me to the cameras and back again. "I recognize you. You're that kid from *The Black Sheep*."

I step forward to shake his hand. "Kendra Bishop."

"Love the show," the guy says. "Especially because it's local. When you said good-bye to your little otter friend . . ."—he pauses to thump a fist against his heart—"it got me right here."

I squirt a squiggly line of ketchup across my French fries and look up at Mitch, who's sitting opposite me in the booth. "Is this okay? Or do you want to demonstrate the proper technique?"

"If you take that attitude, there's nothing I can do to help you," he says, grinning as he bites into a grilled cheese sandwich.

"I don't need help, I'm doing fine on my own," I say, pointing to the row of flyers across the diner's window, plus the ones on the bulletin board behind the counter. "You're the one who almost ended up in custody."

"He wouldn't have called the cops," Mitch scoffs.

"Because I won him over," I say. After I signed the owner's apron and had my picture taken with him, he offered all of us a free meal. Bob and Chili were only too happy to put down their equipment and get busy on a couple of burgers. "I know it hurts to thank me, but—"

"For someone who claims she didn't join the show for the fame, you seem to enjoy the attention."

"For someone with such high principles, you seem to be enjoying your free lunch," I counter.

"You've got a point," he says. After chewing in silence a moment, he adds, "Maybe I overreacted about the whole kayaking thing."

"Overreacted?" I say. "Is that the best you can do?"

"Judy pulled her circus into my private—"

"I know and I felt awful about it," I interrupt. "But you're going to have to lighten up about the crew if we're working on Team Fourteen together. I'm under contract, as Judy keeps reminding me, and I can't control her."

He nods reluctantly. "Okay."

"And would it kill you to be a little less grumpy?"

"Grumpy?" He looks surprised. "That's just who I am."

"That's not always who you are," I say. He tries to sprinkle vinegar on my fries, and I pull them away. "Promise."

"I promise to *try* not to be grumpy."

I push the fries toward him. "Good. Now, promise to take everything I say seriously and admit that I'm smarter than you."

"Who asked what time otters get up?"

Black Sheep Rule Number Thirteen: *Quit while you're ahead.*

The diner's owner plies Bob and Chili with more pie at my

request, thereby giving Mitch and me a little more time to chat.

"Since you're so smart, you must have big plans for your future," Mitch says.

"Plans?" I can't even imagine what life will be like after the show ends and I'm back in New York. I want it to be different from what I left behind, but I'm not entirely sure how yet. "You mean, when I graduate from high school?"

He nods. "You must have thought about it."

"Not really." I wish I had a more interesting answer, because he's known what he wants to do with his life since he was Egg's age. "If I hadn't come to California, I probably would have given in to my parents and become a banker."

"But you did come, so now what?"

"I'm still figuring it out, but banking is officially off the list."

Black Sheep Rule Number Fourteen: *Design your own future.*

"Maybe you could be an art critic for *The New York Times*," Mitch suggests.

I look up to see if he's making fun of me, but he appears to be serious. "An art critic?"

"Why not? You know a lot about art and you have opinions."

He thinks I have opinions! Opinions are good. Opinions mean I have a personality. "Well, I don't know enough for *that*."

"Maybe not yet, but you could study art in college. If you're interested enough, you'll want to learn all there is to know. At least, that's been my experience."

He reaches for the remains of my blueberry pie and finishes it in three mouthfuls. It astounds me how much he can eat, but I'm glad he feels comfortable enough with me now to take food off my plate.

"I'm not sure I'm *that* interested in art."

"Well, think of something else, then. My parents always tell us to 'follow our passion.'"

Passion? I don't even know what passion feels like. But as I watch Mitch drink the rest of my soda, it occurs to me that I might get the chance to find out while I'm here.

Chapter 10

In just a few short days, Team 14 has grown to two dozen members. Lisa has set up the "head office" in the only room at the aquarium big enough to hold us and the equipment we need: the supply room. There are no windows and it smells like stale otter, but it has phones, two computers, and space for everyone to work. At the moment, Carrie and Meadow are stuffing envelopes with flyers, while Tia and a few others are painting posters.

The janitor wheels in another desk. "Where do you want it, Kendra?"

I'm the one in charge right now, because Lisa took Mitch with her to gather more samples. I point to Tia, who is sitting on the floor using an empty otter kennel as a makeshift work surface. "Over there, please."

Judy hops onto the desk to claim it when it comes off the dolly. "Finally!"

Tia stares at her.

"What, you think you've got it bad?" Judy asks. "I thought I'd seen the last of these clammy walls, but if KB insists on running her little campaign out of here, I'm going to need somewhere to keep my things." She sets her coffee cup on the desk and slides her purse into a drawer.

"Judy, off," I say, crossing the room. Tia has absolutely no interest in marine life, but she was kind enough to volunteer her time and her artistic talent. The girl deserves a desk. "You can store your stuff in my desk."

"Excuse me, Miss Bossy Boots." Judy follows me back to my desk. "I am the producer of this show. I should have my own desk."

"I'm the star of your show and I should have my own bedroom, but that didn't happen either, did it?" I ask. "It's a tight squeeze here, so we have to share. Which reminds me, since you're taking up space, how about rolling up your sleeves to help?"

"I'm here to document, not participate, remember?"

"I notice you participate when you feel like it. When there's free booze, for example."

"Well, excuse me if I'm not moved by seals. If you'd found a more compelling cause, I might be stuffing some envelopes."

I slap a pile of flyers and another of envelopes in front of her. "I want to see some paper cuts, fast."

"And I want to see an attitude adjustment, now. This is a supply room, KB, not the White House." She tosses the envelopes back to me. "You haven't been yourself since you joined this group."

I take that as a compliment. If Judy can't accept the new Kendra Bishop—the one who has the guts to transform herself from low-key conformist into hell-raising activist—that's her problem. All I'd seriously aspired to with Black Sheepism was to conquer my fears on what the rest of the flock thought about me. I wanted to become more independent, but I never had any ambition to lead the flock myself. Yet, here I am, with people looking to me for advice and direction.

"Kendra," Meadow says, "can I call the golf club?"

"I think it's better if I keep trying," I tell her. Meadow looks disappointed. Though only ten, she has none of my insecurities. Wait till she hits puberty. "Hey," I say, leaning in for a closer look. "Are those eyelashes fake?"

"They're real," she says, "just not mine. Your *Glamour* magazine said long lashes would make my eyes look bigger." She plucks at the strands of hair stuck to her high-gloss lips.

"Did *Glamour* also say my lip gloss would make your lips look bigger? Or that my blue T-shirt would make your—"

Mitch and Calvin's arrival prevents me from getting more graphic.

"Where's Lisa?" I ask.

"Dropping off samples at the lab," Mitch says. He pushes Calvin toward a computer. "Show Kendra what you've done."

Calvin types a Web address, and the brand new Team 14 Web site pops up.

I click through the site. "This is fantastic."

"How goes the battle on the home front?" Mitch asks.

Eager to prove that I have the skills to do more than arrange desks, I tell him about my calls to the president of the Boulder Beach Golf Club.

"How did it go?" he asks.

I shake my head regretfully. Not only has the president refused to take my call, but the vice president and all manner of lower-ranking plebes have dissed me, too. I ended up delivering my spiel about moving the fourteenth hole to the receptionist in the hopes that she'd convey the message to her higher-ups. That's when she asked me to stop pestering them with "nuisance calls."

"It's so rude," I tell Mitch. "They won't even listen to me."

Mitch nods toward the *Black Sheep* cameras. "Let's talk about it later."

Glancing at Bob and Chili, it occurs to me that there's more than one way to "educate" people about an issue. "I don't care if they're filming this," I say. "I want the public to know that these people are arrogant and ignorant and cold. I swear, I will not give up this fight until things change. They will learn that they can't mess with Kendra Bishop."

"Hear, hear," Carrie yells.

That's all the encouragement I need to climb onto my chair. "Listen up, everybody. I say it's time we take this show on the road. Team Fourteen should go to Carmel! We've got to get them to drop their golf clubs and take notice."

Led by Carrie and Tia, the group begins to applaud.

Inspired to continue, I yell into Bob's camera, "We'll plaster the town with posters. We'll set up a public meeting. We'll go door-to-door with a petition. And we'll picket City Hall if that's what it takes. We will not rest until our demands are met!"

The cheer reverberates around the supply room until an angry voice rings out from the back of the room.

"What the hell is going on?"

Lisa paces back and forth in front of me. We're in her office and Judy's face is pressed against the glass door beside Chili's lens. This time Lisa doesn't bother to close the blinds. "Let's get one thing straight," she says. "Kendra Bishop is not the star of Team Fourteen."

"I never said I was."

"We are a group of people working toward a common goal, which is raising awareness, not causing trouble."

"I know that."

"If you know that, why are you harassing people with dozens of phone calls? If you piss them off, they won't even listen to what we have to say. My plan was to gather some preliminary data and present my findings in a professional way. They would have taken *my* call because I'm an academic."

It's amazing how often she can work that into a conversation. She's going to be one of those Ph.D.'s who insists on being called "Doctor."

"How was I supposed to know you didn't want them to know about Team Fourteen yet?" I ask. "I mean, they'll hear about us eventually. In case you haven't noticed," I lower my voice to a stage whisper, "there are television cameras following me around."

"Oh, I've noticed," she says. "The only reason I let you back in here is that the Mulligans are the bedrock of our volunteer program. As for Team Fourteen, I wanted to get some influential lobby groups on our side before I met with the golf executives. Now those groups are going to think we're rank amateurs."

"At least they're going to know we're passionate about our beliefs," I argue. "Discussing every angle of the problem and analyzing endless data won't help. We need to *do* something."

"What we need is for you to stop acting like you're too important to follow the rules around here."

Chili runs out of tape before Lisa runs out of steam, and by the time I return to the supply room, everyone but Mitch has gone home for the night.

"Where's our favorite set of teeth?" he asks, powering down the computers.

"She went back to the hotel to celebrate because she got enough conflict on tape to fill a miniseries."

"Lisa really came down on you, huh?"

I nod. "Honestly, Mitch, I wasn't trying to take over, and I didn't mean any harm in calling up the club." I'd like to tell him that I think her plan to bore the club's president to death with lectures and statistics is lame, but she is his friend.

"She can't fault you for being enthusiastic."

"Oh, she faults me all right."

"She'll get over it," he assures me. "Give her time."

After locking up, we wind our way through the darkened aquarium galleries toward the exit.

Mitch stops outside an exhibit. "Hang on," he says. "I always say good night to the jellyfish."

"That's one exhibit I've skipped," I say. "It's usually packed with screaming kids."

Beckoning, he goes inside. "You've got to see it."

I follow him hesitantly into the darkness. "Don't you jump out at me."

"I thought you were only scared of sharks," he says from somewhere ahead of me.

"Oh, no, the list is long." I turn to go. "How about we say good morning to the jellyfish instead?"

"Wait," Mitch says, catching my hand and leading me farther into the exhibit. "It's gotta be dark. That's the best way to see them."

My eyes begin to adjust to the dim, but I'm no longer looking for jellyfish. All I can focus on is the warmth of Mitch's hand.

He stops in front of one of the largest tanks. "The sea nettles are my favorite," he says. "Can you believe they have no bones and no heart? They're ninety-five per cent water, which means there isn't much appeal for predators."

There isn't much appeal for humans either, at least from what I can see. It's just a bunch of shadowy shapes in the water. But with Mitch holding my hand, it's by far the best lecture I've had in some time. To prolong it, I decide to show some interest. "They sting, don't they?"

"Only if they get loose," he says. "And if that happens, I'll protect you."

He taps on the glass until I catch his other hand. "Stop it. You'll piss them off."

"I'm just making sure they're awake," he says. He shakes his hand free and reaches for a button. "Watch this."

A light comes on in the circular tank, illuminating dozens of bright orange jellyfish, some larger than dinner plates, against an intense electric blue background. I watch, mesmerized, as they pulse slowly and rhythmically through the water. Below the large bells of their bodies dangle delicate orange tentacles and feathery wisps that look like white vapor trails against a clear blue sky.

I grope for a word that does justice to what I'm seeing, but my mental dictionary overloads and spits out, "Spectaculous."

"Exactly," Mitch says, laughing. "Whatever that means."

I'd be embarrassed, except that he doesn't seem to mind. He's moved in so close to me that his laughter buzzes against my ear and sends a shiver down my spine. Then he steps around in front of me, and I just know that he's going to kiss me. Carrie was right, it's animal instinct. My stomach does a nervous flip. It's not that I haven't kissed a guy before—I have. Earlier this year, Rosa offered to chaperone a school dance so that I could go. I met this guy from another school, and at the end, he kissed me. It wasn't horrible or anything, but I have to admit, it didn't rock my world. I figured it was my fault—that my parents confiscated the how-to manual every other girl gets before it reached me.

Mitch doesn't wait for my warning about the missing manual before kissing me. It's just as well, because animal instinct kicks right in to compensate for the knowledge deficit. So this is what the fuss is about. Our mouths come together like two pieces of the same puzzle, a perfect fit. I open my eyes just long enough to see the jellyfish floating around his head like balloons. Then he wraps his arms around me, and I do the same. Four tentacles, no sting.

Finally Mitch pulls away and looks at me. "Spectaculous," he says.

"Exactly," I say.

Suddenly, I hear Judy's voice echo over a walkie-talkie in the distance. "This is Wolf One. Has anyone found the lamb?"

Mitch and I jump apart, and I smooth my hair with my fingers. "In here," I call. My voice is all spidery and high, a total giveaway.

Mitch begins reading the wall plaque aloud so that Judy will think we're having an educational moment.

"KB?" Judy calls. "What did I tell you about hiding?" She steps into the gallery and shines a huge flashlight into Mitch's face. "What's going on here?"

"We're studying the jellyfish," Mitch says, squinting. "You've got to understand the basics about invertebrates before you can appreciate the rest of the exhibits."

"So you're showing her *the basics?*" Judy asks. "In the dark?"

Her leer could transform a beautiful moment into something slimy, but I'm not about to let that happen. "Oh, look, Mitch," I say, reading aloud from another wall plaque, "jellyfish tentacles are covered with stinging cells that paralyze prey and move it into the mouth for digestion. It sounds just like a producer's job."

Judy jerks her flashlight over to blind me, proving that she moves a lot faster than your average jellyfish.

Max and Mona made only one special request when they

agreed to participate in *The Black Sheep*, and that was for Sunday dinner to be a camera-free event. Judy and crew have respected this request, but after discovering Mitch and me in the jellyfish exhibit, she had no intention of releasing her prey without a few good stings. Over Mona's objections, she invited herself for a vegetarian feast and brought Bob along to document the occasion.

"So, Kendra," she begins in her singsong, ha-ha-I'm-about-to-drop-a-bomb-on-you voice. "Are you excited about going home tomorrow?"

"Tomorrow?" I say, trying to disguise the panic in my voice. She can't pull the plug on this now. My life is just beginning to heat up—in more ways than one. "I have a whole week to go. Plus, you said these things usually hang over."

"I did say that, but your endless complaints haven't fallen on deaf ears, kiddo. I made a few calls and busted you out of here early." She takes a huge gulp of wine and dabs at the edges of her mouth with an otter napkin. "You can thank me later."

I'm sure it's no coincidence that the minute I start to enjoy myself, Judy has to shake it up again in the endless search for conflict.

"You don't have enough footage for the final shows," I point out.

"I've got loads of footage in the bank. We'll be fine."

"What about Maya? She's having a great time and I'm

sure she doesn't want to come home early."

"Maybe we'll have you both in New York for a bit. I'm still working out the details."

I look around the table for support, but everyone appears to be in shock, especially Mitch. "I can't go yet," I say.

"Why not?" She grins around her wine glass at Mitch. "What's changed?"

"What's changed is Team Fourteen. I've never been involved in a project like this before, and I want to see it through."

"You mean, Team Lost Cause. You can't honestly believe that motley crew is going to convince a prestigious golf club to rearrange its multimillion-dollar designer fairway because of a couple of dead seals?"

"That's exactly what I believe. Except for the fact that it's otters." The more Judy disses Team 14, the more determined I am to do whatever it takes to prove her wrong.

Max raps his fork against the table. "You tell her, honey."

"You're welcome to stay here even after filming is done," Mona says.

I smile with relief. "Then I'll be here a while longer."

Judy punches some buttons into the phone and hands it to me. "Let's get your parents' permission," she says.

"Do you mind if I take this upstairs? It's a private conver—"

"Zoom in," Judy tells Bob.

My mother picks up at the other end, and with a last desperate look at Mitch, I say, "Hi, Mom, it's Kendra."

"Kendra?" She sounds confused.

"Kendra Bishop—your daughter."

Judy grabs the phone and presses speaker so that Bob's mike can pick up both sides of the conversation.

Meanwhile, my father comes on the extension. "Is everything all right, Kendra? You're not supposed to call, are you?"

"It's okay, Dad, I have permission to break the rules. But everything's all right."

"Good," he says. "You look well on the show. The Mulligans must be taking good care of you. Please tell them their daughter is delightful."

"Delightful," Mom echoes.

I haven't spoken to my parents in weeks and all they want to talk about is Maya. "I saw what you let her do to my room," I say.

"It can all be changed back," Mom says.

"I didn't change *her* room at all." I don't know why I'm going on about this, since I don't even care anymore.

"Let's not worry about that now," Dad says. "When are you coming home?"

I tell them all about Boulder Beach and Team 14. "Mona said I could stay as long as it takes to get the club to agree to do the right thing."

"Your father and I golfed there last fall after the San Francisco Marathon," Mom says. "It's already marvelous, but moving that hole to the shore would make it even better.

I can't believe my ears. "It won't be marvelous for the otters living in the cove."

Dad cuts in. "I'm sure the Coast Guard can move them along. Get Max to give them a call."

I feel my face flush at their ignorance. "Dad, they're animals. They have the right to live wherever they want."

"Be reasonable, Kendra. Surely there's a compromise?"

"There's no compromise. Besides, the golf club wouldn't take any of my calls."

"You can't pester them like that, Kendra," Dad says, his voice becoming stern. "They're busy people with a business to run."

"I thought you'd be proud that I'm becoming a concerned citizen." I didn't actually think so, but it would have been nice.

"It sounds like bleeding-heart foolishness," he says.

Mom says, "If you're really interested in these . . ."

"Otters," I supply.

". . . you could take a course at the Central Park Zoo. As long as it counts as a science credit, we're in full support."

"You'd be in full support of my jumping off the Brooklyn Bridge if it counted as a science credit," I say, raising my voice.

"You're being ridiculous," Mom says.

"And you're missing the point! You're not listening to me."

"Of course we're listening," Mom says, sounding surprised by my outburst.

"But you still have to come home," Dad concludes. "Judy called earlier to say we should expect you tomorrow night. We can't wait for you to meet Maya—"

I click END and hand the phone back to Judy, wondering how long my cash from the show will hold out if I rent a place of my own in New York. Probably not long enough to make it through high school.

The kitchen is quiet. I scan the table. The only people who meet my eyes are the twins.

"Your parents are mean," Mason says. Matt nods agreement.

"They're not mean, they're just not interested in animals," I say, although I can see why the twins would think so. Why couldn't my parents support my interests for once? Here I am, thrilled to be part of a team that's trying to make a difference, and all they can think about is the busy executives we're bothering.

Mona is watching me with sympathetic eyes. "We know they're good people, dear. They've been wonderful with Maya."

Silence descends once again, broken only by the clatter of knives and forks on china. Meadow is the first to speak.

"Are those real diamonds?" she asks, pointing to the ring on Judy's right hand.

Judy rolls her eyes. "There are no fakes in Judy's life, kid."

That's a laugh. From where I'm sitting, everything's fake in Judy's life.

"Can I try it on?" Meadow asks.

"If you must." She takes the ring off and passes it to Meadow.

Meadow slips the glittery rock onto her skinny finger. "Are you engaged?"

Judy shakes her head. "It's a commitment ring—a commitment to Judy. I don't need a man to buy me nice things."

Meadow is unimpressed. "I'd rather let guys buy the bling. That way, I can spend my money on a great big car." She flings her arms apart to show how big, and the ring flies off her finger and shoots across the room.

Before it's even stopped rolling, there's a flash of silver fur and the ring is gone.

Judy leaps to her feet, knife at the ready. "Which way did it go? I'll fillet that rat."

"Kids, you'd better find Manhattan before Judy does," Mona says.

Meadow and the twins follow Judy out of the room, while Bob documents the Great Ferret Hunt.

"We know how frustrated you must be, Kendra," Max

says after they're gone. "But your parents might come around when they've had a chance to think about it."

"You don't know my parents," I say, still too mortified to look at Mitch. "They just don't get it."

"Remember your parents, Mona?" Max asks.

Mona explains that her parents disapproved of her first protest to protect an ancient redwood forest that had been targeted for destruction by a developer. "Being from Chicago, they'd never seen a tree that's hundreds of years old and twenty stories high—a tree that's survived flood and fire and continued to shelter us."

"A miracle of nature," Max adds reverently. "But if you haven't experienced that kind of majesty personally, it's easier to ignore that it's being destroyed."

"Plus, my parents didn't care much for my Max," Mona says, with a fond pat to her Max's belly. "They thought he was leading me astray."

"Whereas, I was following her lead," he says, nibbling on her ear.

Mona recounts how they invited potential buyers to the woods to see what would be sacrificed for their new homes. Many withdrew their deposits, but it wasn't enough to kill the plan. Finally, Max and Mona organized a rally in which nearly a hundred students—including the mayor's son, the governor's son, and the granddaughter of the developer himself—chained themselves to tree trunks.

"In the end, the government bought the land back from

the developer and declared it protected," Max says. "It was our first win."

"Yeah, but then you were arrested," Mitch says.

Mona and Max exchange uneasy glances. "There was a little trouble with the law," Mona admits. "But my father was a lawyer and he dealt with it. Afterward, we took him up to the forest and then he completely understood. In fact, both my parents became such supporters that they asked us to scatter their ashes there."

"My parents want their ashes scattered in the lobby of Bank of America," I say, glad the cameras are out of the room.

Mona laughs. "Well, honey, everyone has a passion."

"I just wish they understood me the way you do. You know me better than my own parents. I want to stay here forever."

Mona leans over to give me one of her bone-crushing hugs just as Judy reappears in the doorway, looking the worse for wear. Her hair is a mess, and there's a dirty streak running down the front of her white T-shirt. Bob is shooting over her shoulder.

"You sound distraught, KB," Judy says, oozing sympathy. "If you're that upset, Judy has a solution: divorce your parents."

"Divorce them? That's a great idea," I say.

She misses my sarcasm. "Isn't it? The process is actually called *emancipation*, and it's legal at your age in California."

"Judy, don't give Kendra such ideas," Mona says. "I'd be angry if you suggested it to Maya."

"I'd never need to, would I?" Judy says, smiling sweetly. "It's Kendra who's miserable. She wants to play Mother Teresa of the Sea, and her parents are standing in the way. But as you know your contracts give us the right to extend the show by two weeks at our discretion. As a personal favor to you, KB, I just called our VP of programming. He's willing to consider green-lighting the extra episodes if you're willing to consider the idea of emancipation. You'll get to finish the show as planned, and have an extra couple of weeks to boot."

"I'm not going to divorce my parents," I say. "That's crazy."

"I said *consider* it, not *do* it. We just want you to toss the idea around for a while." She rubs her temples and sighs. "Look, kid, we all make sacrifices to get what we want. Do you think Judy's hanging out with you people because she wants to? Hardly. I've got ambitions. Now, do you want to help those poor seals or not?"

"Of course I do. But I think Max has the right idea about getting my parents down here to see the otters. Then I'm sure they'd agree to let me stay."

"Let me put this to you another way," Judy says. "When I said the VP would consider green-lighting the extension, what I really meant was, *he already did*. Like it or not, we're going with the emancipation story line and it's going to be a ratings coup."

Mona opens her mouth to protest, but Judy cuts her off by holding up one bare hand. "And you, Mona Mulligan, owe me a carat-and-a-half diamond ring."

Chapter 11

Calvin turns around in the van's passenger seat and asks, "What's that smell? Did Kendra take another dump?"

Although Calvin wasn't at Paco's Tacos to witness the donkey debacle, the front page photo in the *Carmel Pinecone* circulated the story quickly.

Carrie leans forward to cuff the back of her brother's head. "Don't be such a pig."

Calvin's been meaner than ever to me lately, perhaps because he suspects that Mitch and I have become more than just TV siblings.

Not that we're able to hang out like a normal couple. Thanks to Judy's constant vigilance and the endless supply of Mulligans, our relationship mostly revolves around stolen moments in the jellyfish exhibit. It isn't much, but what we lack in time, we make up for with energy.

Calvin reaches around to slap at his sister. "Someone filled a diaper back here, and I don't see you raising your hand."

Judging by the droop in Egg's drawers, he's the guilty

party. I cannot believe we got stuck with him today. We're on our way to Carmel with some of the Team 14 crew to hang out and do some sightseeing. Mitch and I had intended to give everyone the slip to spend some time alone together, but as usual, I underestimated Judy. When we were about to set off, she swept Max and Mona away in a limo for an all-expenses-paid day at Francis Ford Coppola's vineyard, leaving Mitch and me to babysit the kids.

"Mitch, you'd better pull over," I say. "Someone has to change Egg." It won't be me. Black Sheep do not change diapers.

Before Mitch can answer, Carrie screams. I lean over to see Manhattan tangled in her long hair. In the backseat, the twins are laughing their butts off with the open ferret cage between them.

Meadow tries to detach Manhattan. "Sorry, Carrie," she says. "We don't like to leave him home alone with the dog. But he's supposed to stay in his cage."

"Boys, behave," I say, trying to sound like the leader I hope one day to become.

Mason echoes in a sing-song voice, "Boys, behave." Matt giggles.

A leader must control her temper when the troops rebel. "I'm counting on you guys to be reasonable."

"Let me handle this, Kendra," Meadow says. She hands the ferret to one twin and pinches the other twin until he bleats. "Put the ferret in the cage and leave him there, or we are dumping both of you by the side of the road and telling Mom you drowned."

The boys obey her without delay, illustrating what effective leadership is all about.

Carmel is a pretty town, and strolling around its narrow streets would have been romantic if Mitch and I were alone. Instead, I am toting an irritable nine-month-old, and Mitch is distracted by two active boys and an even more active ferret on a leash. I tried to get Carrie to take the whole brood when we split up, but she drew the line at Meadow, and I can't blame her.

The crew tailed us all morning, but Judy eventually disappeared inside the offices of the *Carmel Pinecone*. According to Bob, she hit it off with a photographer at the Paco's Tacos party and wants to check him out while sober. As soon as she was gone, the rest of the crew broke for lunch.

Mitch and I and the kids are on our way to a family-friendly art gallery when I notice two men stepping into an elegant-looking French bistro.

"Did you see those men?" I ask Mitch excitedly. "It's the president and vice-president of the Boulder Beach Golf Club. I recognize their photos from the club's Web site."

Mitch joins me at the restaurant window, and we peer in at the two men. Both are about Max's age, only, unlike Max, they are well-groomed and stylishly dressed. If they'd had the decency to take my phone calls last week, I might even say they're handsome. One has silver hair and a goatee; the other is balding and has a chiseled face.

"Let's go in there and talk to them," I suggest, proving to myself how far I've come. The Kendra Bishop who touched down in Monterey was incapable of spontaneity.

"We can't do that," Mitch says.

"Why not? It's a public place. We'll tell them about Team Fourteen."

He shakes his head. "Lisa isn't ready for that yet."

"But it's the perfect opportunity, and it may never come again. Lisa said I ruined her chances of getting a meeting with them, and now I can make it up to her."

"I don't know," he says. "It could make things worse."

"How? They're already refusing to speak to us."

He seems to be wavering. "What would we say? We don't have data."

"Science isn't everything, you know, especially with money people. We could talk about how their members will be upset about moving the fourteenth hole if it hurts the environment."

I start to walk toward the door while my courage is still high, and Mitch follows.

"Aren't you nervous?" he asks, pausing to tie the ferret to a post.

I turn and see admiration in his eyes, which spurs me to bluff a little. "No. I may be afraid of sharks and jellyfish, but I'm not afraid of money people."

We enter the restaurant and the maître d' hurries over.

"Let me handle this," I whisper to Mitch, giving the maître d' my Cannery Row celebrity smile—the one that gets me freebies every time. "How are you today, sir?"

"What can I do for you?" he asks as snootily as if he were actually from France, which he isn't. Unfortunately, he doesn't recognize me, which means my minor fame won't hold any currency here.

"We'd like to have a word with those gentlemen," I say, pointing at the Boulder Beach execs.

Snootre d' looks us over with evident distaste. "I don't think so. They've asked not to be disturbed."

"I'm sure they wouldn't mind a brief interruption," I say. "We're kids—what harm could we do?"

Egg reaches out to the maître d' stand and sends a bowl of matches flying in every direction.

The maître d' abandons his proper French manner to gesture rudely with his thumb. "Back it up."

A Black Sheep doesn't give up so easily. I try charm, reason, and mild threats, all to no avail. There's only one card left to play, and I play it shamelessly: "Maybe you've heard of my TV show—*The Black Sheep*? If you let us in, I promise to send the camera crew over later to give you guys a nice plug."

As it happens, sometimes you have to take that "don't let the door hit you on the way out" line literally.

* * *

Mitch and the twins trail after me down the alley beside the restaurant.

"Breaking and entering might be common in New York," he says, scanning the alley nervously. "But around here, people take it very seriously."

"It's not breaking and entering if the door's ajar," I say.

Black Sheep Rule Number Seventeen: *The end justifies the means.* (This one is on loan from some dead philosopher.)

I creep up the back stairs and peer around, trying not to think too much about what I'm doing. Otherwise, I'll chicken out, and I really believe this plan could work. If it does, Mitch might be even more impressed by my courage.

The kitchen is to my left, where several staff are too busy assembling food on plates to notice me. There's a short corridor ahead that probably leads to the dining room. I look back at Mitch and whisper, "All clear. Let's go."

Mitch tells the twins to stay in the alley and follows me inside with Egg on his hip. We sneak past the kitchen door and down the corridor to push open the door to the dining room. In a matter of seconds, we're standing beside the Boulder Beach executives' table.

The men look up at us, surprised. I know from the Web site that the silver goatee guy is the biggest wig, so I direct my smile at him.

"May I help you?" he asks.

"Yes, sir," I say. I've learned from dealing with my parents and their colleagues that money people like displays of respect. "We'll only take a moment of your time."

The maître d' approaches at a run. "I'm so sorry, gentle-men. They slipped past me somehow. Shall I call the authorities?"

Bigwig finishes his last spoonful of soup and dabs at the corners of his mouth with a white linen napkin. "That won't be necessary. I'm sure they don't mean any harm."

The maître d' withdraws to hover nearby, and Bigwig motions for us to sit down.

"You obviously have something on your mind," Bigwig says, as I slide into the chair next to him.

Money people enjoy compliments about their assets. "It's about your beautiful golf course, sir."

Bigwig fiddles with his gold cuff link and smiles. "Have you played it?"

"Not yet, but I've heard wonderful things about its design, and I hope you won't change a thing before I get my chance."

"What are you getting at?" Vice Wig demands abruptly. Up close, he's not nearly as polished as Bigwig. In fact, he looks like a well-dressed thug. "We don't have time to waste."

Bigwig raises a manicured hand. "Now, now, let the lady speak."

"It's about the fourteenth hole, sir. We heard you were planning to move it, and we'd like to respectfully ask that you leave it where it is."

Bigwig turns to Vice Wig and chuckles. "Did you put them up to this?"

Vice Wig shakes his head and drains his martini.

Egg starts to whimper, and Mitch joggles him on his knee. "It isn't a joke," he says. "If you move your fairway closer to that cove, it's going to hurt the environment."

"The sea otter population is already endangered," I add. "Toxic runoff from your course could poison their food chain and affect reproduction."

Bigwig raises his groomed eyebrows. "Do you have any proof of that?"

"Not yet, sir," I say, silently cursing Lisa for being right. "We didn't want to wait for hard numbers." I consider delivering an emotional speech about how losing even one otter would be a crime, but decide against it. Money people hate messy emotions. Instead, I appeal to their wallets. "I know that your members care about the welfare of endangered species."

Then Bigwig leans forward. "You two seem to know an awful lot about us, and we don't even know your names."

I extend a hand and offer Bigwig a firm grip. Money people can't stand weak handshakes. "I'm Kendra Bishop. This is Mitch Mulligan and his brother Egg—I mean, Milo."

"Keira, I want you to listen very carefully," Bigwig says, signaling the waiter for another round of martinis. "I hugged a tree or two myself at your age, but now I run a very large, very successful business. I've acquired this beautiful piece of land, and it's going to make my business even more successful. I'm not about to change my plans just because a girl comes crying to me about otters."

I can't afford to get sidetracked by the crying comment. "I understand your business is important, but maybe you could ask some experts before making the move."

The Vice Wig cuts me off, pointing to the entrance. "What's going on here today?"

We all turn to see Judy pushing past the maître d', with Chili. She has Manhattan's leash in one hand. Meanwhile, Bob is coming in the back door leading the twins.

Perhaps in the hopes of ramping up the conflict, Judy "drops" the leash, and Manhattan scampers across the restaurant toward us. He climbs Mitch's leg and jumps onto the table.

The Wigs rear back in alarm, uttering man-squeals. "Get it off," the Vice Wig says. He doesn't sound so tough now.

Bob raises his camera for a close-up.

"Get that out of my face!" Bigwig shouts, causing Egg to burst into tears.

The Vice Wig jumps up and tries to wrestle the camera off Bob's shoulder, and a couple of busboys arrive to help. One of them stops and points at me. "That's the girl from the reality show—*The Black Sheep*."

Judy, now in the clutches of the maître d', calls, "Indeed

she is." She shakes herself loose and walks over to the Wigs. "I'm Judith Greenberg, the show's producer."

Bigwig stands to get away from the ferret and asks, "Is this some silly prank to embarrass us on TV?"

"No, sir," I say. "We're very serious about our cause." Money people value good references, so I try to strengthen my credentials. "We represent the Monterey Bay Aquarium."

"Wait a second," he says, making the connection at last. "Are you the lunatic who called us a hundred times?"

"He called me a lunatic," I moan. "A lunatic!"

"I know," Mitch says, "but can't you put it out of your mind for a while? It took less effort to plan the American Revolution than it did to arrange a few hours alone with you."

"You're right." I shouldn't be wasting precious minutes complaining when Mitch has gone to so much trouble. It's like bringing the Boulder Beach bigwigs along on our first official date.

Max and Mona were still in wine country when we got home from Carmel, so Mitch tracked down a babysitter and paid double her usual rate to get her to cancel her own plans. To ditch Judy, we cycled to the aquarium. She followed in *The Black Sheep* van, of course, but in the parking lot Mitch told her we were going to the lab to analyze samples, and described the process in excruciating detail. For good measure, he added that Lisa is away at a conference. With all hope of conflict gone, Judy cut the crew loose for a few hours, and booked herself a massage.

Once the coast was clear, Mitch and I left our bikes at the aquarium and skulked over to Cannery Row to Oceans 18. I'd envisioned a dim, romantic restaurant with tiny candles on each table and slushy drinks in martini glasses. The only part I got right was "dim." Oceans 18 is not a restaurant, but a miniature golf course featuring black light and fluorescent fish murals. I would have preferred a movie or a walk, or just about anything else to mini golf as my first real date. By definition, mini golf is anti-romance. But I suppose Oceans 18 is about as cool as mini golf gets. It has a *Finding Nemo* feel to it, so I can see why Mitch likes it.

Mitch steps up to the first hole. "Watch and learn, City Girl."

I wait until he's taken his swing before bringing up the bigwigs again. "Can you believe they just dismissed us like that? We were being totally reasonable."

"Kendra, forget about them," he says, exasperated. "This is supposed to be fun. Plus it's a chance to learn about golf. You can always fight the enemy better if you're familiar with their territory."

Trust a guy to relate to everything in war terms. "So what you're saying is Boulder Beach is just like Oceans 18, but without the black light?"

He ushers me into position. "I'm speaking in generalities."

His grin is eerily yellow in the black light, but even that

can't diminish his good looks. Hopefully he feels the same when he looks at me, because my smile is my best feature and Oceans 18 is totally ruining it. Thank God I wore a white T-shirt, because lint and ferret hairs are standing out in relief on Mitch's dark one.

"More like a general," I say.

I take a savage swing at the ball and miss completely.

When Mitch stops laughing, he says, "Good. You're working out your frustrations."

I take another fruitless swing and turn to look at him. "Do you think I really blew it today?"

General Mitch consoles me. "Losing one battle isn't losing the war."

"But Lisa is going to kill me," I say. "They'll never let her present her findings now."

"Lisa can be pretty persuasive when she wants to be," he says. "And she's probably as smart as they are."

I don't want to hear how smart and persuasive Lisa is during my date with Mitch. Next he'll be saying how beautiful she is. "I feel terrible. I screwed up."

"Quit taking all the credit," he says. "I was sitting at the table with you, and I didn't sway them either." He puts his arm around me and pulls me close. "Just remember what I said about my parents and their battles: it takes years to change the way people think, especially when there's a lot of money involved. What happened today was just our shot over the bow."

"Okay, I'm ready to put the war behind me." I pull the scorecard out of my pocket. "Show me how the game works."

Mitch takes the scorecard and tears it up. "You won't need that," he says. "We're playing Confessional Golf."

"Is that like strip poker?" I ask suspiciously.

"No, but if you're up for that later . . ." He grins mischievously.

"I'm not much of a gambler, actually."

"You can't lose with this one," he says. "It's like Truth or Dare—but without the dare."

He explains that the person who sinks his or her ball in the fewest strokes gets to ask the other person a question. No topic is off-limits.

"I don't know," I say. At the rate I'm going, I'll have to answer eighteen questions, and Mitch, none.

"Afraid?" he says teasingly. "What are you hiding?"

"Nothing," I say, and it's true. I'm trying to hide the fact that there's nothing about my past worth hiding. By the fifth hole, he'll be so bored by my confessions that he'll be chatting up the plastic mermaid. "I just think it might be better to play by the standard rules the first time, so that I get the hang of it."

"So you really want to pass up the opportunity to ask about the time I got suspended from school?"

Perfect Mitch got suspended from school?

"And you don't want to ask about how I got stood up for

a school dance, and my mother insisted I take Maya instead?"

"She didn't!"

He nods with mock sadness. "Maya met some guy at the dance, and I ended up solo anyway."

"Poor Mitch," I say, secretly delighted that his love life hasn't always been smooth sailing.

"Notice I'm giving you freebies," he says, "since you're a novice."

"I don't need your freebies," I say. "I happen to have excellent hand-eye coordination."

I step back to the tee and hit the ball. The game is officially on.

Before we've finished nine holes, Mitch has asked about my favorite food (Nana Russell's fried chicken); my earliest memory (watching Mom and Dad from the front window as they left for a run); my most embarrassing experience (losing my shorts during the kayaking expedition); my biggest lie (telling my mother that a scary man was watching our gymnastics class through the window, just so I wouldn't have to go anymore); and my biggest fear (being exposed as hopelessly dull).

But it's not entirely one-sided. I have scored a very respectable four questions, asking about Mitch's favorite role model (Jacques Cousteau, some dead sea captain); his biggest fear (flunking out of college and disappointing his parents); his worst memory (getting booed while singing in a school talent contest); and finally, his best date ever.

Mitch leans against a fluorescent red octopus and smiles. Somehow my eyes have gotten used to the black light, and his teeth now look as white as they ever do. "The best date?" he ponders. "Hmmmm . . . I'd have to say this one."

"Good answer," I say, trying to sound nonchalant. "And just to save you a question—mine, too."

He comes over and kisses me beside the arc of shark's teeth, and I wonder how I thought this wouldn't be romantic. Romance, it seems, is everywhere—on the high seas, inside a jellyfish gallery, and, however unlikely, at Oceans 18. All it takes is a nautical theme and the right company.

I was wrong about mini golf, too. It's a brilliant game—at least the confessional version. I have discovered an unexpected aptitude for it.

Either that, or Mitch is deliberately missing some shots.

"My question," I say, after the next hole. "How many girlfriends have you had?"

"None."

"None?" I can't hide my surprise.

"Well, I've dated a few girls, but no one I considered a girlfriend."

"Why?" I ask.

He grins. "I'm hearing question marks. You're supposed to *earn* answers, remember?"

Before I can respond, we hear a familiar voice behind us.

"We've only got time for nine holes," Bob says. "We've got to be back at the Mulligans' by eight thirty."

Mitch ducks behind a sunken ship and pulls me down beside him. We watch as Chili leads Bob to the first tee.

"No problem," Chili says. "It'll only take twenty minutes to kick your ass."

"Put your money where your mouth is, hotshot."

"I'll do better than that," Chili says. "Loser goes to L.A. with Judy."

Mitch mouths, "L.A.?" and I shrug to let him know it's news to me.

"Start packing, Red," Bob says. "You're looking at the mini putt champion of Bear Creek, Alabama four years running."

Bob and Chili are so busy taunting each other that Mitch and I are able to creep past them and return our clubs unnoticed.

Outside, we keep running until we're back at the aquarium, unlocking our bikes.

The Black Sheep theme song plays over an opening shot of the family portrait from my parents' living room. A banner scrolls cross the bottom of the screen that reads, *Bishops on the Brink of Breaking Up!*

"Judy," I say, turning to her in disgust, "I told you I don't want to divorce my parents."

"Shhh!" Judy hisses from the sofa, where she's sitting

between Mona and Max. "This is a pivotal episode."

"'Zokay, Kendra," Mona says, leaning over to pat my arm and missing by a yard. She and Max are still feeling the effects of their afternoon wine tour. "You don't haf to do anything you don' wan' to."

"Ssssright," Max agrees.

It's hard to take him seriously when he's wearing Mona's beret.

"Sssssswrong," Judy says, frowning. "I still own this kid." Her frown promptly flips upside down as the screen fills with a close-up of her own face. "Hey, I look *good*."

"For thirty-five," I say.

"Thirty-four," she corrects. "Eyes forward, KB."

On screen, Judy is suggesting to me that I divorce my parents. When it's my turn to speak, the camera remains on her, but my voice says, *"Divorce them? That's a great idea."* There's a cut to a shot of me talking to the Mulligans and saying, *"You understand me better than my own parents. I want to stay here forever."* Then there's a shot of my own parents while my voice-over continues, *"I want the public to know that these people are arrogant and ignorant and cold. They think I'm just a silly teenager who can't stand up to them, but I'm going to prove them wrong."*

Judy has taken what I've said at other points and cobbled it together to sound like a rant against my parents. She applauds her own wizardry. "Now that's great TV!"

When the show ends, I am too angry to speak. In the

dark, Mitch reaches for my hand and gives it a squeeze.

"Well, Mulligans, what do you think?" Judy asks.

Max answers with a loud snore, and Judy stands to turn on the lights. Mona's eyes flutter open.

"It's slander," I answer for them.

"Kendra, don't be such a stick-in-the-mud. Three million people tune in to *The Black Sheep* each week, and it's not to see what you're having for breakfast. They're looking for excitement, emotional turmoil, and life-changing events."

"It's life-changing, all right. It bears no resemblance at all to my real life."

"It all happened, KB, just maybe not in that order. Anyway, let's not get bogged down by details. What's important is that Judy is giving the audience what they want and they're eating it up. So much so that you've been invited onto the *The Nelle DeLerious Show* to talk about the parental divorce angle."

"There *is* no divorce angle. I never said I hated my parents, I'm not divorcing them, and I'm not promoting a lie on a talk show. So you can cancel *Nelle* right now."

Judy shakes her head as she climbs the basement stairs. "Am I the only person with vision around here?"

She slams the basement door behind her. Max lets out a series of snorts, and Mona rises unsteadily to her feet. "Come on, Max," she says, tugging Max's arm. "It's time for bed. 'Night, kids."

Mitch pops a DVD into the player and pulls me onto the sofa beside him. "You okay?" he asks.

"I've got to call my parents," I say. "They're going to hate me when they see this episode."

"It's one o'clock in the morning in New York," Mitch says. "Which means they've already seen it. I'm sure your folks know it's a publicity stunt."

"Do you think so?" I'm not so sure, but I'm ready to be convinced.

"Sure," he says, wrapping an arm around me. "Parents always see through the hype."

I rest my head on his shoulder and consider this. It's true that my parents aren't snowed by much. Like typical New Yorkers, they're skeptical of everything. Who knows? Maybe they've been misrepresented on the show, too.

For the moment, I decide to focus on how good it feels to have Mitch's arm around me. With him in my corner, I feel like I can take on anything, even Judy.

I will simply have to be more assertive. There is no way I am doing that talk show.

Chapter 12

I wince as the limo jerks to a stop in front of Warner Brothers Studio in Burbank. My neck is still stiff today, three days after falling asleep on Mitch's shoulder in front of the television. Fortunately, Meadow didn't even wake up when I crept into our room at four a.m.

Judy slides out of the limo to speak to the security guard, and I lean back against the plush leather seat, struck by an odd feeling of familiarity. It's not being in a limo on a studio lot that feels familiar, obviously. What's familiar is the fact that waiting to gain entrance to the studio where *Nelle DeLerious* shoots feels like just another event in my new life.

I don't know how it happened or when it happened, but at some point over the past month, the unpredictability of my life on *The Black Sheep* magically became the new normal. Even the blinking red light of Bob's camera flashing at me now through the window feels normal. What's more, it feels like it's been like this for a lot longer than a month. The Mulligans are as familiar to me as my own family, if not more so. Even Judy has become familiar in her unpredictability.

"Kendra." Judy's voice disrupts my philosophizing. "Look at me when I'm talking to you."

I swing my body around awkwardly to face her.

"What's wrong with you?" she demands.

"Stiff neck," I say. "The flight was so turbulent."

"You'd better loosen up before you meet Nelle, KB. Thanks to the divorce episode, you're flavor of the week. We've booked you for the full talk-show circuit and Judy won't tolerate your tanking on the first one."

"I'll be doing other talk shows?"

"*Every* talk show. That's what makes it a circuit. And before you start whining, I want you to remember our discussion on the plane."

"I remember my obligation to the network," I assure her. "Publicity is part of the package." But I didn't promise it would be exactly the kind of publicity Judy wants.

"Correct. I appreciate that you've been more cooperative during the past few days. Maybe you've finally realized that being on TV means you have a certain responsibility to the public. Letters and e-mails have been pouring into the network. Granted, they're mainly complaints from parents saying their teenagers want to divorce them because of you, but at least people are watching. Like I always say, any publicity is good publicity."

I'm glad she feels that way. I can't turn my head far enough to see her full-on, but I do my best to look sincere with one eye. "You're right, Judy, I do have a responsibility to the public. I guess I'm almost a role model."

"Not 'almost,' you *are* a role model. People look up to you."

"Really? Do you think so?"

"I know so." She leans in until her teeth block the light from the tinted windows. "I'll let you in on a little secret, kid: you've got presence. And if you play your cards right, you might have a future in television."

"Wow. I hope you're right."

She squints suspiciously. "Are you toying with Judy?"

"Of course not," I say. "I've just realized what an opportunity you're giving me, and I want to make the most of it. I'm going to do my very best on this circuit, Judy."

She seems convinced. "Good girl. Now, on to more pressing matters. Earth tones."

"Huh?"

"Don't let Tess use any on you."

"Tess? You mean the makeup artist who disappeared after the first day of shooting?"

"Don't get smart. You know the network decided you should do your own makeup to keep it real."

The network decided I should do my own makeup to keep it under budget.

"She'll meet you in your dressing room," Judy continues. "I've asked her to blow out your hair as well. You look about ten years old with it that way."

She's referring to my ponytail, and I'll admit it's not

exactly sophisticated. These days, I hate wasting time on a blow out. Maybe it's the Mulligan influence, but I've been less obsessed with my appearance lately. Carrie says I'm just a hairy armpit away from turning into a full-fledged granola type, but it'll never happen. You can take the girl out of New York, but you can't take New York out of the girl.

To be sure of that, Carrie dragged me off on a shopping spree to find an outfit worthy of *Nelle*. It gave me an excuse to avoid the aquarium after Lisa got back from her conference and heard about my encounter with the bigwigs. Mitch downplayed her reaction, but Tia overheard Lisa calling me a "hopeless screwup" and threatening to shut down Team 14 altogether.

Nelle is giving me another chance to turn things around. When Lisa sees how I've used a popular television show to educate the public about our cause, she'll back off. Then Mitch will be able to stop apologizing for me all the time.

The prospect of taking on Nelle DeLerious, a comedian, is daunting, but at least I have the right clothes. Carrie and I debated my look in a succession of changing rooms, finally settling on a modern, edgy outfit that reflects my forward-thinking personality: black knee-high motorcycle boots to show I mean business; a black satin skirt to show that although I'm strong, I haven't forsaken my femininity; a conservative black shirt to show I don't need to exploit that femininity; and a vintage black plaid cap to show I'm brave enough to stand apart from the crowd. I wore everything on the plane today except the cap. Somewhere between the Mulligans' house and the airport I realized that I need to work up to standing apart.

"—with the rest of the schmoes," Judy says. "Got it?"

"Got what?" I ask.

Judy places a hand on either side of my head and cranks it around to face her, ignoring my squeal of pain. "Judy needs you to focus," she says. "When Tess is done, you will make your way to the greenroom, where the guests wait. A flunky will come to take you onstage."

"No earth tones . . . wait for the flunky. I got it."

"And when you make your entrance, you have to dance."

"*Dance?*"

"Don't you watch the show? Nelle's all about the danc-ing."

"I don't know how to dance. I grew up in a museum, remember?"

"Well, try to groove a little. You know . . . feel the music." She lets go of my face and jiggles in her seat to show me how it's done.

It's a good thing I'm so motivated to promote Team 14.

I follow the flunky down the corridor, my heart picking up speed with every step. I'm used to cameras dogging me, but live TV is a whole new ballgame.

The flunky holds a finger to his lips before opening the

door and beckoning me to follow him into the wings. In the silence of the studio, my motorcycle boots clunk on the cement floors. The flunky turns to scowl at me and taps briskly on his lips a few more times. Through a gap in the velvet curtain, I can see Nelle DeLerious shticking for the crowd. When they begin to applaud, I creep closer to the gap, where I can see row upon row of mainly female faces. They are all waiting to hear about my plan to divorce my parents.

Make that Judy's plan to divorce my parents for me. I have no intention of pretending to take the question of emancipation seriously on the air. Sure, I'm still upset at my parents for not supporting my new interests, but that's no reason to make silly threats. I fully intend to go home to New York eventually. California isn't going to work for me forever. Unless Mitch and I get married, that is. But it's too early to think about that.

Beyond the curtain, it's become very quiet. Nelle studies a card in her hand and reads, "Now would you please welcome a little black sheep who's come all the way from smoggy New York City to graze in the sweet California sunshine . . . Kendra Bishop!"

The DJ cues up a song I've never heard before and, just as Judy predicted, Nelle starts to dance. The flunky gives me a shove and I start walking toward Nelle, shaking my shoulders a little. Nelle gives a shimmy and I shimmy back, tossing my head around for good measure. She raises one arm and I shoot mine up, too.

"Are you okay?" Nelle asks, when I finally reach her. "I thought the black sheep got struck by lightening."

The audience howls. Okay, this isn't the best start.

I take the seat across from her and she smiles. It's friendly enough, but her eyes seem a little glazed, as if she doesn't really see me. "That's a nice outfit, Kendra."

"Thanks." The makeover is working!

Nelle turns to the audience and says, "It looks like someone's taking her role a little too seriously." When the laugh subsides, she adds, "But at least she's not wearing her fleece tonight, huh, folks?" Nelle selects a card from the coffee table and holds it up for the camera. Glancing at the monitors, I see it's the *Carmel Pinecone* photo of me on the donkey. "Did you know someone's selling the original on eBay?" Nelle asks. She doesn't wait for me to answer before turning to her DJ. "How much is the bidding up to today?"

The DJ taps into a laptop computer. "Two hundred and four dollars."

"Obviously you have some fans, Kendra," Nelle says. "I guess denouncing your parents on national television has made you the hero of every teen in America."

This time she pauses long enough for me to respond. "I didn't denounce them," I say. "Everyone knows these shows are edited to—"

"Blah, blah, black sheep," Nelle interrupts. "There's no

212

use denying it. We all saw the show, didn't we?" The audience cheers. "You said you hated your parents and divorcing them is a great idea."

I see a chance to exit the divorce freeway, and take it. "I'll admit I was angry with them, Nelle, but only because they wouldn't take Team Fourteen seriously."

"Team Fourteen?" Nelle leans forward in her chair, curious. Ha. Score one for the kid on the donkey.

"It's a public education group. We're letting people know about a threat to marine wildlife in Carmel. The Boulder Beach Golf Club is planning to redesign its course, which could put the sea otter population at even more risk."

I've heard that Nelle is a major animal lover, so I'm half expecting her to announce a drive to save the otters. If she does, Lisa Langdon will be begging this hopeless screwup for forgiveness.

"Do your parents golf, Kendra?" Nelle asks. "Are you a golf orphan who's trying to get even?"

That's not the response I was hoping for. Nelle is trying to set a divorce trap for me, but I'm not that gullible. "My parents prefer running."

"Running away from you?" she asks, without missing a beat. "No wonder you want to turn the tables now."

"I'm not running away from anything, Nelle. I ran *toward* a free vacation in sunny California."

The audience laughs.

Scoreboard says: Black Sheep, one; famous talk-show host, zero.

Before she can reply, I add, "The show has given me a chance to meet some people who really care about the environment. I'm just trying to lend my support."

Nelle turns to the audience. "Sounds like Kendra's got a talent for public speaking. But it doesn't end there, people." She reaches down beside her chair and picks up a flute. This can't be good. "The bio your show sent me said you're a musician, Kendra."

"I've only taken lessons for a couple of years."

"I'm sure your fans would love to hear you play." She turns to the audience and they burst into a cheer.

And the score is tied, folks: one all.

My hand shakes as I take the flute. Music isn't my calling and I know that, but I see an opportunity to turn this to my advantage.

I raise the flute to my lips and do my best rendition of "Bah, Bah, Black Sheep." The audience recognizes the first few notes and applauds.

Rack up another point for the undersheep.

Nelle tries dancing to the song, but I hit so many sour notes that she cuts me off after four bars. "That's all the time we have today, but before we say good-bye to Kendra, we have something for her."

She pulls out a gift bag and hands it to me. I unwrap what appears to be a small black hammock.

"Your very own set of Donkey diapers!" Nelle announces gleefully.

The crazed laughter blows me off the stage and into the wings.

Final score: Famous Talk Show Host, ten; Black Sheep, slaughtered.

When I get back to the greenroom, I head straight to the food table. It's going to take half a dozen chocolate cupcakes to recover from that experience.

"Save one for me," a male voice says behind me.

I spin to find a tall, dark, and very cute guy standing behind me. I've seen his face before. . . . Every single morning as soon as I open my eyes, actually.

"You're Logan Waters," I say, spraying him with cupcake crumbs.

He hands me a stack of napkins. "And you're the Black Sheep."

Nodding, I hold a napkin against my mouth. "My sister—on the show, that is—loves you."

"Meadow," he says. "I know. My agent told me about the shrine, so I tuned in."

I hope he doesn't think that just because Meadow and I share a room that we're equally immature. "She's only ten. She gets carried away."

"Well, tell her I said hi," he says. "I was watching you out there just now. I thought you did a great job. Talk shows can be tough, especially for beginners."

"Nelle totally humiliated me."

"You held your own," he says. "I'm guessing the emancipation thing wasn't your idea."

"How did you know?"

"I've been around the block a few times. There's always someone behind the scenes pulling strings. All you can do is keep fighting. You have to stay true to yourself."

Logan Waters is giving me advice! Wait until Lucy hears about this. She will freak out. I am freaking out a little myself, although I'm working hard to hide it. A Black Sheep must be above hero worship.

Logan is a well-known environmentalist, so when he asks me about Team 14, I give him all the details, even the story about meeting the Bigwigs.

When I finally stop talking, he asks, "How old are you?"

This flusters me. If Logan is curious about my age, he must be thinking of ditching the model girlfriend for me. I wouldn't have thought it possible, given how much younger I am, but I've always been mature for my age. Plus, I'm not the same private-school math nerd who left New York.

Not that I can even think about going out with him. Logan may be one of the coolest, best-looking guys I have ever met, but I do have a boyfriend.

At least, I think I have a boyfriend. Mitch still hasn't come right out and said the word "girlfriend," but he acts as if I am. I catch him looking at me a lot, and he keeps trying to find opportunities to get me alone. And then this morning, he lent me his iPod for the plane and told me he'd downloaded some songs he thought I'd like. That is *such* a boyfriend thing to do.

On the other hand, we've stolen a few moments together here and there since our mini golf date, and Mitch could easily have let me know where I stand. How hard could it be to work that one little word into a sentence? As in, "I am so glad I could lend my iPod to my *girlfriend*." Or, "It's great to be working on Team Fourteen with my *girlfriend*."

Given that Mitch hasn't said the word, I decide to keep my options open with Logan. Mitch is definitely my first choice, but if he's not going to commit, Logan Waters would be a great fallback.

Logan startles me out of my reverie. "Is that such a tough question?"

"Sorry?"

"I asked how old you are."

Since I'm keeping my options open, I exaggerate. "Eighteen."

He laughs. "I wouldn't have put you a day over sixteen."

I'll take it. Now that I think about it, I could totally see Logan and me together. We're both from New York, and he's obviously someone who shares my concerns about animals and the environment. Meadow's magazines haven't said he's hung up about education, either. He probably doesn't believe in getting stuck in ivy-covered bastions of higher learning when he could be out in the world learning by doing. In other words, he might be a Black Sheep, just like me.

Still, I don't feel good about leading Logan on. "Listen," I say. "There's something I—"

Before I can let him down easily, the flunky arrives to collect him. Logan reaches out to rap my hand lightly with his fist and says, "It was nice meeting you, Kendra."

"Wait!" I call as he turns to go. "Could you give me your autograph—for Meadow?"

I offer him a napkin, and while he's signing it, I write something on another one. We exchange napkins and he waves good-bye.

"You tricked me, KB," Judy says, practically shoving me into the limo. "I did not spring for an all expenses-paid trip to Los Angeles so that you could grandstand about some stupid cause on my dime."

"Telling people about a real problem isn't grandstanding," I say.

Judy slams the door and walks around the car, complaining audibly the whole way.

"Don't speak," she says, climbing into the seat beside me. "Just listen. Harry Queen's people called while you were on with Nelle, and he wants you to do his show tonight. Once we set foot in the CNN studio, the word 'seal' will not cross your lips. There's only one animal that Harry Queen wants to hear about and that's *The Black Sheep*. Do I make myself clear?"

"Perfectly." I unfold the napkin Logan gave me. It says, *Meadow, your big 'sister' Kendra rocks, and you do, too! Love, Logan Waters*.

Judy reaches for the napkin but I snatch it away and stow it in my purse. With this to barter, Meadow will never borrow my clothes again.

"I'm serious, KB," Judy continues. "If you keep harping on about Team Fourteen, I won't be the only one in trouble with the network. The divorce is the issue here. That's what talk-show hosts want you to talk about. Repeat after me: From now on, I will discuss only *The Black Sheep*."

"From now on," I say, "I will discuss only *The Black Sheep*."

Harry Queen shakes my hand and turns to the camera.

"Good evening, everyone. Tonight's guest is a young lady from New York City who's joined forces with her new friends and family in Monterey, California, to take on a Carmel institution. Kendra Bishop, I want you to tell me all about Team Fourteen."

Chapter 13

It's quiet inside the limo as the driver rounds the corner onto the Mulligans' street. Judy glances up from her *Enquirer* magazine to make sure I'm aware that she's giving me the silent treatment. Apparently it's my fault that Harry Queen was more interested in discussing Team 14 than *The Black Sheep* last night. Apparently it's also my fault that three radio shows wanted me to talk about the same thing on the air today. I pointed out that I'm just giving the people what they want, but Judy said that if I hadn't "ranted about the damn seals" on *Nelle*, they wouldn't have wanted the wrong thing. Whatever. She's the one who set up the talk-show circuit, not me.

Chili is alone outside with his camera when we pull into the driveway, which is strange. The Mulligan house is usually a magnet for every kid in the neighborhood, but today it looks deserted.

"Where is everyone?" I ask Chili as the driver deposits my bags on the porch.

He shrugs. "Dunno. Place seems pretty quiet."

I dig the house key out of my bag and unlock the front door. "Hello! I'm home!"

There's no response. Judy and Chili trail behind me as I walk through the house and open the door to the backyard. Empty. Not even the dog to greet me.

"Gee, what a letdown," Judy says, breaking her silence to taunt me. "I'm sure you were expecting a hero's welcome after your antics in L.A."

"I wasn't expecting anything," I say, lugging my suitcase upstairs. I was, of course, but it's not like coming home to an empty house is new to me. After my parents fired Rosa, the place was so empty it echoed. I could have screamed my head off and no one would have heard me inside that marble tomb.

When I first came to Monterey, the Mulligan house felt like Grand Central Station, with its constant traffic. It took me weeks to adjust to the noise and frenzy, but now that I have, I realize that one of the things I like most about living here is that there's someone to greet me whenever I walk through the door. Mona always makes a point of asking about my day and discussing the highs and lows as if they're actually interesting to her. She does the same thing with Mitch and Meadow and even the twins. I imagine she learned the technique in some hippie encounter group, but it does make you feel special.

In my room, I sit down on the bed and stroke Manhattan. While I haven't grown to love him, I no longer cringe when I feel his bones through his pelt. Tonight, he's better than nothing. I scratch under his chin and something shiny drops out of his jaws onto the quilt: Judy's diamond ring.

I pick it up as she walks into the room and starts in on me again. "KB, even your seal-whisperer shtick is more interesting than this."

"No one's keeping you here," I say. I change my mind about returning the ring to her and slide it under the pillow. Maybe I can pawn it later and use the proceeds to start up a school to promote Black Sheepism.

"You're right," she says. "Wrap it up, Chili. I happen to know where we can get a free drink. God knows I need one."

Judy must really be steamed over *Harry Queen* if she's skipping out before tonight's *Black Sheep* episode airs, but I don't try to stop her. Instead, I watch out the front window as the limo pulls away from the curb, and then head back into the kitchen to get a soda.

Although I didn't expect a hero's welcome, I did count on Mitch's being here to greet me. Yesterday was a really big day, with more excitement than I've experienced in an entire lifetime. At the very least, he should want to hear about it firsthand. Is it too much to ask to share this experience with my boyfriend? What's the point of even having one if he's not going to be around when you need him? He's probably off doing guy things with Calvin during my time of need, leaving me to confide in a ferret.

Looking around for a pen and paper to write my breakup speech, I find Mona's note on the kitchen table: *Kendra, we're at the aquarium.*

The aquarium has already closed by the time I arrive, but being an activist in residence I have a key. I hurry to the supply room, assuming that there's an impromptu meeting. Maybe the golf club has reacted to my talk-show appearances in some way, and everyone has gathered to brainstorm.

I fling open the supply room door to find more than two dozen people crammed inside. The Mulligans are all here, as well as Carrie and Calvin, aquarium staff and volunteers, and all of Team 14. Obviously something big has happened, and I arrived just in time.

Then I notice the streamers hanging from the light fixtures, and the food laid out on one of the desks. Are they having a party without me?

Mitch is the first to notice me, and he comes right over. If anyone else happened to be watching, they'd probably say he rushed. His smile is wide enough to satisfy even *my* doubts. I don't know what I was thinking earlier. Logan Waters may be rich, talented, and hot, but he's no Mitch.

"Welcome back," Mitch says. His arms rise as if he's going to hug me, but he remembers where we are and drops them again.

I resist the urge to grab his hand. "What's going on?" I ask.

Mona steps forward to do the hugging for us. "Let's hear it, people," she says, turning to the crowd.

Everyone sings "For She's a Jolly Good Fellow." Meadow's voice soars above the rest of the voices and Max's croaking bass sinks below.

A grin stretches across my face. "For me?"

Mona points to a sign on the wall congratulating me. "Do you see anyone else's name? Sorry we couldn't pull off the surprise. We didn't know when you'd get here."

"Oh, I'm surprised," I assure her.

Meadow rushes over and says, "*She* ruined the surprise. *She* said Bob would radio in when you got to the aquarium so that we could turn out the lights and hide." The "she" in question is Judy, who is leaning against a makeshift bar with a glass of red wine in her hand.

"So I forgot," Judy says, draining her glass. "Big deal."

Carrie whispers, "What's her problem? She's been a bitch since she got here."

"Too much otter, not enough divorce," I reply. "As if I would diss my parents on national TV just to make Judy happy. I hope they caught Nelle's show so that they know I'm not buying into the plan."

"Bad news on that front," Carrie says. "Judy mentioned that your parents are running a marathon in Mexico with Maya this week. They probably didn't see it."

Before I can react, Team 14 members surround us. Mitch

hands me a soda and raises his glass to propose a toast. "To Kendra, who really knows how to get the word out."

"To Kendra," everyone echoes, clinking plastic glasses.

Everyone except Judy, that is. I can't help but notice that her glass remains glued to her lips. But then, it takes work to keep a mouth that size full.

Meadow picks up Mitch's camcorder and begins to interview the crowd. "Wasn't Kendra great on *Nelle?*" she asks Judy.

"Fantastic," Judy says, her voice devoid of enthusiasm. "In fact, I'm going to use my network resources so that she can launch a National Otter Tour. Get it? *National Otter Tour?* As in NOT!" She punctuates her remark with a wave of her glass, splashing Meadow's lens with red wine.

Chili lowers his camera. "Maybe you've had enough," he says.

"Did I ask for your opinion?" Judy snaps. "Just plug the damn eyepiece and leave me alone."

Leaving them to bicker, I head over to the food table.

"I saw you on *Nelle* yesterday," Jordan says, joining me. "You looked great—especially in those boots."

"Uh, thanks," I say. I'm no expert, but it appears that Jordan is flirting with me. Given our history, nothing would make me happier than telling him I have a boyfriend, but I can't do it, because it's a secret boyfriend.

"I think it was really cool the way you mentioned Team Fourteen," he says.

I glance around the room warily. "Is this a setup?"

"No." He sounds indignant. "I'm serious. If you don't believe me, check their online petition. I signed it."

"Since when have you had an interest in otter welfare?" I ask.

"Since I saw you in those boots," he says, laughing. "Just kidding! Listening to you convinced me I should. That's why I joined Team Fourteen."

"You did?"

He nods. "Also, I wanted to prove I'm not a total jerk. Every time I see you, I end up looking like an idiot. I guess you make me nervous."

As far as I know, the last time I made someone nervous was when I explained the benefits of capitalism to my first-grade teacher. Obviously Black Sheepism has transformed me not only into an activist, but also a femme fatale.

I hope Mitch appreciates how lucky he is.

Black Sheep Rule Number Twenty, Subsection—Guys: *Where there is sufficient evidence of repentance, second chances are permitted. Note: third chances may not be granted under any circumstances.*

"I'm glad you've joined the team," I say. "We need all the help we can get."

Jordan's smile lights up his face, and I return it, basking in the glow of my influence. I, Kendra Bishop—Plain Jane, Math Nerd, Wallflower—am finally popular! I'm on the radar at last.

Over Jordan's shoulder, I see Mitch watching us. He catches my eye, unsmiling, before turning to walk away.

I peer into the jellyfish gallery. "Mitch? Are you in here?" When there's no answer, I walk farther into the exhibit. The light is on in the sea nettle tank, so somebody must be home. My vision adjusts, and I see him leaning against the wall beside the tank. I can't see his expression clearly, but there's no gleam of white teeth.

"What's going on?" I ask.

"Just taking a break from the crowd," he says. "Being stuck in a room with that many people and no windows isn't my idea of a good time."

I try not to take offense over the fact that he's not enjoying my party. He's a nature guy, more at home on the high seas than in high society. I understand that. In fact, it's one of the things I like about him. So I decide to be the understanding girlfriend. "You don't have to stay if you don't want to. We can catch up at home."

He crosses his arms. "If you want me to leave, just say so."

"That's not what I said!" My voice squeaks in alarm. "I just don't want you to stay if you're hating it."

"I never said I hated it. But you've hardly even spoken to me, so I didn't think you'd notice if I left."

Has he gotten into the wine? "You know we can't talk that much with Judy around."

He shrugs. "You don't seem to mind if she thinks you're with Jordan."

Okay, now I see what's going on here. "I'm not interested in Jordan, Mitch," I say.

"Why would I care?" he asks, turning to watch the sea nettles on their magical journey. "You're not my girlfriend or anything."

Ouch. The nettles couldn't sting any worse than that. "No," I reply faintly. "I guess not." I feel like toxins are creeping through my body, killing me slowly. How could this have gone so far wrong? I shouldn't have gotten my hopes up. Mitch and I have met here many times over the past two weeks, but we've only had one real date. Any other girl would have known he was just leading me on. Any other girl would have recognized that a secret relationship is an imaginary relationship. Any other girl would have realized that guys are not worth the trouble.

The feeling returns to my feet, and I turn to go. Mitch catches my arm. "Wait," he says. "I didn't mean that. I'm sorry."

"It's not like I can tell Jordan that I'm seeing you," I point out. "If that's what I'm doing."

"You are," he says, letting his hand slide down my arm until he is holding my hand. "That's why I'm jealous."

"But you just said I wasn't your girlfriend." This time I will leave absolutely no room for doubt.

Mitch's teeth finally flash in the gloom. "Your boyfriend's a liar." He pulls me in for a kiss.

After a few more reminders of why guys are worth the trouble, Mitch tells me that he's proud of the way I handled myself on the talk shows.

"I guess I was pretty good," I say.

"Pretty good? You have no idea. The Web site has been flooded with e-mails from people who want to help with Team Fourteen. Overnight, we got fifty thousand signatures on the petition."

Fifty thousand! "The Boulder Beach bigwigs will have to change their plans now," I say.

He shakes his head. "They're still ignoring us. Lisa's contacts say the club is holding a charity tournament next week, and the bigwigs are going to unveil a model of the new fourteenth fairway."

"Maybe we should round up those fifty thousand supporters and crash the tournament. That'd be pretty hard to ignore."

Mitch's eyes light up. "You mean stage a sit-in on the fourteenth hole? That's a great idea!"

I was actually joking, but if he wants to give me credit, I'll take it. After all, behind every great man, there's a great Black Sheep.

Lisa has joined the party by the time I return to the supply room. I guess she's gotten over herself now that I've educated a few million people on her behalf.

"Well, if it isn't the girl of the hour," she says witheringly.

She's giving me attitude at my own party? Obviously her massive brain is so cluttered with scientific data that there's no room for the rules of etiquette. "What's your problem?" I ask.

"I heard about how you ambushed the Boulder Beach president at a restaurant and totally pissed him off."

Oh, that. I figured my success on *Nelle DeLerious* would erase that from my record.

Mitch comes over and grabs Lisa's arm. "Did Kendra tell you about her idea?"

I interrupt him. "Probably not a good time, Mitch."

He's too excited to stop. "She wants to stage a sit-in during the Boulder Beach charity tournament."

Lisa's jaw drops. "You've got to be kidding, Mitch. If Kendra wants to star in another publicity stunt, I want no part in it."

"I think it could work," he persists.

"It's stupid," she says, turning to go.

Mitch follows, practically at a run. "But my parents used to stage sit-ins all the time."

Materializing at my side, Judy says, "Those two look tight, but I wouldn't worry, KB. I'm sure Mitch will be true to you."

I can tell she doesn't know anything about Mitch and me; she's just fishing. "Have another bottle of wine, Judy," I say.

"Judy can see that you think you're in love with that boy. It's sweet, really."

I'm surprised at how good I'm getting at refusing the bait. "How much wine does someone have to drink before she's officially an alcoholic?"

"It doesn't count if it's free," she says. "By the way, Chili says Lisa and Mitch were joined at the hip while we were in L.A."

"I hope they got a lot of work done," I say. "Can we go back to your not speaking to me now?"

"No. I can't stand being on the outs with my little black sheep. Especially since your seal-hugging stunt with Nelle and Harry sent the ratings for tonight's episode through the roof." She plants a kiss on my cheek, and I wonder if it's possible to black out from secondhand alcohol fumes. "KB, we are officially the number one–rated show on the Reality Network!"

"Great. Can I go now?"

"Sure, just as long as you let me know where you are. Come to think of it, you were already missing in action for a while earlier. Did you and your pretty brother find a moment to gaze into each other's eyes? Or is he playing hard to get?"

I smile. "Haven't I provided enough entertainment today? I'm off duty."

"Oh, come on," she says. "You can tell me. Judy knows all about boy trouble."

"Actually, I'm going to follow your example and stay single forever. It's the best way to enjoy my independence, don't you agree?"

Judy hesitates. "I'm not *always* single, KB. I just keep romance in perspective."

"I admire you for putting your career first," I say. "Like you say, a girl can buy her own bling."

Judy tips the rest of her wine down her gullet and stares at her bare hand.

At home, Meadow carries the cake into the living room and sets it on the coffee table before me. I wait for the sparklers to burn out and carve the cake into slices.

"Did I tell you Kendra got me Logan Waters's autograph?" Meadow says, passing Judy a piece of cake.

"Only about a thousand times," Judy says.

Mona offers Judy one of the Nelle DeLerious mugs I borrowed from the greenroom. "Coffee?"

"No thanks." Judy shakes her head. "I'd take a glass of wine, though."

"Sorry, Judy, we drained the bar at the aquarium," Max says.

"What kind of people don't have a wine cellar?" Judy mutters.

While we eat, Mona shows us the quilt she is entering at a competition in Garberville next week. It's an elaborate depiction of an otter swirling in a bubbling eddy. Across the bottom she has stitched "Pico 1989." Pico is a legend in Monterey because he was the first orphaned pup ever to be reintroduced to the wild by the aquarium. I'm all for keeping Pico's memory alive, and I know Mona put many hours of work into this quilt, but I'm not sure it's the kind of thing people would want to see on their bed.

Judy, who is rolling her eyes behind Mona's back, apparently agrees.

I am saved from having to comment by the ringing of the doorbell.

Mitch answers it and returns leading a man wearing a dark suit and carrying a briefcase.

"Terrance Burnside," the man says, extending his hand to Max. "VP of programming for Reality Network." He flips Max a card.

Judy stampedes across the room and reaches up to air-kiss Terrance's cheek. "Terrance, sweetie!"

Terrance rears back. "Are you *drunk*, Judith?"

Judy sobers up instantly. "Of course not," she says. "We just had a toast to celebrate the ratings sweep."

Terrance takes off his jacket and tosses it to Mona. It hits her in the shoulder and slides to the floor. She leaves it there.

"To hell with the ratings," Terrance says. "I would never have agreed to extend the show if I'd known you were going to turn it into a joke."

For once, Judy is speechless.

"If you want to save the planet, Judith, get a job at the Documentary Network," he continues. "Our advertisers aren't interested in animal rights." He glances at the row-boat coat cupboard and snorts in disgust. "This place is every bit as ridiculous as it looks on TV."

Max and Mona blink at him in shock. They turn to Judy, waiting for her to defend their home.

"That is no way to talk about this house," Judy scolds him. "Sure it's a pit, but you couldn't build a set this tacky."

Mona gasps. "Judy, how dare—"

Terrance interrupts. "No wonder the kid's turned into a flower child." He looks at me. "We sent you here to make fun of these people, not go over to the psychedelic side."

"Make fun of them?" I ask. "Why would I do that?"

"You're from New York, for God's sake. I shouldn't have to tell you how crazy they are. Between you and me, you were a lot more interesting when you were droning on about art all the time."

"I think you should leave," Mitch says.

"I don't think so, Prince Neptune," Terrance says. "I didn't fly all the way up here to get the bum's rush from a kid."

"Wow, he's really rude," Meadow says. "Have you ever seen anybody this rude in New York, Kendra?"

"He's definitely the rudest," I say.

"You've been brainwashed," Terrance tells me. "This whole otter thing is absurd."

"I believe in what I'm doing," I say.

"You're fifteen years old," he says. "You don't know what you believe. And you"—he turns on Judy—"you should have been able to control this child."

"I am not a child!"

Judy speaks over me. "Terrance, I don't understand why you're so upset. Our ratings are off the charts."

"It's not about ratings, Judith."

"Everything in this business is about ratings," she says, honestly bewildered.

Noticing Chili in the corner for the first time, Terrance explodes. "Turn off the damn camera. What the hell is this?"

"A television show," Meadow explains patiently. "It's called *The Black Sheep*."

Terrance's briefcase twitches, as if he wants to whack her with it, but he controls himself. "Let me draw you a picture, Judith," he says, pulling his wallet out of his pocket and taking out a card. He holds it between thumb and index finger for all to see: it's a Boulder Beach Golf Club membership.

Judy wiggles her eyebrows at Chili, a silent communication that propels him out the front door. Two seconds later, I see the red light through the window. Bob surreptitiously turns on a mike.

Poking Judy with the card, Terrance continues, "I pay more in a year to belong to this club than you earn. You have no idea what I had to go through to get in. They wanted a family history dating back to Roman times, a DNA swab, a dozen references, and a list of favors rendered to other members."

Judy looks a little pale, but she keeps up the fight. "I had no idea you were a member, Terrance."

"So are two of our biggest advertisers, but perhaps not for long." Terrance says. "After *Harry Queen*, the club threatened to revoke our memberships unless we put this to rights." He jabs his card in my direction. "Thanks to this troublemaker, they've been flooded with calls from do-gooders. Some high-profile members have hung up their clubs until this blows over."

"Maybe they've hung up their clubs because they support the cause," I say.

A vein begins to throb ominously on Terrance's forehead, and his face distorts like the guy in that Edvard Munch painting called *The Scream*. "I've had just about enough out of you," he says.

An unlikely protector steps between us. "Terrance, calm down," Judy says. "You know as well as I do that a scandal is as good as minting money in our business. The show could run in syndication for years."

He glares at her. "If you don't call off your kid, neither one of us will be around to enjoy that cash. Anyone who's anyone in Hollywood belongs to that club, Judith. That's where I make all my deals. In fact, that's where I got financing for *The Black Sheep*."

I can see the wheels turning in the back of Judy's head. "Anyone who's anyone?" she repeats. "How much does it cost to join?"

"More than you can afford," he says, bending over to yank his jacket out from under Mona's Birkenstock. "Especially if you lose your job. If you don't want that to happen, you and your black sheep had better do some damage control, ASAP."

"What did you have in mind?" she asks.

"I've booked the kid on *Dr. Ernest* next week. You get her to stick to the parental divorce script, people will forget all about the golf course. Soon, this otter crap will be ancient history."

I step out from behind Judy. "Absolutely not. There's no way I'm divorcing my parents, Terrance. And I refuse to go on *Dr. Ernest*."

Judy gives me a savage elbow to the ribs.

"That's Mr. Burnside to you," he says. "And you will do what I ask unless you want me to sue the asses off your parents and the Mulligans here. Is that what you want?" He glances around the hallway. "How would you feel if they lost this dump because of you? The whole lot of them could end up living out of that." He aims a thumb at the rowboat coat closet.

My stomach sinks like Judy's heart of stone. The last thing I want is for Mona and Max to be hurt because of my big mouth.

The vein in Terrance's forehead recedes as if by magic. "I thought so. Tell Ernest I owe him one."

He throws on his jacket and strides out of the room, oblivious to the dusty footprint between his shoulder blades.

Chapter 14

Judy accosts me in the greenroom as we wait for the taping of *Dr. Ernest* to begin. "KB, this is a very important show," she says. "Would it kill you to be interesting?"

"What do you mean?" I ask, although I know perfectly well what she means. I've taken dull to new heights on the talkshow circuit just to spite Judy and Terrance. As it turns out, by suppressing my inner Black Sheep and tapping into the old Kendra, I can be spectacularly, mind-numbingly boring:

Yes, Meredith, the Mulligans are every bit as nice as
    they seem.
No, Matt, I don't really mind if Meadow borrows my clothes.
    Family is all about sharing, right?
Yes, Kelly, I'm looking forward to going home—
    eventually. I belong in New York.
No, Regis, I don't want to divorce my parents,
    although it's tempting sometimes.
No, Rosie I don't think emancipation should be an
    option for all teens.
No, Kelly, I don't think your kids will divorce you.

Judy's eyes have been rolling back in her head from boredom. "I mean, a dead seal would be more riveting than you've been lately," she says.

I shrug helplessly. "It was Team Fourteen that made me so interesting before. Since you've forbidden me to talk about it, we're back to plain old boring Kendra."

Judy glares at me, knowing I've trumped her. Withholding controversy may be the only tool I have left in my arsenal right now. If there are others, I'm too tired to think of them.

Our three-day trip to promote *The Black Sheep* on the talk-show circuit has meant appearing on nearly twenty shows across five states. At least, I think it was five states. I've spent so much time in planes, hotels, limos, and studios, it all started to look pretty much the same.

Only one city stood out from the rest: New York. I didn't see much of it during our whirlwind visit, and there was no hope of escape, with Judy attached to my side like a big, toothy barnacle. Still, the glimpses I got of my favorite Manhattan landmarks, especially Rockefeller Center and Central Park, triggered homesickness.

Judy must have picked up on the vibe, because she asked the driver to cruise past my parents' house as we left for the airport. It was cruel even by her standards, but I know it's part of her larger plan to wear down my defenses before the *Dr. Ernest* show. Dr. Ernest is all about emotional breakthroughs, and to improve the odds of my snapping publicly,

Judy's been restricting my sleep, keeping me too busy to eat, and isolating me. It's probably similar to the tactics that cults use.

Fortunately, I have a finely honed repression mechanism at my disposal, and Dr. Ernest, the Cult Master, won't find it easy to combat.

I am a vault that cannot be cracked.

Dr. Ernest is so nice when he greets me that I almost feel bad about depriving him of my breakthrough. The guy probably thinks I'm just a regular teen, but he couldn't be more wrong. I am now a self-trained expert in personal transformation.

Maybe Dr. Ernest will be so impressed with my story that he'll ask me to cohost his show. Judy did say I might have a future in television—that I have *presence*. If that's true, I don't even need Ernest. I'll get my own show and use it to promote causes I believe in.

But first, I have to defeat the Cult Master.

"Kendra," Dr. Ernest says as the show begins, "Y'all have expressed a need to divorce your parents. And I want to tell you, this day is about to become a changing day in your life. Are you ready to begin?"

"Why not?" I ask, smiling. I might as well let the guy take his best shot before laying him flat.

"Tell me about your childhood in New York. Were you unhappy?"

I give an exaggerated sigh. Doesn't Ernest watch his competition? I've answered this question twenty times. "It wasn't horrible. I had everything I needed."

He studies me with sympathetic brown eyes. "Except love?"

I feel my back stiffen in spite of my determination not to react. "Families show love in different ways."

"And how did yours show it?"

"By giving me endless opportunities to learn, I guess. My parents believe that by training my brain, I'll be able to get the most out of life."

He pats my arm so warmly that I have an urge to bite it. "But what about training your heart?" he asks.

"Eew," I say, shuddering, "You're turning this into a *cringing* day, Dr. Ernest." The audience murmurs disapprovingly. "Well, come on," I tell them, "this whole divorce thing has been blown out of proportion. All I wanted was a chance to explore some things that don't interest my parents. Thanks to *The Black Sheep*, I got that chance, and it's been a great experience so far. Except for doing the talk-show circuit."

Ernest opens his mouth to ask another stupid question and I cut him off. I am hijacking this interview. "Look, Ernest, I'm *fine*. For once, I feel good about my life. I don't hate my parents, I just don't *need* them. I've come a long way in five weeks."

Ernest smiles. He has small teeth for a guy his size, but

they're still sharklike. "So what you're saying is, you're all grown up."

He's trying to make me look like an immature brat, but he'd have to get up a lot earlier to outfox me. "No, Ernest, I'm definitely a work in progress."

"Well, I'm glad you think so, because I brought in some people to help you with that work."

The panel behind him rises to reveal my parents. I gasp, and I hear the sound echoed throughout the audience as people recognize them from the show.

Okay, so Ernest is good, but I'm better: I recover quickly enough to give my parents a casual wave. If Ernest thinks he can use shock tactics to manipulate me into a bogus breakthrough, he's wrong. I'm going to give his PhD a run for its money. He's not even a real doctor.

"How does it feel to come face-to-face with your parents after being separated for so long?" he asks.

"It's nice to see them," I say, turning slightly in my seat so that I can't actually see them. If I can't see them, I can keep the upper hand. It's just Ernest and me duking it out.

"Look at your body language," he says. On the monitor, I see my arms crossed and my head averted—not quite the image I'd hoped to convey. "I think you need to be a little more honest with yourself about how you're feeling."

Oh, I'll be honest with myself—I feel like I'm going to hurl—but I won't be honest with him. Instead, I uncross my arms and say, "I'm feeling the urge to discuss my activism,

Ernest. Maybe you can help my parents understand why it's important to me."

There's a fleeting glimpse of recognition in Ernest's eyes. Perhaps, like Terrance, he has a membership at Boulder Beach to protect. "Let's chat about your relationship with your parents more generally," Dr. Ernest says.

Why should Ernest and Terrance call all the shots? If they're going to spring my parents on me to induce an emotional meltdown, I'm going to launch evasive maneuvers. "But the activism issue is way more interesting, Ernest. You see, I've joined this group called Team Fourteen, and we're trying to save endangered sea otters in Carmel. Unfortunately, we haven't been able to get the right people to listen."

Ernest's smile is fixed and more sharklike than ever. "It sounds like you're directing the anger you feel for your parents into this cause," he says. "How's that working for you?"

"I'm pretty happy with the way things are going so far."

"Why don't you tell us what your parents did to make you so angry that you'd want to divorce them?"

"The divorce wasn't my idea." He's clinging to the whole divorce thing like a ferret to a diamond ring.

"Does your anger have anything to do with our other guest?" he persists.

Another panel rises to reveal Rosa. She's wearing her favorite multicolor cardigan, as if it were just a regular day.

"Oh, no," I say. If anyone can crack this vault, it's Rosa.

"Tell everyone who this is, Kendra," Ernest says.

My mouth has gone dry. "Rosa—my former nanny."

Rosa leaps out of her chair and hurries over to crush me in a bear hug, muttering in Spanish.

"Care to translate?" Ernest asks me.

"She says I'm too skinny, too pale, and too mouthy."

The audience laughs.

"And in big trouble," Rosa adds, still clutching my arm.

Ernest beckons my parents. "Come over and join us, Mom and Dad."

My parents silently take their seats beside Rosa. Up close, I see they're both wearing a thick layer of makeup, which has pooled in the lines around Mom's eyes. The bright lights show the silver in Dad's hair. They look almost as old as Mona and Max.

"Well, go on, Mom and Dad," Dr. Ernest says. "Give your daughter a big ol' hug."

Mom steps forward and puts her arms around me gingerly.

Dr. Ernest shakes his bald head. "You call that a hug?"

To demonstrate proper form, he comes over and crushes me against his chest. "She's not a porcupine, she's your daughter. Put a little heart into it."

When he finally releases me, I can feel the imprint of his tiepin on my cheek.

"We're not demonstrative people," Mom says, "but that

doesn't mean we don't love our daughter."

"In our family, we have unspoken communication," Dad supplies.

Dr. Ernest crosses his arms and leans back in his chair. "The daughter you say you love wants to sever her relationship with you. So how's the unspoken communication working for you?"

"It isn't working at the moment," my mother admits. "But that's because of this silly TV show. Until Kendra got involved with *The Black Sheep*, everything was fine."

"See?" I tell Ernest. "We were fine."

Dr. Ernest turns to Rosa and she shakes her head. "Not fine," she says.

My mother spins to stare at Rosa. "Excuse me?"

"I'll thank you not to comment on my family's business," Dad says.

"I was invited to comment," Rosa tells Dad. "I'm part of Kendra's family, too."

"Now, now, Dad," Dr. Ernest says. "Rosa is only trying to express how she feels. And God bless you, Rosa, for claiming that right."

Rosa beams at Dr. Ernest.

"I understand you keep your daughter on a very strict schedule," Dr. Ernest continues.

"Too strict," Rosa says.

"Maybe Mom and Dad can tell us why—" he begins, but Rosa cuts him off.

"I'll tell you why." She jumps up off her seat and comes to stand beside me. "Because they'd rather work than spend time with their child. It's always been that way."

Even though I've said the same thing myself, it hurts to hear it coming from Rosa—and in front of an audience.

"That's not true," my mother objects.

"We work hard to give Kendra all she needs to have a good life," my father adds. "A nice home, private school, tutoring, music lessons . . ."

Dr. Ernest says, "I think that's a valid—"

"You're her parents," Rosa interjects. "You should be raising her yourself, not outsourcing the job."

Rosa is speaking my parents' language now.

Mom appeals to Dr. Ernest. "We invest plenty of time in our daughter. Kendra and I go to art galleries all the time."

"Once a month," Rosa says.

Dr. Ernest turns to me. "Do you enjoy visiting art galleries?"

Sometimes I do, but Rosa doesn't give me a chance to say so. "She calls it 'Torture Day.' They never ask her what she might like to do."

"We have a plan for cultivating her mind," Dad says.

"She has a mind of her own now," Rosa says, pacing in front of my parents.

To my knowledge, Rosa never argued with my parents in all the years she worked for them. I can see her relief in being able to say how she really feels. Part of me wants to

cheer her on, but another part wants to leap to my parents'
defense. The two parts cancel each other out, leaving me
paralyzed.

"We don't always enjoy the things that are good for us,"
my father says.

"My point is that you don't want Kendra to think for
herself because she might realize that she doesn't want the
life *you* want for her," Rosa says.

The audience bursts into spontaneous applause, and
Rosa looks around, startled, as if she forgot they were there.

My mother doesn't wait for the applause to die before
responding. "Kendra can live whatever life she chooses."

Rosa puts her hands on her hips. "Then why aren't you
supporting her decision to take a stand against that golf
course in Carmel?"

"That's just some foolishness the Mulligans dragged her
into," Dad says.

"It's not foolish to Kendra," Rosa says. "It's important to
her."

"Kendra isn't the type to challenge authority," Mom
says. "Someone has been feeding her ideas."

Rosa throws her arms in the air and utters a string of
Spanish expletives. "You're the expert," she tells Dr. Ernest.
"Why don't you say something?"

Dr. Ernest mugs for the camera, and the audience howls.
"I think Doctor Rosa has made a good case, here. Mom,
Dad, you're not listening to your daughter, and you're not

taking responsibility for what's going wrong with your family. Does your daughter look happy to you?"

Three cameras zoom in for close-ups of my face, and I see on the monitors that while I was distracted the vault began to leak. Dr. Ernest takes a tissue out of his pocket and hands it to me. I'm ashamed of myself. Bishops don't cry—especially not on TV. Obviously, my defenses have been weakened by exposure to the Mulligans.

"Why assume it's our fault?" my mother asks. "Some people are actually happy living with us."

Mom points to a familiar head of shiny black hair in the front row of the audience.

"That's different," Dr. Ernest says. "Anyone can get along with a houseguest for a month. Unless y'all are willing to take ownership of the problem, you're not going to be able to move ahead as a family." Ernest turns to Rosa. "Any suggestions?"

"Maybe a taste of their own medicine," Rosa says. "Parenting lessons."

Ernest smiles. "I like the way your mind works, Doctor Rosa. Boot camp for the parents it is."

I know she means well, but Rosa's gone too far. She's made my parents sound much worse than they are. After all, they didn't turn me into a psychopath.

Dr. Ernest turns to the crowd. "Do y'all agree with us?"

"I don't," I say, but my voice is drowned by the crowd's cheer.

Dr. Ernest rests a hand on my parents' arms. "Mom, Dad, this train was heading for derailment, but I think we caught it in time. We need to reeducate you. We need to help you let go of your old thinking and open your minds to new ideas. We need to tear you down so we can build you up to become the best parents you can be."

"Parenting lessons?" my father says. "I don't think so."

Mom shakes her head in mute solidarity.

"You may not *want* to attend my boot camp but I am telling ya, ya'all *need* to. In two short weeks, America is going to be voting on whether your daughter should divorce you. You'd better build your case now if you want to hold on to her."

"Wait a second, America can't vote on my future," I say. "That's unfair."

"That's ridiculous," my parents chorus.

"That's crazy," Rosa says.

"That's show business!" Dr. Ernest says.

Like magic, my barnacle has disappeared. It takes a while to find her, but I finally spot a pair of flip-flops under a restroom cubicle. "Judy?"

Silence.

"Judy, I recognize your feet."

The toilet flushes and Judy emerges. "Oh, hi, KB."

"What was Dr. Ernest talking about?"

"You mean the boot camp? Better talk to your beloved

nanny about that." She turns off the faucet and hits the button on the hand dryer.

I raise my voice to be heard over the noise. "I meant the vote."

"Oh, that." The dryer stops and Judy turns to me. "Didn't I mention it? Terrance thought it would be great to let America decide about the divorce."

"This is a free country, Judy. I get to make my own choices."

"Sure you do," she says, patting my arm with a damp hand. "Just as soon as the show ends."

The only good thing that's happened today is that I've discovered Maya isn't nearly as pretty in person as she is on TV. Her hair is definitely amazing, but her eyes are mere pinpoints of blue, unlike Mitch's. Plus, she's built like a linebacker from all those years of lugging her own kayak. There's no place for that kind of muscle on Fifth Avenue.

When I find her outside my parents' dressing room, she doesn't even pretend to be nice.

"What do you want?" she asks.

"Nice to meet you, too," I say, reaching for the door.

Maya's hand closes like a steel clamp over mine. "You're not going in there."

"My parents don't need a bodyguard."

"But they do need someone who cares about their feelings. Unlike you."

"You don't know anything about me."

"I know everything about you—just like the rest of the country. I've seen how mean you are to them."

"Yeah, well you're not known for your sweet personality in Monterey, either."

She tosses her hair and glares at me. "I bet you're trying to turn everyone against me. You totally suck up to my parents."

"I don't suck up to your parents. I don't need to, because they already like me."

"They like anyone with a cause. Don't think you're special."

"Maybe not, but the cause is special."

"Yeah, yeah, Team Fourteen . . . That's all you ever talk about. I volunteered for seven years at that aquarium, and no one made a big deal out of it. Now it's all about selfless Kendra saving the otters."

"I don't know why you're so bitter. You've had it pretty good in Manhattan. 'Oh Mrs. Bishop, let's go to another gallery. If I could drown in culture, I'd die happy. Oh, Mr. Bishop, let's run another ten-K this weekend before I lose my endorphin high.'"

Maya's eyes narrow until they virtually disappear. "I call them Deirdre and Ken. They asked me to."

"Well, good for you. I call them Mom and Dad, and if you don't mind, I'm going to speak to them."

"I do mind." She blocks the doorway. "You've hurt them enough for one day. Deirdre is crying, you know."

Crying! Impossible. It's never happened in my lifetime. "She's just embarrassed."

"Embarrassed to have a daughter like you."

I'll be getting nearly five grand from the show, thanks to the extension, and that might be enough to hire an assassin.

"I wouldn't put *my* mother in a position like this," Maya continues.

"The divorce wasn't my idea," I say. "I only agreed to explore it because I needed more time in Monterey to finish what I started."

"You shouldn't put a cause above your own family," Maya says.

Now I see what's bothering her. "Maya, if you feel your parents are involved with too many causes, you should take it up with them, not me."

"I was just trying to give you a bit of friendly advice," she says. "You keep saying you want more freedom, and I'm telling you to be careful what you wish for."

Maya was obviously on the receiving end of all the bad personality traits in the Mulligan gene pool. "I don't need advice from someone who listens to Britney Spears."

Maya's eyes widen in shock. "Keep your hands off my things!" she says. "Including my ferret."

"Manhattan loves me. He sleeps with me every single night." I stop short of mentioning that I'm almost as close to her brother.

I try to push past her, and she pushes back. "If your

parents disown you—and they're talking about it—don't think you can steal mine," she says. "I'm moving home soon, and there won't be room in that house for both of us."

"No kidding," I say, turning to walk away. "I'll tell Meadow your ego needs a king-size bed."

"You're going to end up all alone in the world, Kendra Bishop," she shouts after me.

"That's fine with me," I shout back. She opens the door to my parents' dressing room, flounces in, and slams it behind her.

My parents are not going to disown me, I'm quite sure of that. In the unlikely event that they do, however, I have a Black Sheep Rule to sustain me: *From independence comes strength.*

I hope.

Chapter 15

While I was away doing the talk-show circuit, Lisa came up with the idea of holding a rally during the Boulder Beach charity golf tournament tomorrow.

It's pretty similar to an idea I had last week, only back then it was called a sit-in and Lisa thought it was stupid. By renaming it, she gets to take full credit. There must be more educational value in a rally, although I can't see how.

What *is* stupid is Lisa's idea of holding an overnight campout on the actual site of the fourteenth hole. I don't understand why we have to rough it overnight when we could just get an early enough start to beat the golfers, but no one asked my opinion. Obviously, Mitch goes along with whatever Lisa suggests. I guess that's because she's his mentor, whereas I am merely his girlfriend.

The only reason I'm not complaining about it as we rattle along toward Carmel in the Mulligans' van is that I don't want to ruin the short time we have alone.

Mitch isn't nearly as thoughtful. "So, how was Maya?"

It's the third time he's asked the same question. Every

time he takes a break from talking about Lisa, he talks about Maya. It's frustrating, because I begged Carrie to take Meadow with her so that Mitch and I could talk about *me*. Two days ago I allowed Dr. Ernest to break me down in front of millions of viewers. It was such a sad lapse of Black Sheepism that I still haven't recovered, and I could use a little moral support from my boyfriend.

"She seemed fine," I say. My vague answers haven't been cutting it, but what am supposed to do when the truth—that his sister is a bitch—isn't pretty? Lie, of course, as any good girlfriend would do. "I think she's having fun in New York."

He looks unsatisfied. "What else did you talk about?"

"Music, pets . . . nothing important."

"I get the feeling you're not telling me the full story," Mitch says.

I sigh. "Maya said something that upset me, that's all."

He glances over at me. "What?"

"She overreacted about the divorce thing. She said I was mean and that she'd never do something like that to Mona."

Mitch smiles, apparently satisfied. "It sounds like the trip's been good for her."

What?! He's totally missing the point, which is that his sister said I'm mean. He should be defending me like a normal boyfriend and reminding me that everyone hates Maya. Then he should reassure me that my parents will never disown me, no matter what. And that even if they do, he'll always be there for me.

Maybe he agrees with Maya that I am a bad, ungrateful daughter. Or maybe he saw my parents in action on *Dr. Ernest* and realized I'm damaged goods. He's probably going to dump me before it gets any more serious.

Unless I dump him first.

Mitch reaches over to take my hand. "I missed you," he says. "I thought you did great on *Dr. Ernest.*"

On the other hand, there may be hope for us yet. "I can't believe he brought my parents onto the show," I say.

"I know." He squeezes my hand. "I felt bad for you."

He did? That's so sweet! I won't tell him I locked myself in the hotel bathroom after the show for so long that Judy threatened to call the fire department to break down the door. He'll see that on *The Black Sheep* soon enough. For now, I can put on a brave front. "It was okay. I was mostly in shock."

"How come you never told me about Rosa?" he asks.

The problem with confiding in guys is that sooner or later (in my case sooner) it gets uncomfortable. This discussion may be what I thought I wanted, but now that I have to ante up, my words have receded to the primitive part of my brain. I stare at a crack in the van's windshield. "I don't know."

He waits for me to say more before adding, "It seems like you were close."

I can't lie to him when he's holding my hand; he would feel it. Which means I have to tell the truth, no matter how lame it is. "We are close," I say. "She's the one who raised me."

There's no time for more, because we've reached the center of Carmel, and Mitch has to let go of my hand to guide the van into a parking spot. I'm simultaneously relieved and disappointed to end the discussion.

Mitch cuts the ignition, and a well-dressed couple turns to stare as the van continues to gasp and sputter for a few seconds longer. Eventually it releases a great belch of smoke that blocks the couple from view.

"How long has this heap been in your family?" I ask Mitch as he claws through the camping gear to find what we need for our day at the beach.

"Longer than I have," he says. "With so many kids and only one income, my parents can't afford a new one." Lowering his voice to a whisper, he adds, "Don't call her a heap. If you offend her, we might have to walk home."

"You're right, I should just be grateful that your dad let us take it for the day."

"He was glad to have an excuse to rent one for the drive to Garberville," he says.

"I figured your parents would give up the quilting show to join us tonight. They love a good tent rally."

He winces. "I know, but I didn't mention this one, because they only attend protests held on public property. Dad says their trespassing days ended when they became role models. They want us to use our voices, but they also want us to stay out of trouble."

"It's just a peaceful sit-in," I say as we climb out of the van. "What could possibly go wrong?"

Mitch doesn't answer because he's scanning the street for the source of an odd sound. It falls somewhere between human and animal vocalization.

Our eyes light on *The Black Sheep* trucks, and Mitch pulls me behind the van so that we can spy on Judy, who is eating a Popsicle while chatting to someone I recognize from the Paco's Tacos opening. She directs tooth wattage at the guy and touches his arm with her free hand. Then we hear the noise again.

"Is she . . . giggling?" I ask.

"It's a mating call," Mitch says, smiling. "That's Ted Silver, a photographer from *The Carmel Pinecone*. He felt so bad about the photo of you in the sheep suit ending up on *Nelle* that he came by the aquarium and offered to help with Team Fourteen. Judy took such a shine to him that I keep inviting him back."

"You're matchmaking?"

Mitch returns my incredulous look. "I'm trying to distract her. I'm sure she's already heard about the rally and has something up her sleeve. Maybe Ted can keep her out of the way."

"So you're pimping him for our cause?"

"He's a consenting adult," Mitch says, shrugging. "Besides, Judy doesn't try to hide what she's really like."

Not normally, but that isn't the Judy I know, listening to Ted with such rapt attention. "It doesn't seem fair to Ted," I say. "She's evil."

"Yeah, but she's hot."

I stare at him, horrified. "How could you say that?"

"I'm just being objective," he says. "I can hate her and still see that she's hot—in that librarian-with-a-wild-side sort of way."

I must have been imagining our connection earlier. I don't know this guy at all. How could he possibly find me attractive if he finds Judy attractive? Sure, she's got good features, but that smile is something else. And she's *ancient*. "Is that how guys really think?" I ask.

"What do you mean?"

"I mean that when a girl thinks a guy is evil, she can't see anything attractive about him, even if he's the hottest guy on the planet.

Mitch smiles. "All I'm saying is, Ted knows what she's like and he isn't complaining."

He certainly isn't. When I look over again, he's taking a bite from Judy's Popsicle.

Carrie tosses me a tube as we spread our towels on the sand. "Sunscreen?"

I pass it back to her. "Thanks, but I'm already covered."

"I'd add some more," Meadow says, moving my towel so that she can put hers next to Carrie's. "You're pretty pale."

I move my towel back. "Remind me why I agreed to let you come today?"

"Like you had a choice," she says. Max and Mona packed Meadow into the rental van with the rest of the kids this morning, but at the last minute she convinced them to let her stay behind, and we got stuck with her.

I squint to examine her face. "I hope that's not my eyeliner you're wearing."

"No," she says, "it's mine."

"Good. Because I have one just like it and it gave me conjunctivitis."

"Conjunctawhat?" she asks, looking nervous.

"Pinkeye. Never seen so much pus. I meant to throw it out."

Meadow races off to find a washroom, and Carrie gives me a high five.

"Kendra!" Mitch calls from the water, where he and Calvin are bobbing in the waves. "Come on in. The water's warm and Calvin will keep the sharks busy."

"Later," I call, pulling a magazine out of my beach bag. For Carrie's benefit I add, "Like, in my next life."

"Maybe a swim would help you relax," Carrie says, lying back on her towel.

"What makes you think I'm not relaxed?"

"The magazine's upside down," she says. "You're thinking about *Dr. Ernest* again, aren't you?"

I nod. "What if America votes 'divorce,' and I have to

emancipate from my parents?"

"You won't let that happen," she says.

I'm not sure how I'd be able to stop it, but I let it go for now. "Will you visit me in New York?"

"I'd love to, especially since we wouldn't have a camera crew tailing us. Speaking of which, where's Judy? Did you slip her a sedative?"

"Don't give her any ideas," Judy says. We turn to see her behind us, holding a camcorder. She unclips a walkie-talkie from her belt and speaks into it: "This is Wolf One to Little Red Riding Hood. I've got the lamb. What's your twenty, Red Riding Hood?"

Chili's fuzzy red hair emerges from a cluster of girls nearby. He lowers his camera and raises his walkie. "Stop calling me that."

"Camera guys are so touchy," Judy says, motioning me to move to the edge of my towel so that she can sit beside me. She pretends to be blinded by the glare off my legs. "Jeez, KB, have those sticks ever seen the sun? I hope you've got a little SPF going on."

"The sun shines in New York, too, you know. I'm not an idiot."

Judy powers off her camera. "Don't get snippy with Judy. Especially not when she's doing you a favor by letting you join the seal rally."

"I can do whatever I like. It's a free country."

"*The Black Sheep* is a country unto its own," she says.

A country with unjust legislation. They get to make up all kinds of lies about me, but if I make a single decision for myself, they threaten to sue.

Judy leans over and lifts my sunglasses. "Don't think for a minute that you're doing anything I don't want you to do, KB. Even on her worst day, Judy is smarter than you are."

She probably is smarter than I am, and worse, she has no conscience to slow her down. If Judy decides to keep me away from the rally, she'll find a way.

After staring at me for another moment, Judy drops my glasses and says, "As it happens, I've decided to stay true to my journalistic integrity and let events unfold as they may."

Virtually nothing in my life has unfolded naturally since I arrived here, thanks to Judy. "But you're a reality show producer with a nasty boss to please," I say.

"I was a journalist first, KB. And Terrance doesn't scare me."

"Then how come you've kept me on such a short leash this week?"

"Sometimes you've gotta look like you're playing the game, kid. But Judy's journalistic integrity will not be compromised under any . . ." Her voice trails off as Ted Silver walks by. Carrie and I grin at each other, but Judy is too entranced to notice. Eventually she turns back to us and asks, "Where was I?"

"Your integrity won't be compromised," I prompt.

"Right. Terrance has no idea what the people of

America really want, because he's been stuck behind a desk too long. I used to want his job, you know, but I've realized that I can do more by getting my hands dirty in the field." She sifts a handful of sand to illustrate her point. "For some reason, 'Joe Average' relates to your seal cause, KB. He wants nothing more after a long day at the factory than to watch little Kendra Bishop try to fight the Establishment. It gives him hope that he can do more with his own sorry life." She pauses to reflect for a moment. "I owe it to Joe Average to deliver on this protest, and I refuse to let Terrance Burnside derail it simply because he wants to cut deals at some stuffy old golf club."

I prop myself on one elbow to look at her. "So what you're saying," I summarize, "is that the Boulder Beach execs turned down your membership application."

Judy flings herself down on the towel in disgust. "I don't want to talk about it."

"A body like that is wasted on a scientist, isn't it, KB?" Judy asks, after a short sulk.

I lift my head to see Lisa, tanned and clad in a sporty bikini, heading toward the water. "Why would I care?"

"Because *he* does." She points to Mitch, who has stopped roughhousing with Calvin to wave to Lisa. Picking up her camcorder, Judy zooms in on him.

"What are you talking about?" Carrie asks.

Judy takes her eye from the eyepiece. "Those two have

salt water in their veins. Call me a sentimental fool, but when two people have a bond like that in common, it transcends the age difference."

"I've heard that opposites attract," Carrie counters.

"Maybe," Judy says, getting to her feet and strolling away, "but it never works."

Carrie and I sit up to watch Mitch and Lisa throw themselves into a big wave and bodysurf into shore. Mitch offers Lisa his hand and helps her to her feet. Her bikini clings to her perfect body and they are both laughing.

"Judy's right," I tell Carrie. "Mitch and I have nothing in common. I can't even talk to him. At least, not like I talk to you." I drop back onto my towel with a sigh. "Why can't this be easier?"

Carrie reaches for her cooler. "You know what you need? Food. And fortunately, I was baking all night." She stares into the cooler and then roars, "Calvin!"

Calvin jogs over, followed by Mitch and Lisa. "You rang, sweet sister?"

"What did you do with my food?" Carrie asks. "The cooler's practically empty."

"*Your* food? Dad financed that and he knows I'm still growing."

Mitch says, "Kendra and I can go and pick something up."

Lisa chooses this moment to lift one sand-speckled hand to pluck seaweed from Mitch's damp hair.

"That's okay," I say. "You guys stay. Carrie and I can take care of it."

If he wants to frolic with an old mermaid, far be it from me to hurl the first harpoon.

Carrie and I take a booth in the crowded café and order burgers and milk shakes.

"I know what you're doing," she says. "You're trying to reject Mitch before he rejects you."

"I'm just trying to give him some space," I say.

"He didn't want space," Carrie says. "He wanted a few minutes alone with you."

"What's the point? I'm going home soon anyway."

"Last week you were crazy about the guy. Did I miss something?"

The waiter delivers our milk shakes, and I stir mine for a moment before confessing, "I don't think he's that into me, Carrie. You saw how he was with Lisa. And earlier, he said"— I lower my voice as she leans toward me—"that Judy is *hot*."

I expect her to shriek in dismay, but she laughs instead. "Kendra, that's just how guys are. Take my word for it. I have two brothers."

"We've only been seeing each other a few weeks. If he's already noticing other girls, what will happen when we're on opposite coasts?"

"I think you're looking for trouble," she says. "And if you look too hard, you'll find it, even if it isn't really there."

Oh, it's there, I'm sure of it. It's just a matter of time before it surfaces.

Carrie reaches over, grabs both my hands, and says, "Listen to me: he likes you. Do not—I repeat—do not vote yourself off the island."

The door opens and Jordan walks into the café with Aaron, Tia, and several other Team 14 members joining us for the overnight campout.

"Hey," Aaron says, noticing that Carrie is still holding my hands. "Girl-on-girl action. All we need now are the cameras."

"You missed your chance," I say. "The crew's on lunch."

He looks momentarily disappointed and then brightens again. "Hey, is Kelly Ripa as hot in person as she is on TV?"

Carrie raises her eyebrows at me and says, "See what I mean?"

Tia leads the others to a free table, but Jordan hangs back and slides into our booth across from me, pinning Carrie to the wall. "How's it going?" he asks me. "I saw how upset you were on *Dr. Ernest*."

I nod. "It was a bit of a shock to see my parents, but—"

"Do you want to go drinking some time?" he interrupts. "I've got a couple of fake ID's."

"I don't think so, but thanks."

"Come on," he says. "How many times do I have to say I'm sorry before you'll go out with me?"

"You can't count that high," Carrie says.

Jordan turns to Carrie as if noticing her for the first time and says, "She'll come around." He looks back at me. "Am I right?"

"Nope." I shake my head. "Sorry."

Jordan appears to be stunned, but recovers in time to take a parting shot as he leaves the booth. "Aaron must have been right about you two."

Before Carrie and I have a chance to make fun of him, I hear a voice I've quickly grown to loathe, saying, "How does this make you feel, Dad?"

There's a small television over the bar showing *Dr. Ernest*. The shot widens out to reveal that the dad in question is my own, and he's hugging a life-size, inflatable doll. Looking up at Dr. Ernest, he answers, "Foolish, Ernest."

"It'll get easier," Dr. Ernest says. "Hugging is a natural expression of affection."

Carrie reaches over to pat my arm, but my eyes are glued to the screen.

"Now," Dr. Ernest continues, "I wasn't surprised to hear y'all grew up as only children in emotionally distant families. The apple doesn't fall far from the tree."

That's the first I've heard anything negative about their families.

"And I understand you were dirt poor, as well," Ernest says. "No wonder you're obsessed with financial security."

Is this some kind of desperate bid to gain public sympathy? Did my parents hire a spin doctor? If so, neither one looks very happy about it. My mother is standing beside Dad, wearing a grimace of shame.

"Growing up without emotional or financial security is tough," Dr. Ernest says, "and you're obviously trying to make up for some of that with your daughter. But you're going to have to give her some space to grow, and for God's sake, show her the love. Even if you never experienced affection as children, you're going to need to show some to Kendra." He passes the inflatable doll to my mother. "Mom, why don't you have a go?"

My stomach gives the milk shake inside a good spin. This exercise must be killing my parents.

"Woo-hoo!" Aaron yells, as my mother gathers the rubber doll in her arms. "Like mother like daughter!"

"Now what do you say?" Dr. Ernest asks. My mother looks at him with pleading eyes. "Go on, Mom. Pretend this is your daughter. What do you say?"

"I love you," my mother croaks.

"I can't hear you," Ernest says, cupping big hand around his ear. "Why don't you help her out, Dad?"

Together, Mom and Dad mumble "I love you" to the rubber doll.

Aaron whistles and stomps his foot on the wooden floor.

I look at Carrie. "I have to call them. I have to tell them they don't have to do this."

* * *

Mitch catches up with me at the drugstore, where I'm buying a long-distance calling card. "Carrie told me what happened," he says.

I rush past him into the street. "I've got to find a pay phone," I say.

Passing a sidewalk café, we see Judy having coffee with Ted. She takes one look at me and raises her walkie-talkie. "Wolf Two, get over here, stat. The lamb's on the run at Ocean and Casanova." She abandons Ted and starts after us.

Taking this as my cue, I start running. Mitch keeps pace, but Judy soon falls behind because of her flip-flops.

After a couple of blocks, Mitch grabs my arm and forces me to stop. "Use Calvin's cell phone," he says, pressing it into my hand. "Let me cover for you."

I slip the phone into my purse just as Judy runs up to us with Bob. "What's going on?" she demands.

"It's Maurice," Mitch ad-libs. "I think he's been reinjured. Lisa's renting a boat and we're going to try to recapture him. Kendra, you get the binoculars from the van, and Bob and I will head back to get some footage." He walks away, beckoning Bob.

Judy hesitates. "You look upset, KB."

I take a deep breath and pull myself together. "Of course I'm upset. It's Maurice."

"Coming, Judy?" Mitch calls.

She shakes her head and starts back to the café. "My

latte's getting cold. It's just a seal, KB. Get over it, already."

When she turns the corner, I duck into an alley and dial my father's cell phone number. It's not Dad who answers, but Maya. Attempting to disguise my voice, I ask, "Ees Meester or Meesus Beeship in, *por favor?*"

"Oh, hi, Kendra," Maya says. "I sent your parents out for a run. After boot camp, they needed it, poor things. So, adios, amigo. I won't bother to tell them you called."

She hangs up before I can say another word. I hit redial, but before the call goes through, Judy grabs the phone out of my hands.

"I'm disappointed in you, KB," she says. "Judy's been so supportive of your little protest, and this is the thanks she gets? Don't expect a mention when I win the Realie Award for best show on the network."

I try to wrestle the cell phone from her, but she holds it behind her with one hand and biffs me with her sun hat.

I stop fighting to glare at her, breathing heavily. "Don't you dare make this sound like you're doing me a favor," I say. "The only reason you're not telling Terrance about the protest is because you want to get him kicked out of the golf club. And you also want those advertisers to pull out so that he loses his job."

"Sshhh, KB," she says soothingly. "You're overwrought."

I may be overwrought, but I notice she isn't denying it. "You'll do whatever it takes to bring in good ratings, and you don't care who you hurt in the process," I say. "But I won't let you sacrifice my family for your career, Judy Greenberg." Turning, I see that Bob has returned with his camcorder. "Are you getting this, Wolf Two?"

The camera nods.

"Good. Because the day after tomorrow, I am going home," I say. "My parents and I may have some things to sort out, but that's none of America's business. I am not divorcing them, and I am not putting them through any more of that horrible boot camp. Find yourself another sucker, Judy."

Chapter 16

The full moon makes the white sand glitter underfoot as we trudge along the beach toward the golf course. I'm not thrilled about being out here in the wilderness, but at least the light from the moon means we won't lose any of our supporters along the way—especially the two grannies hobbling beside me. Somehow I never envisioned seniors supporting the cause, but a love of otters apparently knows no bounds.

There is a long line of shadowy figures ahead of us, lumpy with backpacks and rolled-up sleeping bags. Yet any sound the procession makes is swallowed by the gentle crash of waves on sand. Even Meadow is silent for once.

Mitch is leading the group. It wouldn't bother me that he stuck me with the kid and took off, were it not for the fact that Lisa is currently nowhere to be seen. I bet she is marching by his side, pretending to be Queen of the Rally. Last time I checked, that crown belonged to me—and so did the King.

I give myself a mental shake. Why am I always looking for

a fight with Mitch? Just this afternoon he tried to help me evade Judy so I could call my parents. It was a very romantic gesture, even though it failed. Carrie is right that I'm looking for trouble, but I can't seem to help myself. It's like I have to turn everything into a test, just as my parents do.

Tonight will be different. It has to be, because it could be our last night together. If I make good on my threat to go home after the protest, I may never see Mitch again. Sure, we'll instant message, text message, e-mail, and call now and then, but it won't be enough, and Mitch is too hot to stay single for long. If it isn't Lisa, it will be someone else. Meanwhile, I'll go back to my girls' school and never meet another guy until college—and that's only if my parents unlock the prison door to let me pursue a higher education.

I am going to get things on the right track with Mitch tonight even if I have to take the initiative. There's already one thing working in my favor: no crew. At this very moment, Judy is having dinner with Ted Silver at Carmel's swankiest restaurant. It wasn't his idea, but she doesn't know that. This afternoon, I went to the restaurant and charged a hefty gift certificate to Mom's credit card. I presented it to Ted as a thank-you for his help with Team 14 and suggested he use it with Judy tonight. She's so hot for Ted that she jumped at the offer, even though Ted invited Bob and Chili along. Maybe he has better taste than I gave him credit for.

At any rate, Judy isn't here barking orders into a walkie-talkie, chasing us with cameras and bright lights, and generally making a commotion that could attract the attention of Boulder Beach security and the local police.

We leave the beach and clamber up a hill onto the course, where more than a hundred people are already milling around. It's a huge turnout, and it makes me feel good to know that I contributed to bringing everyone together. And as much as I hated the idea of camping, I'm excited to be out here trespassing on private property under a starry sky. I have never felt so alive. Especially because my sunburn is so hot my T-shirt is about to detonate.

Leaving Meadow with Carrie, I set off in search of Mitch, eventually finding him near the cliff, setting up a small tent. He hammers in the last stake and turns to me.

"I trust the lady will find this evening's accommodation satisfactory?" he asks, smiling.

"This is my tent?" I ask.

"*Our* tent," he corrects me.

Ours? Well, this I didn't expect.

Mitch holds back the flap for me to enter. "Check it out."

I climb into the tent, and my romantic illusions evaporate with a pop. There are three sleeping bags, one of which is pink and covered with images of Barbie.

When I tell the story back home, I will definitely edit Meadow out of it.

"It's not five-star, but the view is amazing," he says,

gesturing to the moon that is seemingly floating just off shore.

"It's great," I say, lowering myself warily onto the middle sleeping bag. "Can spiders chew through canvas?"

Mitch sits down beside me. "Not a problem: they couldn't get a club membership."

I giggle nervously. "Ants?"

"The anteater just left."

"Snakes? Bats?"

"This tent is the deluxe pest-proof model. You're perfectly safe."

Maybe so, but I probably won't sleep a wink. Even if I could ignore land and airborne hazards, there's a rock the size of my fist digging into me. I won't complain, however, because I am a supportive girlfriend. If Mitch likes outdoorswomen, I can rough it. A Black Sheep is low maintenance.

"Air mattresses are available," Mitch says, setting the flashlight down beside him. "But you'll have to blow up your own. I'm saving my lips for better things."

I scan the tent for multilegged adversaries and turn back to face Mitch. Remembering my vow to take the initiative, I lean over and kiss him.

He pulls away, saying, "I'm getting a second-degree burn from the heat off your face."

"I put sunscreen on this morning. And before you say it, no, I did not reapply, and yes, I now realize how stupid that was. If it makes you feel better, I'm in pain."

"It doesn't make me feel better, but it does explain why you whimpered as you sat down."

"The backs of my knees are the worst," I say. "It's hard to bend."

He takes a first-aid kit out of his backpack. "Doctor Mitch to the rescue."

I watch suspiciously as he opens a small plastic container. "What is it?"

"An old Mulligan family secret," he says. "Roll over."

"I don't think so—it's going to hurt."

"Look, if you can't trust your own boyfriend, who can you trust?"

At the sound of the magic B-word, I obediently roll onto my stomach and Mitch spreads a deliciously cool substance on the back of my knees. I can almost hear the sizzle.

"Aloe gel," Mitch says. "Squeezed from the plant with my own hands—just for you."

"Is that a pickup line?"

"Sure," he says, continuing to skim the gel over my calf. "Is it working?"

It's definitely working, but I don't plan to admit it just yet. "I'll get back to you on that."

"Dad thinks aloe is the natural wonder drug. We never go camping without it."

I'm more interested in Mitch's touch on my leg than I am in the healing properties of aloe. When he stops, I turn to face him, disappointed. "Done, Doctor Mitch?"

"Just getting started," he says, pulling another container from the first-aid kit. "Witch hazel." He soaks a cotton ball in the liquid and dabs it lightly all over my face. As it dries, my face feels cooler. "Better?"

"Better."

He picks up the aloe again and strokes it onto my face with his index finger.

"That stuff isn't green, is it?" I ask.

He smiles. "You'll never know—unless there's a mirror in your backpack, which I highly doubt."

Then he doesn't know me as well as he thinks he does. There is a mirror, and I'll be using it at sunrise. Roughing it is fine, but why risk scaring off a boyfriend so early in the relationship?

Mitch stares at me intently as he runs the aloe along my jawline. If this is supposed to be clinical, it *so* isn't. There's a chill running down my back.

"You're really good at this," I say, just to say something. "Maybe you should forget about saving wildlife and become a doctor."

"But I like animals better than people," he says, sweeping aloe along my nose. "Except for you."

This is the kind of talk I had hoped to hear tonight, and I kiss him again to encourage him to say more.

"Ouch," he says, drawing back. "Splinters."

Okay, not romantic.

He bites the end off a vitamin E capsule, squeezes the oil

onto a cotton swab, and runs it over my chapped lips. "Try it again," he says, and I kiss him once more. "Nice," he pronounces, lying down beside me and pulling me close.

It's amazing how much more a boyfriend feels like a boyfriend when you're horizontal—even if there's only a thin layer of canvas separating you from a hundred people.

This time Mitch takes the initiative, and his lips seem to melt into mine until I can't quite figure out where he stops and I begin. I feel like a sea nettle, cast adrift in a timeless, weightless universe. The thought makes my eyes open in search of the familiar backdrop of jellyfish.

What I see freezes my blood in its veins: the red eye of a camera at the mesh window of the tent.

Mitch pulls away. "What is it?"

Sitting up, I point soundlessly.

He lunges instantly for the door flap and hauls the perpetrator into the tent in one swift motion. There's a high-pitched squeal as he pushes someone onto his sleeping bag beside me.

"Jump on her," he says.

I pin Meadow to the sleeping bag before she can bolt.

"I'm sorry," she squeaks.

"Sorry for what?" Mitch demands. "Sorry for spying, or sorry you got caught?"

Meadow looks to me for support, but I'm just as mad as he is. "What are you doing with that camera?"

"I told you about my movie—*The Making of* Black

Sheep. I sort of forgot about it, but now I want to finish it before you go home. How was I to know you'd be in here making out?"

"We weren't making out," I say. "Mitch was treating my sunburn."

She smirks. "Right, he was kissing it better." She turns to him. "You were totally making out."

Mitch's lip twitches. "We were totally making out," he confirms. "So why didn't you turn off the camera when you realized that?"

"I was surprised, I guess," she says, staring up at him. "Hey Mitch, if you marry Kendra, she'll be my sister for real."

"Don't be stupid," he snaps. "We are not getting married!"

It's not like I've ever seriously considered marrying him, but hearing him reject the idea as if it's the dumbest thing he's ever heard hurts more than my sunburn. I let go of Meadow and sit back with a sigh.

Meadow looks hopefully at me. "Come on. I could be your bridesmaid."

I change the subject quickly. "Meadow, you've got to promise not to say anything about what you saw. Judy would make our lives a living hell."

Max and Mona probably wouldn't be impressed either. I've noticed that they're more liberal when it comes to the rest of the world than they are with their own kids. I wouldn't want them to think we've been messing around under their roof, especially when they've been so kind to me.

Mitch gives his sister's shoulder a little shake. "Promise, Meadow."

She raises a hand and solemnly swears that our secret is safe.

"What secret?" Carrie asks, appearing at the door of the tent. Meadow looks so guilty that Carrie laughs. "It's okay, Meadow, I don't even want to know. I'm just here to report a miracle: Calvin the tech nerd actually managed to get a bonfire going."

"Where were you?" Lisa asks Mitch when we join everyone by the fire. "I've been looking all over for you."

Mitch takes her aside to offer an explanation. I'd try to eavesdrop, but unfortunately Tia has chosen the same moment to tell Carrie and me about her day in town. I can only catch snippets of Lisa's comments when Tia pauses to breathe, but what I hear alarms me: "too much time with Kendra" and then "you promised" and finally "—share a tent."

Did Mitch promise to share a tent with her tonight? Was the aloe intended for her perfect, tanned body? Does he see *her* as bride material?

"Kendra, did you hear me?" Tia demands. "Jordan asked me to share a tent with him tonight!"

"He did?"

"Don't sound so shocked," Tia says.

"I'm not, it's just that . . . I thought he liked someone else." My femme fatale status sure didn't last long.

She tosses her head. "So what if he did? He likes me now."

"Be careful, Tia," Carrie says. "The guy's a player."

Tia flounces off. "You're just jealous because you're bunking with your brother, Carrie Watson."

Carrie sighs. "Some girls won't believe a guy's a jerk until they experience it first hand."

I glance at Mitch and Lisa. "Is that a hint?"

Carrie follows my gaze. "Of course not. They're talking otters over there." I fill Carrie in on the fragments I overheard, but she doesn't buy it. "You're letting Judy poison your mind," she says. "If you'd just talk to Mitch, you'd know that."

"I've been trying, but we keep getting interrupted."

"Then why don't you let me take Meadow to my tent tonight? I'll promise her a makeover or something."

It's a tempting offer. If Mitch and I spent six hours alone in a small tent, I could work up to telling him how I feel about him. And yet, if I'm not already sure where I stand, should I really be spending the night alone with Mitch and his magic first-aid kit?

After a couple of moments, I shake my head. "I don't think so. Besides, this is your chance to get to know that new guy who's been volunteering at the aquarium."

"Luke?" Carrie asks. "What's the point? He's only here for the summer."

I shake my head. "Didn't you shoot down the same argument when I used it earlier?" I give her a little shove. "Go talk to him."

"Okay," she says. "Then we'll both make the most of tonight." She gives me a quick hug. "Deal?"

"Deal."

When Mitch returns, Carrie goes off in search of Luke. Beckoning, I lead Mitch to the edge of the cliff to watch the moon on the water. I reach out and wrap a tentative arm around his waist.

Behind us, there's a disapproving cluck from the grannies. "Young ladies didn't make the first move in my day," the one with the cane says.

Mitch calls over, "I'm all for it, myself."

I drop my arm hastily, but the grannies totter off to find a better view anyway.

"Don't let them bother you," Mitch says.

"I'm not, I just want to—" I pause, struggling to find the right words. This is it, my chance to say something romantic and elegant and poetic. To tell him how much it's meant to me that he has supported me this summer. To confess that I couldn't have survived *The Black Sheep*—or become one myself—if it weren't for him. "I want to tell you something."

"Sure," he says. "I have something to—"

"Well," Judy interrupts him. "Izn't thiz cozy!"

She is weaving her way toward us, one arm around Bob and the other around Chili. I should have known she wouldn't let a guy get in the way of her career for long.

"Where's Ted?" Mitch asks Judy.

"Pazzed out," she says. "Great guy, but he can't hold his liquor. Plus, we mizzed our spunky KB." Judy releases the guys and lurches forward unsteadily. She shoves Mitch toward the fire and says, "Go away, little hottie. I need a moment alone with my sheepy."

Mitch mouths *Good luck* and leaves with the guys. Flopping onto the grass, Judy pulls me down beside her. "Judy forgives you for the nazty things you said today," she says.

"Tell Judy I didn't apologize," I say. "I meant what I said. I'm going home soon."

"*Soon?*" She kicks off her flip-flops and runs her toes through the damp grass. "I could swear I heard you say the day after tomorrow."

And I could swear she had a slur two minutes ago. "I was making the point that I'll go home when I want to go home."

Judy gives up the fight. "Whatever. It doesn't matter." She drops back onto her elbows and stares up at the stars. "I'm going to get fired after taping this protest anyway."

"Then why do it?" I ask suspiciously.

"I told you. Judy is working for Joe Average now, and she

isn't going to let Terrance Burnside stop her from delivering the truth."

"What's in it for Judy?" I ask.

She looks at me, and the distant campfire is reflected in her pupils, as if it's flickering within. "You know me too well, KB," she says. "This protest is going to make for spectacular TV, and the ratings will be my ticket to any job I want."

That sounds more like my Judy. "Are you shooting all night?" I ask, sensing the end of romance.

"Nope. Just wanted to be on-site early."

"Hey, Judy," Aaron calls from the fire. "I Googled you yesterday and saw you worked on *Pimp My Ride*."

Since Judy enjoys nothing more than talking about Judy, she immediately ditches me for Aaron's crew.

After she's gone, I resurrect my hopes for the evening. While the rest of the camp dreams, Mitch and I can explain away all the mysteries and misunderstandings, snuggled up in our cozy tent.

If there's one thing I've learned in the past six weeks, it's that ten-year-olds sleep very soundly.

"Jeez, when's the last time you trimmed your toenails?" I ask.

Meadow rolls over, pushing my half of the Barbie cocoon off the air mattress, which I blew up after an hour of tossing uncomfortably. Twin beds are sounding good right now.

"Sharing a sleeping bag with you is like being wedged into a tinfoil jacket with a baked potato," Meadow says.

Beside us, in my sleeping bag, Judy rips out a loud snore.

Mitch lifts his head on the other side of Judy. "Quiet, guys, I'm trying to sleep."

I wrestle Meadow to reclaim my spot on the air mattress, and the tent falls silent. Then another sound emanates from Judy's quarter. It isn't a snore.

"Kendra," Meadow says, "Please tell me that wasn't you."

"Of course it wasn't me," I say, scandalized.

Judy giggles. "Oops! Must have been the onions."

Mitch opens the tent's flap, and the remnants of romance float out on a wave of toxic gas.

Chapter 17

"Offither," Judy says, pulling a blood-soaked towel out of her mouth and sticking her bruised, swollen face between the bars of the holding cell. "Where the hell ith the dentitht?"

Desk Sergeant Newman reluctantly shifts his eyes from the small TV in front of him. "Lady, I already told you, there's no one local on call. Someone's coming in from San Francisco, but it's going to take a couple of hours."

"A couple of hourth? I could bleed to death by then. Jutht let me out of here and I'll take care of it mythelf."

"No can do," he says, turning back to the television. "You're here until someone bails you out, or Boulder Beach Golf Club drops the charges."

"I don't need bail for a charge of trethpathing," Judy says.

"True," the sergeant replies. "You need bail for the charges of failing to disperse and damaging personal property. And if you drip blood on those bars, I'll add damaging police property to the list."

Judy puts the towel back to her mouth, muttering something in which the word "pig" figures largely. She gives a muffled oink.

"Don't push your luck," Sergeant Newman says. "You're in enough trouble."

We certainly are. The rally turned out to be a textbook case of civil disobedience gone wrong. It started with Judy getting the crowd riled up to maximize conflict, and ended with the Boulder Beach bigwigs calling the cops. In between, everything is a blur. The wigs flipped when they saw the cameras and started yelling. The crowd yelled back, and then one of the grannies took a swing at the plastic model of the new fourteenth fairway with her cane. In trying to capture the shot with her camcorder, Judy stepped right into the line of fire.

Ultimately, the police hauled everyone off to jail except Bob and Chili, who pretended they were reporters. They offered to take Meadow, but she insisted on coming with us and has been sitting with Sergeant Newman watching TV.

More than thirty of us are crammed into this large holding cell in Carmel. The others are in the Monterey police station, which is apparently a palace compared to this hellhole. Judy has commandeered the one bench, on medical grounds, so the rest of us are sitting cross-legged on the grimy floor—a sad echo of our earlier protest. There is a toilet in the corner, which some people have actually used. I'd have to be here a year before that ever happened.

My stomach is another matter, however, and if I am hungry, the rest of the team must be, too. I nominate myself cell spokesperson. "Could we get something to eat, please?" I call to Newman.

"A waiter will be along any moment to take your order," he replies.

"But it's one o'clock and we didn't even have breakfast."

"You gave up the right to regular meals when you broke the law."

It wasn't enough to strip us of human dignity; now they're going to starve us as well.

My wrists still hurt from being cuffed at the golf course and herded roughly into police cruisers as if we posed some sort of threat to national security. My pride hurts even more, because the Bigwigs and their followers applauded as we were carted away (the grannies, now in Monterey with Carrie and Calvin, blew raspberries back).

At the station, the police frisked everyone for weapons, fingerprinted us, and confiscated our personal possessions, including belts and shoelaces. They even took my lip gloss. I explained to Newman that because of my sunburn it was a fundamental human need—that without it, my lips would crack like the paint on an old Rembrandt—but he said I might as well get used to it, because luxuries like makeup aren't allowed in "the big house."

It was a blatant attempt to intimidate, but I didn't buy it. There is no way I'm going to do time for attending a rally.

I'm a minor. My lawyer will point to my clean record and argue that I'm incompetent to stand trial due to raging teenage hormones.

Still, I'm in a bind today, and I really want to think of a way to get everyone out of here. I tried slipping Newman Mom's credit card to bail us out, but he said we'd need an adult to sign the paperwork. So then I asked Meadow to make some calls, but she doesn't have any quarters, and Newman is such a hard-ass that he refused to let her use his phone unless it's to call her parents. Max and Mona are at the quilting show until tomorrow, and naturally, they scorn such modern conveniences as cell phones.

It's almost enough to make me wish I were a regular white sheep again, content to graze in fenced pastures and follow the flock without question. My old life may have been dull, but at least I was never behind bars. If I'd stayed on the sidelines, like a good Banker in Training, none of this would have happened.

But it has happened, and the truth is that I don't regret coming to California. If it weren't for *The Black Sheep*, I wouldn't have experienced the thrill of working with a group toward a common goal. I wouldn't have learned how to stand up to my parents and fight for the right to make my own decisions. And, I wouldn't have ended up with a boyfriend like Mitch Mulligan.

Not that he's behaving much like a boyfriend right now. In fact, he's sitting in the corner with Lisa, who's crying so hard her eyes have puffed into slits. What does she have to cry about? Sure, she organized the rally, but she made it perfectly clear when we got locked in here that it went south because of me.

To be honest, I agree. Because I was there, the cameras were there to set the wigs off and Judy was there to stir up trouble. Still, none of that is *directly* my fault. I feel like having a good cry myself, but I won't. You've got to be tough to make it on the inside.

A little sympathy would be nice. I know Mitch can't make a big show of supporting me in front of Judy, but would it kill him to throw me a smile to show that he doesn't blame me for what happened? As far as I know I'm still his girlfriend, even if no one is aware of that fact except Meadow and Carrie.

He is so lucky we're in jail right now. Otherwise I'd be throwing a tantrum that would make this morning's riot look like a pillow fight.

Aaron is standing behind Judy, massaging her shoulders. Tia says Aaron has set his sights on a career in reality television and sees Judy as his ticket in. Since she isn't refusing the massage, she must have agreed to let him start paying his dues as her personal slave.

She looks up as I approach. One lens of her glasses is missing, the other is cracked. "What?" she asks.

"I want to know if there's anything you need. Other

than a dentist and an optometrist, I mean."

She raises her eyebrows. "And if I did?"

"I'd implore Newman to show a little compassion and get it for you."

She closes her eyes and sighs. "What do you want, KB?"

"I want you to get us out of here, and I'm prepared to do whatever it takes to make that happen."

Her eyes pop open again, proving she hasn't lost her will to live—and make trash TV. "I'd love to take you up on that offer, but I have no idea how to get uth out."

"You could bail us out."

"My lifethtyle doethent leave a lot of room for thavingth," she says, holding up the diamond ring that recently reappeared on her finger. I left it in the drawer of my bedside table, so either Judy or Meadow went snooping.

"You could get Bob to pawn it for us," I suggest.

"No way," she says. "It might be the only diamond I ever get."

"So ask the network to bail us out."

"Are you kidding? Burnthide ith laughing his ath off right now. For all I know, I might already be fired."

"Well, think of something. You said you were smarter than me on your worst day."

"That was before I had a concuthion," she points out. "You got uth into this meth—you get uth out."

"Me! If you hadn't riled everyone up, it would have been a peaceful protest."

"Peathful proteth don't make good TV. Bethides, pathive rethitanth never workth, KB. Remember what happened to Gandhi?"

"No." That was decades ago.

"Murdered," another voice supplies. It belongs to the sole resident of the station's third holding cell, a tall, bald man in jeans and a denim shirt. If it weren't for the tattoos peeking out from his shirt cuffs, he'd look like a regular guy. "So was Martin Luther King."

Judy lifts her head to look at the guy and drops it back on the bench, knocking her glasses awry.

"Get up," I say. "Talk the officer into letting you make a phone call. You must know someone who can get us out of here."

"Yeah," the bald guy tells her. "You're the adult. Do something."

"Thut up, you," Judy tells him.

The guy laughs. He's got a nice smile for a felon. I wonder what he's in for.

After a moment, Judy does get up. "Offither, I demand to know what ith going on."

"We're still processing paperwork," Sergeant Newman says, keeping his eyes on the TV. "The ringleaders will be the last to go, so expect a bit of a wait."

I join Judy at the bars. "You've been processing paperwork for four hours," I say. "Meadow, get out your camcorder and shoot Sergeant Newman on the job. The people of

Carmel won't be impressed by how their tax dollars are being spent."

Meadow squirms in her seat before whispering, "It's gone."

"Gone?" My voice rises a couple of octaves. "Gone where?" There's incriminating footage of Mitch and me on that camera.

"I don't know," she says. "I lost it when they were loading us into the van."

Judy watches me shrewdly. "Why tho worried, KB?"

"It's Mitch's camera," I say. "He won't be happy."

Judy turns to get a look at Mitch through her cracked lens. "Litha will conthole him."

"You were going to try to get us out, remember?" I say.

Shaking the bars of the cell, Judy says, "I demand my phone call."

"Is that the best you can do?" the bald guy asks her.

"Keep it down, Walter," Sergeant Newman says. "I'm trying to watch the news."

"Sorry, Mike," Walter says. If they're on a first-name basis, Walter must be a regular here. "But can't you let the toothless one make her call now? The whining is getting painful." Walter winks at me.

Sergeant Newman reluctantly unlocks the door and lets Judy out of the cell. They disappear into another room.

"Thanks, Walter," I say, winking back.

"No problem," he says. "You're famous, kid. Newman

watches your show all the time." He points to the TV. "Hey, you're on the news now."

A local reporter I recognize from the rally is standing on the golf course, saying, "A riot broke out today when Boulder Beach Golf Club unveiled plans for a new fourteenth hole. Ringleader Kendra Bishop is the star. . . ."

In the cell behind me, a couple of people boo.

Walter shouts, "Shut it. Incoming badge!"

"Look," Newman says, "you kids give me any grief and I might misplace your paperwork. You're supposed to be using this time to think about what you've done."

He pushes Judy into the cell and we crowd around her to find out what happened. She shakes her head to signal failure. "Bob thaid Terranthe threatened to fire him and Chili if they bail uth out."

Someone calls, "Kendra's the one who should fix this."

A ripple of agreement spreads throughout the cell.

"Whiners," Walter calls to them.

He's right. These people are taking prison way too hard. It's a life experience, and if they knew more about Black Sheepism, they'd value that.

Mitch finally emerges from his corner to check on me. "How are you doing?

"Fine," I say. It's more or less true. My life may be spiraling downhill, but I'm hanging in there. "We haven't come up with an escape plan, though. At this point, our best bet is your parents."

"I'm not sure they'll bail us out," he says. "At least, not until they're good and ready. Like I told you before, they don't approve of breaking the law."

"They've broken the law themselves."

"And they paid a price for it." He explains that the redwood forest incident wasn't their only arrest. At another protest they organized, a police officer was injured when violence broke out, and they were charged with assault. "My grandfather couldn't get them off. Later, they couldn't get a credit card, or buy a house, or travel outside of the country because of their criminal records. My dad couldn't get a job, and he couldn't find anyone to insure him when he tried to start his own business."

"That's awful," I say.

"I know. That's why Lisa's so upset. Berkeley could kick her out, or she could lose her scholarship, which would amount to the same thing."

Oh.

"But don't panic," Mitch continues. "A good lawyer will probably be able to convince the golf course to drop the charges, and we can apply to have our records expunged later."

"Max and Mona are still going to freak out," I say.

"They are."

"I'm partly to blame for getting us into this, so I have to get us out. I'm a mature adult. I can handle this."

He smiles. "Gonna call your folks?"

"Absolutely."

* * *

"Sergeant Newman?" I ask. "Can I make a phone call?"

"Nope."

"Please? Pretty please? I'll get you profiled on the show."

Judy oinks behind me. "Like hell you will."

"You trying to bribe me, kid?" Newman asks.

"Of course not. Although, everyone knows the system is corrupt."

Walter laughs. "Let her make a call, Mike."

"Nope," Newman repeats. "She's got too much attitude."

"It's not about me," I say. "It's about Meadow. Look at her, she's terrified."

Meadow puts down the Snickers bar Sergeant Newman gave her and tries to look terrified. "I want to go home," she says.

"See? She's young and impressionable. She could be scarred by this experience."

"Especially by being exposed to people like me," Walter says.

Detecting a trace of doubt in Sergeant Newman's eyes, I persist. "Usually when she's this upset, she starts crying. And once she gets going, man, she never stops."

Sergeant Newman looks at Meadow, and she rubs a sleeve across her eyes.

"It's brutal," I add. "But if you can stand it, we can."

Sergeant Newman gets to his feet and unlocks the door.

* * *

"Hi, Dad."

Silence.

"I wanted to apologize about the whole divorce thing," I say.

"You're only apologizing now because you're in trouble," Mom says on the extension.

"How did you know I'm in trouble?" I'm so relieved that they already know that I forget to mention I've tried to contact them before.

"Terrance Burnside called two hours ago," Dad says. "He said he's going to sue us because Boulder Beach is apparently going to sue the network for slander."

"It's not slander if it's true," I say.

"You'll have a hard time proving your case in court," he says. "Kendra, we told you not to take on Boulder Beach and you did it anyway. What do you want us to do about it?"

A week of *Dr. Ernest* boot camp and they still aren't capable of supporting me. But now is not the moment to point out their deficiencies as parents. "I was hoping you'd post bail for me. And for the rest of the group, too."

My mother actually laughs. "I have better ways to spend my life savings."

"Do you want me to rot in jail?"

"No, but we want you to take responsibility for your own actions," Dad says.

The man is cold. He could afford to clock a few more hours with Ernest's rubber dolls. "Well, if I can find an adult to sign the papers, can I at least charge bail to your credit card?"

This time it's Dad who laughs. "We canceled it."

Mom says, "I'm surprised you'd turn to us after telling the whole world we're such horrible parents."

"Not the whole world, just North America," I say. "And I never said you were horrible. You know that half this show is a lie. The divorce is just a stupid publicity stunt, and I told both Judy and Terrance that I wouldn't agree to it. I'm coming home soon."

There's another silence I can only read as a lack of enthusiasm over my return. I consider asking if I'm welcome, but I'm afraid of the answer. Instead I ask, "Aren't you worried about me at all?"

"What could be safer than a police station?" Dad asks. "I'm sure you'll be fine, Kendra. Good luck."

I put the phone down and follow Sergeant Newman blindly back to my cell. My parents are devoid of emotional vital signs. I understand that they're disappointed, but it's not like I stabbed someone or pushed drugs or anything. I shouldn't have wasted my one phone call on them. I should have called Rosa.

Walter pats my shoulder through the bars as I pass. "I guess I don't have to ask how that went."

I appreciate Walter's sympathy, but what I really need is

some support from Mitch. Unfortunately, he's returned to Lisa's side.

"Poor little Black Theep," Judy lisps, as I enter the cell. "All alone in her time of need. I think you're finally figuring out Mitch's game."

Judy's the one playing games, so I let this go.

"They're obviouthly a couple," she continues without any encouragement from me. "And they uthed your thelebrity to promote their cauthe. Remember how they avoided the camerath at firtht? Then, after you got all riled up about the plight of the th-th-th-"

"Seals?"

She nods. "They warmed right up. Particularly Mitch."

"We're just friends," I say. In spite of myself, I start reviewing the timeline in my head. My heart contracts when I realize that the timing supports Judy's theory.

I glance over again, and Lisa's head is resting on Mitch's shoulder. Could Judy be right that he used me to get media attention for the otters? No. He may not be a classic Romeo, but he's a compassionate guy who cares for his family and friends, animals and the environment. Sure, he pimped Ted for the cause, but he wouldn't do it to anyone else, especially me.

On the other hand, it would explain why Lisa disliked me from the beginning, and why she freaked out about my sharing a tent with Mitch last night. It would also explain why things have always been awkward between Mitch and me: it was fake—on his side—all along.

Judy smiles as I reach my conclusion, baring three broken front teeth.

"Close your mouth," I say. "You're scaring people."

Sergeant Newman slams the phone down and opens the cell door. "You're free to go."

"All of us?" I ask, scared to believe it's true.

He nods as if he can't quite believe it either. "All of you."

"My parents came through?" I ask. Maybe Dr. Ernest did emotional CPR and brought them back to life.

"Nope. A guy by the name of Logan Waters. He was surfing at Big Sur and drove into town when he saw the news. He signed the papers and picked up the tab. You are one lucky girl."

I am indeed. Who needs a second-rate Romeo when you've got Logan Waters on your side?

Chapter 18

Mona paces around the kitchen with the phone to her ear, while Max keeps Mitch and me pinned to our seats with a glare.

"We didn't know about the protest in advance, honestly," Mona says. "I am so sorry that your daughter was arrested. Trust me, they will be punished."

Faster than you can say "hypocrite," Mona and Max have transformed from liberal, tolerant citizens of the world into conservative banker wannabes. All that's missing is dollar signs where their pupils should be.

Hanging up the phone, Mona says, "That makes twenty calls. Apologizing for you two is becoming a full-time job."

"We're very disappointed," Max says. It's the fifth time he's said that since getting back from Garberville.

"I don't know what we'll do if Boulder Beach decides to sue us, too," Mona says.

"We'd be in serious trouble," Max says.

Cue the dollar signs.

"Your parents might be able to afford it, Kendra, but we'd have to sell the house," Mona concludes.

There's an explosion of light at close range as Judy exposes her shiny new crowns in a nauseatingly happy smile. Far from being fired for shooting the protest, she has become the network darling overnight. The CEO—Terrance's boss—was so impressed by the footage of the episode that he's already nominated her for a "Realie."

There's no justice. Mitch and I have explained what happened over and over, but nothing is getting through to his parents.

"It was just a rally," Mitch repeats.

"A *peaceful* rally that got a little rowdy in the end because of Judy," I add. "Someone smacked a display, that's all."

"You should have known that would happen," Mona tells me.

How? It's not like a crystal ball came with my contract. I expected a little more support from Max and Mona. Once upon a time, their rally went further off the rails than this one.

"You were *arrested*," Mona says, as if it might have escaped my notice that I spent half a day behind bars. "And you're acting like it's no big deal."

"I know it was a big deal," I say. "But look on the bright side: it brought a lot of attention to the cause, so maybe it was worth it."

"The end does not justify the means, young lady," Max says.

"Have you thought for one moment about how your life will be affected if the charges aren't dropped?" Mona asks.

I decide not to respond, because it will only prolong the agony.

When Mona doesn't get an answer, she resorts to hurling quotes from *The Book of Parents*:

"We thought you had more sense."

"Did you think you wouldn't get caught?"

"Breaking the law is not something we tolerate in this house."

"What are we supposed to tell the other parents?"

Please. No one wearing otter barrettes and a caftan really cares what other people think.

"Calm down, sweetie," Max says, patting her shoulder anxiously. "Maybe Kendra doesn't know any better."

This is the worst insult yet. Of course I know better! I was raised by nerds, not wolves.

"Well, Mitch certainly knows better," Mona says, focusing on her son. "You lied to us."

"I didn't lie," he says, shifting uncomfortably. "I just skipped some details."

A nervous grin twitches on my lips, and Mona raises her

hand as if she'd like to cuff both of us. She remembers the hippie inside her just in time. "How could you expose your little sister to a violent situation?"

I take this one. "The only person who got out of hand besides Judy was two hundred years old."

Mona shuts me down. "I was talking to Mitch. This is a family matter."

A family matter? When did I lose my family status? She certainly has no problem treating me like one of her own when it comes to the chore roster.

"But you're still grounded for as long as you're here," Max adds.

Great. I get all of the crap that comes with being part of the family, but none of the benefits.

Meadow appears at the kitchen door and says, "I think Kendra's getting a bum rap."

"You do," Mona says. It's a statement, not a question, but that subtlety is lost on Meadow.

"Yeah. It's not like anyone took a dirt nap."

Max stares at his daughter. "A *what?*"

Chili looks around his eyepiece to translate, "Prison slang for 'died.'"

"Meadow, where did you pick up that sort of language?" Mona asks.

Judy beats Meadow to the answer: "The kid hit it off with the thug from the next cell."

As Mona gathers herself to blow, I interject, "Meadow

was sitting with Sergeant Newman the whole time. We asked her to go with Bob and Chili but she refused."

"She's ten," Mona says. "You don't ask her to leave jail, you tell her."

Mitch finally decides to chime in again. "Mom, we were cuffed and in the cruiser when Bob left. There wasn't much we could do."

His mother deflates faster than a slashed tire. "Our son was taken away in handcuffs," she says. "We have failed as parents."

"Now, now," Max says. "Some of them are turning out all right. Maya's a wonderful girl."

Mitch rolls his eyes and Mona wags a finger at him. "We warned you that a criminal record could ruin your life, but you wouldn't listen," she says. "Whose idea was the sit-in?"

"Kendra's," Mitch says before I can even open my mouth.

I stare at him, stunned. Sure, I threw the idea out there, but he's the one who formalized it, and Lisa put the wheels in motion. This girl merely went along for the ride.

Meadow punches him in the arm. "Quit bitching up Kendra."

Max escorts her to the door. "Unless you'd like to rinse out your mouth with dish soap, I suggest you go to your room."

The phone rings and Meadow picks up in the hall. "Mitch, it's Lisa. She wants you to come to the aquarium right now."

Max shakes his head. "Grounded."

"Tell her I'll call her later," Mitch says.

"Okay, but she says someone vandalized her office."

Mitch waits until his father nods reluctantly and then bolts out the door without so much as a backward glance at me.

Mona and Max sit down on either side of me. "What on earth possessed you to do such a crazy thing?"

I'm tempted to shift the blame to Mitch, but unlike him, I know the meaning of loyalty. "You told us about your sit-in to save the redwood forest and we thought it might work here."

Mona offers the all-time parental classic: "That was different. We cared about that forest, Kendra. We weren't staging an event to get television ratings."

Judy makes a motion of someone twisting a knife in her gut and pretends to die. If only it were true.

"How can you say that?" I ask. "You know I care about saving the otters."

"And you know you won't be around to deal with the consequences of your actions. You're running back to New York and leaving us holding the bag."

"But the show is ending! I have to go home."

"That's my point," she says. "For you, it's a show. For us,

it's our lives. We've worked hard to establish good reputations for ourselves and our children in this community, and with our history, it wasn't easy. People have very long memories."

Max gets a stab in too. "It's probably not a coincidence that someone broke into Lisa's office today. If computers were damaged, we may lose valuable research."

"It's a shame you didn't think things through before deciding to play the hero," Mona says.

What's really a shame is I didn't know that TV parents could be worse than real ones before agreeing to be part of this show. The only thing that's keeping me in my seat right now is the knowledge that a Black Sheep must display grace under pressure.

That and the fact that they have me surrounded.

I try one last time to reach them. "I thought you'd be happy we were trying to help the otters."

"We *were* happy—when you were acting sensibly," Max says.

Mona stands and beckons to Max. "This stress is putting a kink in my chi. I'm in need of your healing hands."

He follows her out of the kitchen, rubbing his palms together to warm them.

I am alone in the basement when Meadow tracks me down.

"What are you doing?" she asks.

I'm watching "When Nature Kills" on the *Animal*

Planet. In this episode, a pride of lions is stalking a graceful gazelle. "What does it look like I'm doing?"

"Sulking?"

One good thing about going home will be that I'll have solitude whenever I want. I don't know why I didn't appreciate that before. "What do you want?"

"To see if you're okay. My parents came down pretty hard on you."

"Yeah, well, that's life."

"Where's Mitch?"

I shrug. "Who cares?"

"He should be here cheering you up."

She is already more insightful than her brother. "That's life," I repeat.

"Maybe we could go down to the aquarium and help them."

"I don't think so. I've had enough of the aquarium."

"But you can't just give up. You have to—"

I crank up the volume as the lions lunge at the gazelle. There's a horrible screech, and Meadow covers her ears. "Turn it off!"

"I can't. That's what real life is like, Meadow. Someone's always circling for the kill. The sooner we accept it, the better off we'll be."

"So true, KB," Judy says, coming down the stairs. "It's the story of my fabled career. She pauses to watch the disemboweling of the gazelle before popping a disc into the

DVD player. "I've got something even more exciting to show you—not as gory, but X-rated."

Meadow's eyes light up. "Cool."

Judy pulls me off the couch to make way for Max and Mona, who look as pinched and disapproving as a couple of bankers I know. Standing beside the TV, Judy does a little curtsy. "And now, I present to you the teaser for my Realie-nominated episode of *The Black Sheep*. Chili, lights, please."

The screen goes black for a moment and then, in fifty-two-inch living color, we see a couple making out.

"Oh my God!" Meadow exclaims. "Judy stole my camera."

In retrospect, I suppose it could have been worse.

First, Mitch and I could have been naked.

Second, Judy's teaser could have been longer. It felt like an eternity, but it's probably only five minutes. Even so, Mona's increasingly labored breathing throughout had Max pretty worried. I looked over to see him trying to move the chi along, and Mona actually slapped him.

And third, I could have come off as the villain. Instead, Judy structured the segment to depict me as a naive, overprotected city girl who stumbled into the Mulligans' web of free love and deceit. She built her case with carefully layered shots:

• Kendra prancing about her parents' art collection in

blue-and-white pajamas, looking like the biggest
nerd on the planet
- Mitch in the buff, staring down the camera
- Mona tossing condoms into Maya's suitcase
- Mitch hugging Lisa
- A montage of the Mulligans fighting environmental
causes as a family
- A montage of my parents in Dr. Ernest's boot camp
- Mitch and Kendra kayaking among the otters
- Kendra giving Team 14 a pep talk, while Mitch looks
on admiringly
- Kendra on a series of talk shows
- Mitch hugging Lisa again
- Lisa in her bikini
- Kendra and Mitch making out
- Mitch hugging Lisa yet again
- Kendra running, crazed, down the streets of Carmel
- Mitch and Lisa in the back of a squad car
- Kendra alone in the back of another squad car

It was so well done that Judy's voice-over describing
how Mitch used me to gain attention for his pet cause
wasn't necessary, although it did add drama. Meanwhile, a
message scrolled across the bottom of the screen: TUNE IN
TO THE SEASON FINALE TO CAST YOUR VOTE. SHOULD KENDRA
BISHOP DIVORCE HER PARENTS? CALL 1-800-U-DECIDE!

I have to admit, Judy has a flair for storytelling. Not that being depicted as the puppet and pawn of the Mulligans is a high point of my life. On the contrary. But at least it's a change from being portrayed as the ungrateful, disrespectful daughter. It's time someone else took some heat.

Judy shuts off the TV and looks to us for a reaction. "What do you think?"

"I think I'm going to be sick," Mona says faintly. "Kendra, we welcomed you into this family with open arms and we tried to give you space to find your own way. We thought you were a nice, misunderstood girl, but you've obviously been manipulating all of us. I can see why you were having trouble at home. You have no respect for your parents, no respect for us, and no respect for yourself."

Now I'm the one gasping for breath. How could they have taken that message from the piece? They've been manipulated by Judy, not me.

Defending myself would take too much energy—energy I am going to need to make a classy exit—so I decide to take the high road. Standing to face them, I say, "I know you're upset and I can't really blame you, but it isn't as bad as it looks. I want you to know that I think of you both as second parents. I have nothing but respect for you."

Judy chortles. "And I have nothing but respect for the way you've learned to shovel it, KB. All that public speaking has paid off. You're celebrity material now."

"I don't want to be a celebrity," I say. "I want to be Kendra Bishop, a nobody from New York. And by this time tomorrow, that's what I'll be."

I start up the stairs, and Judy grabs me by the shirttail. "That's up to America, remember?"

"You can't stop me from getting on a plane," I tell her.

"You can't get on a plane without a ticket, and if Judy recalls correctly, your credit's dried up."

I glance at Max and Mona, hoping they want to get rid of me enough to offer the money, but they won't even look at me.

Judy releases my shirt. "I guess you'll have to wait and see what America decides."

Halfway up the stairs I realize classy exits are overrated. "America can bite me!"

"Hi, Mr. Watson, is Carrie at home?" I ask, when Carrie's dad answers the door.

"Carrie and Calvin are grounded," he replies, with none of his usual warmth. "I don't think I need to tell you why."

"Okay, well, I'll just say good-bye, then. I'm going home tomorrow."

"I wish you well, Kendra, but I can't say we'll miss you," he says, closing the door gently but firmly in my face.

I suppose asking for a loan to buy a plane ticket is out of the question.

Seated on a swing in the backyard, I dial my parents' home number on Judy's cell phone, which I snatched from the kitchen counter on the way out.

"You've reached Kenneth, Deirdre, and Maya!" a trio chimes in unison. "We can't come to the phone right now because we're out doing something fabulous. Leave a message and we'll call you back!"

I pitch the phone into Mona's marigolds and push off on the swing.

If only I'd ignored that stupid magazine ad. Now, just about everyone I know hates me, including my own parents. What kind of a loser alienates two sets of parents, a good friend, dozens of acquaintances, and a boyfriend all in the space of twenty-four hours?

Of course, this was all part of Judy's master plan. Carrie once said that the show would only accept Maya if Mitch agreed to participate. Now I see why. Judy knew I was too naive to see through him, and I played right into her hands. She got exactly what she wanted—conflict and great ratings. If the kid from New York had to fall under the wheels of the network machine and get her heart crushed in the process, so be it.

Part of me still can't believe that it was all fake, though. Surely I would have seen some signs that Mitch didn't care about me. Surely I am not *that* gullible. If I am, Black Sheepism has some gaping holes I'll have to plug very carefully before I ever date again. *If* I ever date again.

"Hey, slow down," Mitch says, walking across the yard toward me. "You're going to tip the swings."

I pump my legs harder to gain some height. "Like you care what happens to me."

"What do you mean?" he asks.

I throw my whole body into the upward swing and enjoy three seconds of relief during the freefall. "Nothing."

He accepts my answer too easily. "It wasn't as bad at the aquarium as we feared," he says. "The computers weren't damaged and we didn't lose any research. So Lisa is fine."

"What a relief," I say.

He completely misses the sarcasm. "How'd it go here?"

"Just peachy," I say, driving again toward the sky. Suddenly, one of the supports at the base of the swing set lifts out of its hole and the entire structure rocks violently. I cling to the chains until Mitch steps forward to steady me.

"Are you okay?" he asks.

I get off the swing and storm over to a lawn chair. "No, I am not okay. I haven't been okay since you abandoned me in jail yesterday."

"What do you mean, abandoned you?" he asks, following me. "I was locked in the same cell."

"You spent the whole time comforting Lisa. I could have used some support too."

"But you were fine," he says, looking confused. "You didn't seem upset at all."

"I was IN JAIL," I shout. "That should have been your first clue I wasn't fine. Didn't it occur to you that I might feel terrible about getting everyone locked up? And this morning, you let your parents think the sit-in was all my fault."

"That wasn't what I meant," he says. "I was trying not to take credit for your idea. You know I was all for the sit-in. I still think it was a great idea. It almost worked, too."

"Well, your parents have a better reason for hating me now anyway." I meet his eyes for the first time. "Judy got hold of Meadow's camera."

It takes a moment for this to sink in. When it does, he picks up a garden gnome and hurls it at the fence. "Shit."

"While you were helping Lisa, I got to sit with your parents as they watched the rough cut."

"I'm sorry." He tries to take my hand but I jerk it away.

"Judy put this story together about how you used me to promote your environmental agenda. Meanwhile, you've been involved with Lisa the whole time. She's calling it, 'Pimping Kendra.'" The last bit is my invention, but it fits.

Mitch laughs. He laughs!

I get out of the deck chair and charge back to the swings again. I don't care if the whole set collapses around me, I have to swing right now. Mitch comes after me and holds on to the chains so I can't move.

"Don't tell me you believe Judy's story," he says. "You've got to be kidding."

"If you saw it, you wouldn't waste your time lying about it."

"You mean I'm convicted without a trial?"

"You missed your court date." I pry his fingers off the chain one by one and then shove him back so that I can swing. "I am going home tomorrow anyway."

He anchors the pole so that I don't catapult into the rosebushes. "You're going to leave just like that?"

"On the first plane out."

"Fine. If you're the type to take off as soon as the going gets tough, I'll drive you to the airport."

"Don't bother. I'm sure you and Lisa want to get right to work on a new plan for saving the world."

He snorts. "And obviously you need to hurry home to shop on sparkly Fifth Avenue."

I try to kick him as I swing past, but he ducks out of the way.

He opens his mouth but I jump off the swing and speak first. "Don't. There's nothing you can say. "

I run out of the yard before the tears come. Mitch has broken my heart and my confidence, and there's no Black Sheep rule to tell me how to mend them.

I shine the flashlight over the marigolds until I find Judy's cell phone. Then I creep back into the house and lock myself in the basement.

Turning up the volume of the TV, I watch as the

commercial ends and Harry Queen's face appears on the screen.

"And now," Harry says, smiling at the camera, "I have a little surprise. Kendra Bishop is on the phone from Monterey. Apparently, she wants to set the record straight about behind-the-scenes shenanigans on her popular show. Let's hear it, Black Sheep."

Chapter 19

"Take your seats," the judge commands, pounding the gavel so hard that her cheap plywood bench wobbles. "Court is in session."

In other words, we're live. Judy had a last-minute inspiration to shoot the final one-hour season finale of *The Black Sheep: California Edition* live in a courtroom. Since courtrooms are in short supply in Monterey, we had to settle for a TV studio that is normally home to *Nutty's Playhouse*, a children's show featuring a man in a green squirrel suit.

The set decorators worked overnight to create the courtroom, and in typical Reality Network fashion, they cut a few corners. For starters, the American flag hanging over the judge's bench doesn't fully cover the enormous green mural of Nutty. Second, my seat behind the "witness box" consists of an uncomfortable plastic oak tree stump. And last, there are foam peanuts scattered everywhere that squeak when you step on them.

I'm not impressed by the judge, either. As there was no one suitable on such short notice, our very own Judge Judy is presiding, in a voluminous robe adorned with a fuzzy black sheep. She can't even be bothered to look impartial.

To begin the broadcast, Judy introduces herself and all the key players in the courtroom. Then she urges viewers to pick up the phone and vote. Once the polls are officially open, she cuts away to highlights of past episodes and pretaped interviews.

That leaves me with nothing to do but squirm in the witness box while my fate is being decided. After my call to Harry Queen, I'm reasonably confident about the verdict. My eloquent appeal to send me home probably did the trick, but if not, the "Pimping Kendra" episode that aired a few days later surely would have. Viewers couldn't help but realize I've been ill-treated by the Mulligans in general and Mitch in particular, and they'll be eager to return me to the overprotective arms of my parents.

While hundreds of thousands of strangers call in to the panel of producers in the jury box, I sit under the watchful eye of two dozen familiar faces. Rosa, Carrie, and Tia are in the front row of the visitors' gallery alongside Max, Mona, and Meadow. Behind them are Mitch, Lisa, Ted Silver, Sergeant Newman, and Walter, now out on bail. The back two rows are given over to Team 14 members.

Beside the jury box is the defense table, behind which sit my parents and Maya. I haven't been able to bring myself to take a good look at them yet. Oddly enough, I don't feel their eyes on me, either.

Eventually, Judy bangs her gavel and asks, "Has America reached a verdict, Mr. Chairman?"

Aaron approaches the judge's bench, smiling directly at the cameras. His apprenticeship with Judy is obviously coming along nicely. "No, My Lady, we had to do a recount." He corrects himself. "I mean, *Your Honor*."

Carrie rolls her eyes at me, and I try to smile back. It means a lot to me that she defied her parents to attend today. She even slipped me a note through Meadow, saying that we're friends forever and that she's sure today will go well.

I need all the support I can get, especially after what happened with Mitch. Mind you, I've adjusted surprisingly quickly to life without him, perhaps because he moved in with Calvin right after our fight. Why the Watsons don't hold him equally accountable for their kids' arrest is beyond me. Maybe what they're really worried about is that emancipation could be contagious. But whatever. My point is that Mitch is welcome to avoid me for the rest of his days. I am *so* over him.

Just the same, I'd hoped he wouldn't appear in court today since I've already got enough to worry about. It helps to see that his looks have really gone downhill in the past week, probably from living in that cave with Calvin. His hair is unkempt, there are circles under his eyes, and he's wearing a ratty T-shirt. I don't know what I saw in him.

321

Not that I'm in a position to throw stones. My sunburn has taken its natural course, and I am now dropping more flakes than a New York blizzard.

Mona and Max are here not to support me, but to meet their contractual obligations. Although they haven't been openly hostile in the past few days, I know they share my hope that America will send me home. What they will do if I am forced to emancipate myself, I don't know. At one time, they would have welcomed me into their home permanently, but I doubt that's an option now. Maybe they'll let me sleep in the garden shed and forage in the compost for grubs.

Meadow will be the only Mulligan who is sorry to see me go, and even her affection has diminished since Maya arrived in California with my parents. They are staying in a hotel until the show is officially over, but Meadow was allowed one visit and came home with one thing on her mind: Maya's new Manhattan wardrobe.

Fortunately, my association with Logan Waters will help to sustain Meadow's good opinion of me, especially now that he's e-mailing me all the time. Well, twice to be exact. He obviously kept the napkin I gave him with the Team 14 Web site address, because he sent me a note through the site to say he was sorry about what happened at the rally. Naturally, I e-mailed back to thank him for bailing us out. Then he sent another note saying no problem.

I highly doubt Maya made these sorts of connections in

New York, which is probably why she looks especially sour today. She is perched between my parents at the defense table, as if she's their attorney. If she thinks that suit she's wearing is disguising the hippie within, she's much mistaken.

My parents are immobile, as if carved from stone. I had hoped that Judy's episode portraying me as the Mulligans' pawn may have softened them, but apparently the fact that I was making out in a tent with Mitch during the same show offset that. I have tried to sneak out to their hotel, but Judy is so annoyed about the *Harry Queen* "stunt" that she's been sticking to me like cheap underwear ever since.

"Permission to approach the bench, Your Honor?" Aaron asks. "America has reached a verdict."

Judy accepts the envelope he hands her and looks down at me from on high. "The votes are in, KB. Do you have any last words?"

Last words? Am I dying?

"I have full confidence that the voters have made the right decision," I say. And I do. There's no reason why people would want to break up my family.

She pulls the card from the envelope, and her smile expands to fill the courtroom. That's when my heart starts to pound. She wouldn't look that happy if it were good news for me. "Are you ready to hear the verdict?"

"Just read it already."

She pauses a little longer for dramatic effect before

announcing: "By decree of the fair citizens of the United States of America, you, Kendra Bishop, will emancipate yourself from your parents!"

A commotion erupts in the visitors' gallery. Judy bangs her gavel, but that only adds to the din. I sit in shock, seeing nothing but Judy's teeth. There is only one clear thought in my mind: What am I going to do? There was no backup plan.

After more hammering of the gavel, the clamor subsides enough for the judge to speak. "Give Judy a reaction, KB."

Bob closes in for a tight shot as I summon my wits. I am aware of dozens of eyes staring at me. Finally I croak out a question. "What was the final tally?"

Judy's features freeze for a second. "Never mind. That's irrelevant."

"It's relevant to me. I have a right to know."

I stand up and snatch the card before she can chew it up and swallow the evidence. The letters and numerals swim on the page before finally taking shape: TO THE QUESTION OF WHETHER KENDRA BISHOP SHOULD EMANCIPATE FROM HER PARENTS, WE THE PEOPLE VOTE: YEA—453,480; NAY—453,443.

My mental calculator is sluggish, but it works. I lost by thirty-seven votes. Thirty-seven! I can only assume that viewers got caught up with the idea of emancipation and wanted to set me loose on the world. Either that, or they really didn't like my parents.

It isn't fair. I never wanted this. All I wanted was a little more time to be with Mitch and enjoy my independence. But I let myself get crushed under Judy's steamroller, and because of that, my life is going to change forever. I will be all alone in the world, with very few allies.

So that is what it really means to be a Black Sheep. All of sudden, the idea has less appeal.

At the moment, however, Black Sheepism is all I've got. Fortunately, it's just enough to help me realize that, while I am down, I am not quite out. According to Nutty's big acorn clock at the back of the studio, there are seventeen minutes left to the show.

I stand in the witness box. "Permission to approach the bench, Your Honor."

"Denied," Judy says.

I do it anyway.

Judy makes a slashing gesture at Chili and Bob, but I call, "Keep shooting, guys. You've pretty much destroyed my life. I figure you owe me sixteen and a half minutes."

They keep the cameras rolling.

"Your Honor, I have a question. Did the people in this courtroom get a chance to vote?"

"Irrelevant," she repeats. "Sit down."

"I would argue that it is relevant. Everyone I love in the world is in this courtroom—except my friend Lucy and I guarantee you she already voted 'no.' In fact, I would argue that the only people qualified to weigh in on my fate are in this room. I insist that they be given a chance to vote."

"It's over, KB. Give it up."

"It's not over. We have fifteen minutes left in the show. As I see it, you have two options: I walk out of here right now and you fill the dead air somehow; or I give my closing argument and we let people vote one by one."

Judy eyes flick around the room as she does a quick head count. Realizing that there are forty-one people in the room, she shakes her head. "No. I'll go with reactions for the rest of the show."

"Come on, Judy, I'd need thirty-eight votes to break the tie. You know and I know this would make for great TV. Think of the possibilities for conflict."

At the magic word, her eyes start to glitter. "Maybe you're right."

Carrie and Meadow applaud wildly in the gallery, and Judy hammers the gavel down. "Silence," she says. "Although it is highly unorthodox, I will allow the witness to address the courtroom today. Said witness has three minutes to prepare—during this commercial break."

Aaron offers me a long black robe that immediately makes me feel like a legitimate Black Sheep. I walk across the courtroom and bow first to the defense table, and then to the gallery. Focusing on Carrie to stay calm, I begin.

"Good evening. Being on *The Black Sheep* has been the best experience and the worst experience I ever had, all at the same time. Most of you have been behind the scenes with me, but I bet you were as shocked as I was to see what happens to thousands of hours of raw footage. Editors cut and restructure events into whatever story the producer wants you to see. Although it's a version of reality, it isn't the truth."

Judy waves her gavel to attract attention. "Blah, blah, blah," she says. "If we aired every minute of your life, KB, viewers would have tuned out long ago."

"That was an admission of guilt, in case you didn't recognize it," I say. "But recognizing the difference between entertaining TV and the truth isn't the only thing I learned this summer. Living with another family has taught me a lot about my own. My parents are numbers people. They're all about rules. They see cause and effect, profit and debt, black and white. The Mulligans have taught me to see shades of gray. They taught me about living with passion and commitment. Yet, I also learned that even the most open-minded parents want their kids to do as they say."

"KB?" Judy says. "Snoring."

"It's *my* argument," I tell her. "I get to be boring if I want." I continue, addressing the gallery. "Being a teenager means exploring options. We can't always accept what adults tell us at face value. Sometimes we have to figure things out on our own. If parents teach their kids to think for themselves, then those kids should be able to make sound decisions. Some of you think my decisions weren't very sound, but I'm fifteen and I can't get it right all the time. I'm more worried about the decisions that were made *for* me. I never wanted to divorce my parents; I just wanted to spend more time in Monterey. But when the network came up with the idea—" Judy tries to cut in here but I walk back to the bench, seize her gavel, and keep talking. "When the network came up with the idea, I didn't fight hard enough against it. I allowed myself to be railroaded. As a result, I've learned that I have to speak up when I know something is wrong."

Aaron creeps up behind me and snatches the gavel back, giving me a second to catch my breath before going on.

"It was a hard lesson, especially now that I'm potentially facing life on my own. I don't have a plan yet, but I know I'll survive somehow. That being said, I want to go home. I've realized that my parents have done their best. They've given me a good brain, good values, and some practical rules to live by."

"Ticktock." Judy bangs the gavel. "Wrap it up already."

I turn to my parents at last. "I'm sorry I—"

"Let the voting begin," Judy interrupts. "I don't want to influence anyone—judges are supposed to be impartial— but my vote is 'Yes' to emancipation. Aaron?"

"I vote 'Yes,'" Aaron says.

She starts with the show's other producers, and to my surprise, each votes "No."

"I'm not worried," Judy says. "I only need two more votes."

She moves on to the back row of the visitors' gallery, where again everyone votes against emancipation. Now I dare to hope.

With the second row, I breathe a littler easier. As expected, Lisa votes "No" because she wants me in New York so that she can have Mitch all to herself. Mitch also votes "No," which irritates and pleases me in equal measure. Sergeant Newman votes "No." Walter also votes "No," and offers me a place to stay if it doesn't work out.

Judy is starting to get nervous. Her gavel hand twitches.

The first row starts well with Carrie, Rosa, and the Mulligans quickly voting down emancipation. But then Ted Silver mutters an apologetic "Yes." He and Judy must be closer than I thought.

One more "Yes" and I'm done for. I look around and realize the odds are against me. Bob and Chili will very likely support their boss. And Maya, well, Maya could go either way. My parents, with their faces of pale marble, give nothing away.

Judy says, "We have four minutes left, so let's make this fast. Chili, Bob, you're 'Yeses,' I presume?"

The guys look at each other and shake their heads. "Our vote's with Kendra," Chili says. "'No' to emancipation."

Judy gives them the evil eye. "Maya?" she asks, her voice now all high and nonjudicial.

Maya glares at me for a long moment. Then she looks to her parents, and they give an almost imperceptible shake of the head. Her shiny hair swishes from side to side. "No," she says.

"Okay, Bishops, it's up to you," Judy says. "Do you want this piece of defective baggage back or not?"

In unison, my parents chime, "No."

Judy's face cracks in two, all toothy joy. "No?"

For a moment, it seems as if my lungs have calcified. I look around, panicking, and somehow my eyes find Mitch's across the room. They lock on mine, and I see that he is sorry for me. My chest expands in a great gasp.

My mother clutches my father's arm and he shakes his head, "I mean, we *vote* 'No.' Of course we want our defective baggage back."

That's the nicest insult I've ever heard. My parents are already on their feet, smiling as they come around the defense table. We meet halfway, and if we were the crying type, there would probably be some tears on both sides. Even so, my mother gives me a bone-crushing hug, worthy of Dr. Ernest himself. Dad settles for a hearty handshake that more than suffices.

There is a flurry after that, as everyone hugs everyone else. Rosa is honking into a handkerchief, and Mona looks a little misty, too. I look around for Mitch, but he's standing with Lisa.

My father clears his throat. "Permission to speak, Your Judiness."

Is that a joke? My parents don't make jokes, they make rules.

"You've got ninety seconds," Judy snaps.

"My wife and I want to thank the people in this courtroom, as well as the 453,480 who voted to keep my family together. We also want you to know that we never had any intention of abandoning our daughter, regardless of any decision made in the court of reality television. However, we're relieved to know the feeling is mutual. We hope to get to know many of you better—particularly the Mulligans—as we'll be spending the rest of the summer in this area."

"We will?" I ask. "Why?"

"Consider it a gesture of goodwill—toward the southern sea otter," Dad says. "You need more time to win the war."

I smile at them. "What about the bank?"

"We're taking a leave of absence," my mother says. "The bank will still be there in September."

"And by then our colleagues may have forgotten about the show," Dad adds, proving he's still Dad under this new veneer.

"It was our idea, but Rosa agrees," Mom says. "She's helped us realize that we have to put our own pasts behind us and give you the freedom to explore what you want out of life."

"So I don't have to become a banker?" I ask.

"I think the criminal record pretty much eliminates that option," Dad says.

I wave my hand airily. "Don't worry, Dad. If Boulder Beach doesn't drop the charges, we'll have our records expunged later."

"We should have taken you seriously from the beginning," Mom says. "I'm ashamed to say we'd forgotten what it's like to be young and fueled by passion."

Rosa is a genius. I have my doubts my parents were ever fueled by anything but dollar signs, but it's time I started cutting them some slack. "It's okay, Mom. I realize that this whole thing has been a nightmare for you. Believe me, it will never happen again."

I turn to glare at Judy, who lifts her lip to expose a hint of fang. "Oh, boo hoo," she says.

"We're proud of what you accomplished with Team Fourteen," Dad says, "even if it ended badly."

"If you're proud of me, why wouldn't you bail me out of jail?"

"There are different ways to achieve a goal, many of them legal," Mom says primly. "If you're going to go leaping off the deep end, you'd better learn to swim."

And they're back. The New and Improved Parents were too good to last. "You wouldn't let me take swimming lessons," I point out.

Mom ignores this. "Have you forgotten everything we taught you?"

"What ever happened to Rule Number Four?" Dad interjects. "Remember, *Think before you act.*"

"I should have made burning *The BLAH* a condition of my returning home," I say.

Rosa comes up behind me and jabs me in the ribs. "Behave."

Judy hammers her gavel so hard the fake bench snaps in two and crashes around her. "In case you hadn't noticed, we're already off the air. Clear the damn set."

Chapter 20

I flail through the water, choking and sputtering as wave after wave hits my face. Someone should have warned me about the treacherous conditions so that I could wear a life jacket. Sure, it would have been humiliating, given that I'm in the shallow end of the pool, and the other two students in the class are half my age. But the water is extremely choppy, and even the swimming instructor agrees that I have buoyancy issues.

But I must persevere. If I don't figure out how to turn my aimless thrashing into forward motion, my parents won't let me go on the otter-watching expedition I read about. I mentioned it at dinner last night, and Mom had enrolled me in swim class by morning.

It's not how I'd planned to spend day one of our first real family vacation. In fact, I was tempted to throw some foul language around, until Mom said, "But only yesterday you complained that we wouldn't let you take swimming lessons. We're *listening* to you, Kendra, just as you asked." There was a slight twitch to her upper lip that suggested a smirk, but I reminded myself to keep an open mind.

Despite this minor setback, I believe they are trying to lighten up. After all, they offered to come on the otter-watching trip with me—just as soon as we've completed a boating safety course with certified professionals.

Swimming they've already mastered. Who knew bankers are immersible? Yet there they are in the pool's fast lane, creating so much churn I'm taking on water like a leaky kayak. It turns out that they are in training for next year's Ironman competition. This news might have annoyed me if they hadn't invited me along to Hawaii with them.

I drag myself out of the pool, and Rosa rushes over to wrap me in a robe. If I'd known that the swimsuit I bought with Carrie would see active duty, I'd have chosen something that isn't transparent when wet.

Rosa is staying with us for a few days in the cottage my parents rented. It sits high above the shore, not far from where Maurice was released. My bedroom is gorgeous, with the pale, washed-out quality of tide-worn pebbles and sun-bleached driftwood. The best thing about it, however, is that it is mine alone. There are no cameras, no ferrets, and no bratty little sisters to bother me. To be honest, I sort of missed Meadow and Manhattan last night. I've grown fond of them in the way hostages sometimes grow fond of their kidnappers.

"What a natural," Rosa says, leading me to a deck chair. "Your breaststroke was excellent."

I snort, partly to expel water from my brain. "That was the front crawl. I think I'm too old to learn to swim."

"You're never too old to learn something new."

"I learned enough this summer to last me till college."

"So why do I have to remind you to put this on?" she asks, handing me a tube of sunscreen. "I was proud of the way you handled yourself in that courtroom yesterday. You've really blossomed. I used to worry that you'd hide in the shadows forever."

"No one can shoot you in the shadows," I point out. And black sheep aren't as bulletproof as I once thought.

Rosa takes the chair beside mine while lamenting, "You're all grown up. You don't need me anymore."

I lean over and give her a one-armed hug. "Maybe not as a nanny, but I'll always need you as a friend."

"Your parents are doing better, no?"

I nod. "So far, so good. They'd already booked my flight to Hawaii. If they're taking their defective baggage with them, I guess they were serious about not giving up on me."

"They won't give up," she says.

"They even got me a telescope so that I can keep a look-out for Maurice. I can't believe they thought of it."

"Actually, they didn't."

"Who did—Carrie?"

She shakes her head, grinning. "A boy with eyes as blue as the Caribbean Sea."

I lift my shades to stare at her. "I am *so* not ready for jokes about Mitch."

She settles back in her chair and lowers her shades. "Fine, Miss Snippy. If you don't want to hear the story, that's up to you."

I get out of my chair and perch on the edge of hers. "Tell me everything you know."

"I know he's a nice boy."

"Cough it up, Rosa, or I'm boycotting the sunscreen."

"Well, he showed up on the doorstep with a brand new telescope two days ago. I let him in and he set it up for you."

"Why would he do that?"

"To help you see better?" she says, smiling as if she's quite the wit.

"Mitch and I are through. He *used* me."

"Baloney," she says. "He cares about you."

I get back into my own chair, sulking. "If he cared about me, why did he move to Calvin's after our fight?"

"That's what men do. Don't ask me how their minds work."

"Well, what makes you think he likes me?"

"Duh! He told me so."

"I'm the only one who 'duhs' people around here," I say. "And why was he telling you that and not me?"

"Because I listen. He said he tried to talk to you and you 'shut him down.' That doesn't sound like the polite girl I raised."

"Rosa, he's obviously involved with Lisa. You saw the episode."

"I saw some images Judy cobbled together that prove nothing. On the other hand, a boy who spends hundreds of his hard-earned dollars on a girl proves something."

"It proves that he feels guilty. Mitch hasn't exactly been there for me, you know."

"You need to tell him *how* to be there for you. That's what a girlfriend does."

"If there was nothing between them, why was Lisa pissed off when he shared a tent with me?"

"I imagine she thought it was inappropriate," Rosa says. "If so, she was right. You're fifteen."

I don't need a chastity lecture, especially when there's no longer any threat to it. And I don't understand why this has turned into a discussion of my shortcomings, when Mitch was far from the model boyfriend. "Whose side are you on, anyway?" I ask.

"Yours," she says. "Always. But that doesn't mean I won't tell you what I think. And I think you should use the next month to get to know this boy better."

"We're not speaking to each other. *Duh.*"

"Kendra," my mother calls from the edge of the pool. "I heard that. You know I don't like that word."

Rosa grins. "You can start speaking to Mitch at the wrap party tonight. You'll be working with him on Team Fourteen this summer, so you might as well get along."

"What's the point? It's over."

"Just see where it goes," she says. "A Black Sheep always keeps an open mind, right?"

I look at her quickly, surprised. I shouldn't be, because Rosa has always been able to read my mind. *The BLAH* wasn't the only thing that kept me out of trouble.

Settling back into my chair, I end the discussion. "Whatever."

Lisa is already on the small stage when we arrive at the aquarium for the *Black Sheep* wrap party, and she steps to the mike when she sees us.

"I have an announcement," she says. "Boulder Beach Golf Club has decided not to move its fourteenth hole!"

She waits for the commotion to subside before continuing. "They've given in to the pressure generated by national television coverage." She glances over at me and I feel less of an icy stab from her eyes than usual. "They held out for a while because they'd sunk so much money into the property, but two savvy bankers from New York advised them to set up a charitable conservation area on the land that will help recoup their losses—and, more important, improve their public profile."

My parents wave away the applause modestly. I'm thrilled that they supported me by joining the battle, but I'm also curiously disappointed that the fight with Boulder

Beach is ending so soon. I was looking forward to working on it this summer.

Lisa continues to hog the mike. "The Boulder Beach executives have also dropped the charges against us, which means my academic standing is rock solid. I'm hoping to publish an article about the experience."

Trust Lisa to turn every event in her life into an opportunity to educate.

She calls my parents and me to the stage, and the Mulligan twins come toward us carrying the ugliest trophy I've ever seen. It consists of a ceramic otter attached to stacked tin cans with a lot of glue. The shaky inscription reads, TO THE BISHOPS, PROTECTERS OF THE CALIFORNIA SEE OTER.

My parents nudge Lisa out of the way so that I can use the mike. "My parents and I would like to thank you for this unique tribute," I say, raising the trophy. "After yesterday's speech, I don't have much left to say, other than that I've decided to donate half my earnings from *The Black Sheep* to the aquarium's otter-rehabilitation program."

Amid the cheer that follows, I glance at my parents and see that the dollar signs have popped right out of their pupils to jitter in the air before them.

"Someone catch my parents before they faint," I say. "Mom, Dad, don't worry, I'm putting the rest in the bank for college."

"You certainly are," Dad says.

Rosa starts the applause and most people join in. Maya, however, doesn't even pretend to clap; Judy, and Ted Silver are too busy groping each other to bother. Finally, Judy looks up from the clinch and calls, "Did I miss my thank-you, KB?"

I roll my eyes and everyone laughs. "Thank you Judy for giving me a platform to promote a good cause."

The music cranks up and the crowd breaks into smaller groups. Max and Mona come up to me carrying an oversized gift bag. Inside is a quilt that Mona made, but it's nothing like her usual country kitsch. She has transferred photographs onto fabric squares and used them to depict my life in California, and my life in New York. A Team 14 poster and a bright yellow kayak sit beside Rockefeller Center and the Henri Bendel department store on Fifth Avenue. In the center, is a great big black sheep.

"Wow!" I say. "This could hang in the Museum of Modern Art."

"Or you could just use it and think of us now and then," Mona says.

"I'll think of you more often than that," I assure her.

"And we'll think of you every time we drive our new minivan," Max says. "Thanks, kid."

"Don't thank me." I smile. "The network put up the money. I just decided how to spend it."

"Well, you couldn't have chosen better," he says.

I wish Maya had put as much thought into how she

spent my family's portion, instead of donating it to the Museum of American Finance History. It just shows how little imagination she has.

"We're glad you won the fight," Mona says, hugging me. "And we're sorry we were so hard on you. It's difficult to watch your kids repeat your mistakes."

"We shouldn't have blamed you for Mitch's involvement," Max adds. "After a lot of meditation, we realized we were in denial about the fact that our son had defied us."

"And we should have taken our share of the blame," Mona continues. "We filled your heads with stories of our triumphs and neglected to mention the failures."

"I'm sorry I wasn't up front with you about . . . everything."

Mona's smile fades. "You mean the tent business."

I nod sheepishly. "We just wanted to keep it private from Judy."

Max puts a hand on his wife's backside. "I think we overreacted, don't you, Mother? We were younger than they were when we found each other."

I interrupt before they can go too far down memory lane. "Am I welcome to visit this summer?"

"Of course," Max says. "You'd always be welcome in our home, even if you weren't our son's girlfriend."

I examine the quilt as an excuse not to look at them. "I'm not his girlfriend."

"Give it an hour," Mona says, and hugs me again.

* * *

"You must be getting dizzy."

"Excuse me?" I ask.

"I said, you must be getting dizzy from the way the world revolves around you." Maya leans over the bar and adds a shot of rum to her Coke when the bartender isn't looking. "Figures you'd turn the wrap party into an All About Kendra party."

"I didn't know that was going to happen," I say.

"Of course you didn't. Just like you didn't suck up to my parents by donating your earnings from the show to the aquarium."

"I donated that money because I wanted to," I say. "*You're* the suck-up."

Maya takes a sip of her drink and adds a little more rum. "I can't help it if I have more in common with your parents than you do. Besides, showing interest in that stuff was the only way I could escape the morgue you people live in."

"Our house is not a morgue!"

"It is, and there's a pair of stiffs running it."

"My parents loved having you visit. How can you be so harsh?"

Laughing, she raises her glass to me. "I learned from the master."

I decide to teach her something else by walking away without lowering myself to her level. If she couldn't learn as much from this experience as I did, it's her loss.

Black Sheepism is totally wasted on some people.

Carrie deposits me at the door of the jellyfish gallery and says, "Try not to screw it up this time."

One successful date with Luke and she's all superior. I start down a path marked with tiny votive candles that leads to the sea nettle tank.

"I wanted to make sure you could find your way," Mitch says.

"But will anyone be able to find the buffet table you stole these from?" I ask.

He shrugs. "It's a romantic gesture. The end justifies the means."

"I would have settled for an apology."

He looks at me incredulously. "I thought you'd be the one apologizing."

This is a two-way street and I'm willing to do my part. "You first."

"Fine," he says, shaking his head. "Then I'm sorry you accused me of using you."

"You call that an apology?"

He leans against the nettle tank and crosses his arms. "I call it the truth."

"You've got to admit, it looked suspicious."

"I don't care what it looked like. It wasn't true and it wasn't fair. And you didn't let me explain."

I can see that he is hurt as well as angry, and that nearly paralyzes me. "I'm sorry," I say. "It got so that I honestly couldn't tell what was real and what was fake anymore. I was . . . upset." That's putting it mildly, but it's a start.

"Why couldn't you just *tell* me you were upset?"

"Because I don't do that. My way is to stew about things for a while and then explode."

"That's not going to work," he says. "I'm not a mind-reader."

I notice he says "going," as if there is a future between us. It gives me the courage to continue. "I know. I'll try harder." Just in case he thinks I'm too eager, however, I add, "You could afford to communicate better, too."

He thinks about this before nodding. "Yeah, I guess I could. I'll try harder, too."

And that's it. I can tell by his smile that we are boyfriend and girlfriend again. If I'd known it would be that easy, I'd have done it sooner.

"I have a romantic gesture, too," I say, handing him a package.

He unwraps the binoculars and laughs. "It's about time."

"I figured you'd need them to come otter-watching with me."

He wraps his arms around me just as Meadow's voice rings out. "Kendra?"

It figures we can't have a moment alone. "In here!" I call.

She races into the exhibit and hops with excitement.

"You're never going to believe who just showed up! Logan Waters! He said you invited him."

I feel Mitch's arms stiffen ever so slightly. It might be nonverbal communication, but it's pretty clear just the same. "Okay," I say. "We'll be there soon."

"Not soon—*now!*" she exclaims. "What if he leaves?"

If he leaves I'll be disappointed, but after all, this is real life and Mitch is my boyfriend. "Don't worry," I tell Meadow. "You go keep him entertained until we get there."

She runs out, hollering over her shoulder, "Hurry! You guys can make out any time."

"Don't you want to go?" Mitch asks when she's gone.

"Not yet," I say. "With my parents around, we won't get much time alone and—"

Mitch's lips are on mine before I finish, and the world quickly slips away. Before long, I realize that we are being bathed in a mysterious warm glow that's brighter than the votives should be. Maybe that's just what happens when you kiss the guy you're meant to be with forever. Maybe I'm having an out-of-body experience.

Or maybe it's just a nasty flashback.

"Judy, turn off that camera," I say, opening my eyes as I pull away from Mitch. "The show is OVER."

The light turns to focus on her as she addresses Chili's camera. "You saw it here first, folks. Kendra and Mitch are together at last. But will their love stand the test of time and distance? Tune into to *American Lovebirds*, the Reality

Network's new show about the making of a relationship to find out. We'll follow our young couple as they—"

"Cut!" I say, stepping in front of Chili's camera. "My contract is done, Judy. That's a wrap on Kendra Bishop."

Black Sheep Rule Number Twenty-five: *Never make the same mistake twice.*

"KB, come on, you love the camera and the camera loves you," she says. "Besides, Judy's got a gap to fill. The network wants a love story."

"I've got an idea," I say. "Hit me, Chili." He turns the camera on me. "You saw it here first, folks: a Hollywood producer falls for a small-town newshound. Can Judy Greenberg and her Teddy Bear make a go of it? Will Ted sacrifice his integrity to become a paparazzo? Or will Judy go legit? Tune in to *American Lovebirds* to find out."

"Great idea!" someone says. We turn to see Terrance Burnside at the gallery entrance.

I whisper to Mitch, "Our place has been desecrated."

"My personal life is not for public consumption," Judy tells Terrance.

"You promised to deliver a show, Judith," he reminds her. "I can tell you from personal experience that the network president doesn't like to be disappointed."

I lead Mitch away to rejoin the party, clutching his hand even tighter as we approach our parents.

"You must be so proud of your daughter," Max says to Mom when we join them. "She could have a future as an environmental attorney."

A look passes between my parents when they see Mitch holding my hand. Dad's Adam's apple bobs before he responds to Max. "If that's what she wants, it's fine with us. It's a long program, so I'm glad she's saving for college."

Mom smiles at me sweetly. "I hope there's something left for tuition when she's paid her credit card bill."

"Hey, look," I say, escaping with Mitch to the dance floor, "Meadow's dancing with Logan. We'd better get over there and chaperone."

Judy rushes past, dragging Ted behind her. "We've got to get out of here. Somebody hail us a cab!"

Bob is right on their heels with the camera. "Zooming in!" he calls.

Terrance brings up the rear. "Bob, stay on Judy and get into the cab with them," he calls. "Chili, you find out where Ted lives and get a crew over there. Talk to the neighbors and see if you can get any dirt. This is going to be great! When *American Lovebirds* airs, no one will even remember *The Black Sheep*."

"I'll remember it," Mitch assures me, as the door closes behind them.

"Me too," I say, smiling up at him. "Always."

Acknowledgments

Thanks to Jennifer Besser, Jenny Bent,
and our usual cast of supporters.